BLITZ PAMS

POLICE AUXILIARY MESSENGERS

BY JOHN ORTON

First published in Great Britain as a softback original in 2016

Copyright © John Orton 2016

The moral right of this author has been asserted.

Typeset in Dante MT Std and Anodyne

Design and publishing by UK Book Publishing

UK Book Publishing is a trading name of Consilience Media

www.ukbookpublishing.com

ISBN: 978-1-910223-82-6

Cover photos:
Market Place – 3/10/41 – courtesy of Shields Gazette *www.shieldsgazette.com*
Barrage balloons – https://commons.wikimedia.org – Public Domain

Also by *John Orton*...

THE FIVE STONE STEPS

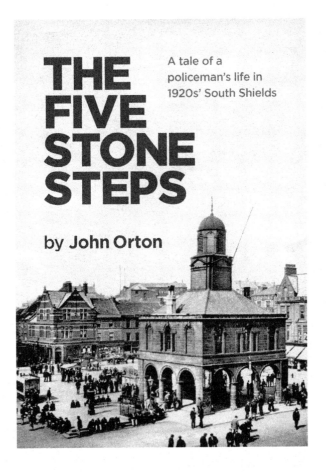

THE
FIVE
STONE
STEPS

A tale of a
policeman's life in
1920s' South Shields

by John Orton

(UK Book Publishing – 2014)

SOUTH SHIELDS 1941

RIVER TYNE

NORTH SEA

NORTH FORESHORE

PIER

St STEPHENS

MILE END RD

St ALDENE ST

FERRY

MARKET PLACE

KING ST

OCEAN RD

DENMARK ST

SEA ROAD

BENTS PARK

St HILDA'S

GAS WORKS

TOWER STREET

TOWN HALL

WESTOE COLLIERY

MIDDLE DOCKS

COMMERCIAL ROAD

LAYGATE LANE

VICTORIA RD

WESTOE RD

MOWBRAY RD

INGHAM INFIRMARY

HORSLEY HILL RD

TEMPLE TOWN

DEAN ROAD

STANHOPE ROAD

CHICHESTER

MORTIMER RD

BRINKBURN FIELDS

CEMETERY

SUNDERLAND ROAD

KING GEORGE RD

THE NOOK PUB

TO MARSDEN

BOLDON LANE

HARTON LANE

GENERAL HOSPITAL

WRIGHTS BISCUITS

PRINCE EDWARD ROAD

QUARRY LANE

TO CLEADON HILLS

Not to scale and diagrammatic only

KEY TO MAP

Sept/Dec 1940

1. Keppel Street Police Station
2. Maxwell Street
3. Frederick Street
4. Claypath Lane
5. Percy Street
6. Napier Street
7. Winchester Street
8. Pinckney's (Volunteer Arms)
9. South Eldon Street

Dec 1940/Feb 1941

10. Brodrick Street
11. St. Aidan's Road
12. Robertson Street
13. Fort Street
14. Fawcett Street
15. Queens Theatre
16. Cockburn Street
17. Oliver Street
18. Lascelle's Avenue

Sept/Dec 1941

19. Mount Terrace
20. Charlotte Street
21. Power Station
22. Trinity Schools
23. Union Alley
24. Barrington Street
25. Livingstone Street
26. Morton Street
27. Grosvenor Road
28. Tynedale Road
29. Erskine Road.
30. Wharton Street
31. Hyde Street
32. Hepscott Terrace
33. Tadema Road

CONTENTS

LIST OF ILLUSTRATIONS

www.southtynesideimages.org.uk/newsite

Blitz Pams tells with astonishing vividness and compelling
verve a story from a forgotten world – a North Eastern town
during the Blitz. John Orton makes this lost world real again.
Through the voice of the narrator, he succeeds in recreating
the life and struggles of young people in conditions where
they could feel they were making a difference. Anyone
who wants a fresh look into what it means to live in a time
of crisis will enjoy this arrestingly well written book.

John Gray

Author of 'Straw Dogs: thoughts on humans
and other animals' (Granta Books)

"All Air Raid warnings had to be responded to, on occasions twice a night, incidents attended to and long hours spent in off duty hours, and no time off or over-time, no canteens, and as was more important, no complaints from the Police."

Thomas Renton Gordon *(1894-1980)*
Station Sergeant
South Shields Police

Market Place – before 1939

Market Place – 3/10/41 – courtesy of Shields Gazette

CHAPTER 1
SEPTEMBER 1940

M e Mam was standing outside wor back door talking to one of the neighbours when she saw me coming yem on me own. I was cycling carefully ower the cobbles. I think she could tell by the look on me face that something was wrong.

"That was quick. Where' your mates?"

I said nowt and just got off the bike and pushed it into the yard. Me Mam followed me in.

"What's the marra, Mossie?"

"They wouldn't take me."

"Why not?"

"The polis said they only wanted British lads and not coloureds."

"But wharraboot your mates?"

"They were sent through to see the Sergeant."

"We'll see aboot that." She went into the house and came back in two secs with her coat on. "Come on then, Mossie," and off she went with me following behind, pushing me bike. It was nae use arguing with her.

When we got to the Keppel Street Police Station me Mam told me to leave me bike by the railings, and we marched up the steps. The same polis who had sent me away was standing there. He was an auld fella and he had a little red epaulette on his shoulder – War Reserve Police – they were men who didn't de any other work that was necessary for the war - they thought they were

1

very important and they were ten times worse than the ordinary bobbies.

"What d'ye want?" he almost snarled.

"I'm taking my Mossie in to sign him up as a messenger."

"Naw you're not. I've already telt him that we don't want his sort."

Me Mam just pushed past him, dragged me with her through the doors, and started doon the five stone steps. The auld bobby came after us shouting blue murder, and for a minute I thought he was going to push us doon the steps. I'd heard that that's what they did in the Shields Police if you got on the wrong side of them.

A door opened just opposite and a big fella with grey hair looked oot. "Keep your voice down, Constable, there's a war on, you know." He looked at me and me Mam. "You must be desperate if you're trying to break into a nick. Now what's the matter?"

"Me son here came doon with his mates to sign on as messengers – the PAMs like. This fella sent him packing – he told Mossie that he wasn't British."

Just then another polis came doon the corridor – he'd heard the disturbance. It was Sergeant Duncan. He'd known me Mam and Da' for years - as well as being the beat bobby doon Maxwell Street years ago he'd also been Aliens Officer and had kept the Register of Coloured Seamen, which me Da' had to sign after each voyage.

He'd heard what me Mam had said. He looked at the grey haired man. "It's alright, Super, I'll sort it out." He turned to the auld polis. "And what's the problem, Constable? I'm the one who decides which of the volunteers we accept, not you."

"Aye, well I didn't want him wasting your time, like – with him being an Arab."

"Where were you born, son?" he asked me.

"In Maxwell Street, South Shields."

"So you're as British as Constable Douthwaite. And where's your Dad?"

"He's away at sea in the Atlantic convoys – that's why me Mam wouldn't let me gan to sea – she didn't want us both away."

He looked at me Mam. "I'm sorry about the misunderstanding, Mrs. Hamed. You go and get your bike, laddie, take it round to the yard at the back so it can be inspected, and then I'll take your particulars. There's no need for you to wait, Mrs. Hamed, young Mossie will be all right."

He turned to the auld fella. "Get back on your beat, Constable Douthwaite, and when you've finished, you come and see me." There was a distinct menace in his voice and auld Douthwaite started to look very worried as he walked up the five stone steps.

There was another auld bobby in the yard but he was a lot friendlier – he had a good look at the bike, checking the brakes and the tyres. It was the delivery bike from Bates' Fruit and Veg where I worked – there was a big metal frame in front of the handlebars where the basket went, but it was solid. "That'll do fine – I'll give you a cover for the front light – they're easy enough to fit but if you have any trouble let me know. It's for the blackout." All cars and vans had to have covers ower their lights so that they couldn't be seen from the air – it meant that they didn't give much light for the drivers either. With all the street lights off the only thing to stop you driving into trolley bus poles was the white tape roond the bottoms - traffic crawled aboot at neet.

I went back to see Sergeant Duncan. It didn't take long – I just had to give him my full name which is Mohammed, not Maurice as you're probably thinking. Mossie is short for Maurice in Shields, but when I first started at Laygate Lane School the lads found Mohammed a bit of a gobful, so Mossie it was. He knew where we lived and when he asked my age I said sixteen – I was only fifteen and three quarters, and he probably guessed as much,

3

but he didn't say owt. You were supposed to be sixteen, but I
knew big fourteen year aulds who'd been taken on.

"I can't put you down for Laygate or Frederick Street with your
mates, as we've got all the messengers we want in those areas -
but we can always do with an extra pair of hands here. I'll take
you down to the storeroom to get you fitted up with a uniform,
and you can report each Sunday for a month for training. Be here
eight sharp and you'll be able to get home for your dinner. After
that you come down here as soon as you hear the air raid sirens."

We were only used when there was a raid, but you got paid 1s
and 6d if you had to turn oot, whether any bombs dropped or
not. The uniforms were army surplus dyed black. Mine was aboot
ten sizes too big and the troosers were like chetty sacks - but me
Mam would soon sort it oot. I had a beret, but also a tin helmet to
wear if there were any bombs flying aboot. As I was on the way
oot with me uniform under me arm, Sergeant Duncan looked
out of the Charge Office. "I forgot to ask you where you worked,
Mossie."

"At Bates' Fruit and Veg in Frederick Street - Mrs. Hussain
runs it what with her husband away in the Navy." Me Da' used
to lodge in Geordie Hussain's father's boarding house before he
married me Mam. His family belonged to the same tribe in Ta'izz
– that's where me Da' and Geordie's Da' came from although
their passports said Aden.

Sergeant Duncan nodded. "I know Geordie and Alice Hussain.
You better tell her that you might be in late if you have to be on
duty most of the night when there's an air raid on."

I just nodded – I did the early morning collection with Mrs.
Hussain from the warehouse doon by the docks, and then we
made wor deliveries to the few boarding houses that were left,
and to hotels and cafés in the Laygate area. With Geordie away in
the Navy she drove the van. She could have got petrol tickets as
she was collecting and delivering groceries, but she reckoned she

wouldn't have got very far with what she'd be allowed, so she had a geet big canvas bag on top of the van filled with gas.

I had to help her with the humping – not that she needed much help as she was a strong woman. She couldn't de it all on her own though, and her brother Nobby was a useless nowt. He ran their shop at the Nook, which meant that he just stood aboot all day in-between visits to the *Winter Gardens* at the *Nook* pub, while his wife Edie worked her socks off. I'd just have to gan in anyway, and ask her if I could put me heed doon later on if I was too tired.

I couldn't wait for Sunda' and I was in the back yard of the Keppel Street nick at half past seven. Another lad who was starting just like me arrived a few minutes later. He was called Matty Lightfoot - he was a big solid lad nearly twice my size. He lived in Fort Street, and he was working on the river with his Uncle who was a waterman. All the Lightfoots worked on the river or went to sea, but his Mam wouldn't let her Matty gan to sea with the war on. His Cousin Billy Duggan had had a narrow escape when his ship, the *Sheaf Crest,* had hit a mine in the channel – Billy had been picked oot of the briny by a warship. "It was his first trip an' all," said Matty, "but it didn't put him off, and he signed up on another ship as soon as he could. I'm just ganna' wait, and when I'm called up I'll join the Navy." I told him me Da' was a fireman away on the Atlantic convoys, and we hit it off straight away. Two other lads turned up for training – Jackie Hansen and Freddie Skee. Jackie was a canny bike rider but he didn't say owt at all that day. Freddie Skee made up for it - he had a high pitched voice and spoke so quick you could hardly make oot what he said - and he said a lot - most of it sh**e.

By eight o'clock we were all inside the nick with Davey Corbett and Jimmy Clay, two of the longest serving police auxiliary messengers, or PAMs as everybody called them, and they worked full time. There was a room in the basement where we would stay when we came on at neet – it had a switchboard and phones and was used when there was an air raid. Davey and Jimmy both worked shifts, like the polis, but were expected to turn oot when the sirens went off. There had been the odd false alarm in Shields when planes went ower, but we'd only just started having raids.

When the War had first started there'd been air raid drills and gas mask drills; air raid shelters had been built all ower the toon – people who lived in the new houses along Mortimer Road and by the Redhead Park had built shelters in their gardens. In the auld part of Shields you didn't have a garden, just a yard for the coal house, the netty, and the washhouse, if you were lucky enough to have one - so the Council had built public shelters for most streets. After spending half the neet shivering in a shelter with people coughing and farting, and sometimes even pissing in the corner, with no sight or sound of a bomb, most folk just stayed yem. Some slept under the table, and some had bought those Morrison shelters that looked like little tables but were made of steel with mesh round to stop any shrapnel getting in. Me Mam had said we weren't having any coffins in wor hoose - not many could afford them, anyhow. All the bairns had been sent to Cumberland and Westmorland and nowt had happened, so most of them had come yem. Me little sister Mary had gone, but when they got to the other end nae one wanted the Arab children, so she ended up staying with one of the teachers - the same as Mrs. Hussain's three children. When they came yem for Christmas they didn't gan back.

Then after Dunkirk the raids started – there weren't many at first but in August a bomb knocked doon some houses up the Lawe Top at Pearson Street. Then there was a raid at the end of August when fifteen bombs were dropped. The alarm went off just after one o'clock in the morning – I was fast asleep and I didn't hear the sirens. Me Mam didn't wake me up at first. She thought it was going to be another false alarm, but after the first bombs dropped she dragged me and Mary oot of bed, half asleep. We pushed the table against the wall and then dragged the sideboard ower in front of it, and all huddled together underneath. We heard more planes coming ower – you could tell they were German because the engines made an uneven sort of sound whereas wor planes' engines were steady. There were then two or three geet big bangs, and they weren't far away as the whole hoose shook, and one of me Mam's vases fell off the mantle shelf. Wor Mary started crying and me Mam had to cuddle her tighter. We then heard a knocking on the back window – it was the Rutherfords from the upstairs flat. "Gan and let them in, Mossie and be quick aboot it." I dashed oot and opened the door - they all came piling in – Mr. and Mrs. Rutherford and their son Jimmy. He was a pitman doon Westoe Colliery like his Da', and was just waiting until he was eighteen to join up. Mining was a reserved occupation, but nae one in their reet mind would stay doon the pit for any longer than they had to. Ye just got on a train to Newcastle or Sunderland, said ye were a milkman or suchlike, and they signed ye up – once in they never hoyed ye oot.

The Rutherfords all squeezed in with us – they'd come doon stairs into the yard to shelter under the steps, but when the last explosion happened half a dozen tiles fell off the roof, and they were starting to get worried.

After aboot an hour things seemed to have quietened doon, and the ack-ack guns fell silent. Mr. Rutherford, who had been oot at the *Auld Mill*, and smelt worse than a brewery, said he had to gan oot to the netty. He climbed oot from under the table – the next we heard was the guns blazing away, and an even louder explosion shook the hoose. Mr. Rutherford came running back in and threw himself under the table, barging into his son Jimmy, who started to have a go at him, and then suddenly stopped. "You're all wet," he shouted. "Is that blood?" Bella Rutherford started shaking her husband to see if he was all reet, and then called him a daft nowt when he told us what had happened. He'd just started having his piss when he heard the guns - he'd ran straight back in with his thing still dangling oot of his fly, and he'd wet all doon his troosers.

The sirens sounded the all clear at quarter past five. Mr. Rutherford said "thank Christ for that", and dashed oot to the netty – he'd been holding it in for more than two hours, but hadn't dared leave the shelter under the table again.

The next morning we found oot that Claypath Lane, Derby Terrace, and Percy Street had been badly hit. Auld Mrs. Stobbart had been killed - she was found by the rescue services stone deed, sitting on the toilet with her drawers roond her ankles, and without a mark on her. The bomb had badly damaged the house, and she had been killed by the blast. Two hundred people had lost their homes. It had been the worst raid so far, and the polis realised that things were starting to get serious so they had decided to recruit more lad messengers.

"It's only a matter of time before they're coming over every night," Davey Corbett said. "My brother Archie's a spitfire pilot." Me and Matty paid attention. The pilots were heroes. "Last time Archie was home he reckoned that the Gerries would start bombing the towns heavily when they realised that they couldn't take on and beat the RAF in the skies over Britain. He says they'll come at night. I'll be eighteen in twelve months' time and I'll be joining the RAF. I already go to the Air Cadets two evenings a week and they say they'll put me straight into pilot training." Davey Corbett was a tall, fair haired lad, and didn't speak with much of a Shields accent – he'd been at the Boys High School but had left to become a PAM.

"Right," he said, "you lads are going to have to know how to get to all of the Police sub-stations, all the ARP shelters, all the auxiliary fire and ambulance service depots, and you'll have to know this part of Shields like the back of your hands. Jimmy will take Jackie and Freddie, and I'll take Matty and Mossie."

Freddie started laughing. "Ye sound a right pair, ye two – Matty and Mossie. Ye could de a double act at the *Queens* – the only trouble is that in double acts one of ye has to look stupid and ye both de."

Matty started walking ower to where Freddie was. "Are ye callin' me and me mate stupid?"

Freddie stepped back, and then Davey looked at him and said sharply, "Put a sock in it, Freddie - and you, Matty, wait until the war's over before you thump him; and then we can all give him one." He paused and then continued, "We'll put you through your paces for the next three weeks, and on the fourth Sunday from now we'll have a competition. The losing team will buy ice-creams for the rest of us at DiBresci's Café." He paused a minute and then added, "Wally Duncan's a PAM and he works there. He lets us have extra red sauce on our ice-creams. He's Sergeant Duncan's son but he's a good lad."

I got yem at half past twelve worn oot and starving for me dinner. Roast joints were a thing of the past, but me Mam was used to cooking meals that didn't always contain meat as me and me Da' were Muslims. We were having Jarra' duck – stuffed marra' to ye. She'd made some lovely thick gravy, and we had roast tatoes and butter beans – it was tapioca puddin' for afters so I didn't gan hungry, and there was enough left to have on Munda' when me Mam did the washing.

I must have ridden miles that morning and Davey Corbett only let us stop if we had to have a piss. We'd first ridden to Tyne Dock, to Napier Street, to Laygate, along Frederick Street and then away to the Nook. We had to kna' where all the Police out-stations were. Davey would shoot ahead and then wait for us to catch up – he had a brand new Raleigh racing bike with a four speed Sturmey-Archer gear hub. I had me delivery bike with the big iron frame for the basket ower the front wheel and Matty's wasn't much better. At the Nook Davey stopped ootside the *Winter Gardens*. "If you ever have to come out here, and there's no one in the station, try the *Winter Gardens*. If they've been in a while they might buy you a glass of beer." With that we were off again – this time to visit all the outside shelters where we would find the air raid wardens, and then the depots for the auxiliary fire and ambulance services, the first aid stations, the Home Guard HQ, the rescue teams and the mobile canteens; there were also buildings where the head fire watcher for an area was based. Then we were back to Keppel Street and Davey would give us an address to go to – it would usually be one of the ones we'd already visited. He'd then point to the map on the wall and say that there'd been an air raid, and one of the roads leading to where we wanted to go to was blocked – he'd give us a minute to look at the map and then we'd be off, on wor own this time.

When we'd finished the bike riding we had to practise using stirrup pumps. They were used to put house fires oot if an incendiary bomb had come through a roof or a winda; but you wouldn't throw watter on the bomb itself unless it was nearly oot anyway – you'd either use the long shovel they gave to fire watchers to hoy it oot the winda or you'd cover it in sand.

We did this every Sunda' for three weeks and Davey had told us to do as much riding in the dark as we could as well. "If there's no moon you can't always read the street names so you need to know them by heart." I didn't fancy riding in the dark on me own, so as we were gannen oot I asked if any of the others fancied deein' any neet ridin' with me – Jackie Hansen, who lived up Winchester Street, said he would and we agreed to meet up on Tuesda' in front of the Town Hall. When I got there Freddie and Matty were waiting as well – after that we'd often meet up, and we started hanging round together. We'd have races to see who could get to the place we'd chosen first. Jackie nearly always won unless there was a short cut doon a back lane that Freddie knew.

One neet Freddie Skee pulled oot a paper bag with five

Woodbines in – tabs were scarce like everything else and you couldn't always buy a packet of ten or twenty. He didn't have any matches so we waited outside the *Pier* until a fella came oot and Freddie asked for a light. The windas were all boarded up in case of an air raid and the man had come oot first through a blackout curtain, and then through the door. "Ye can't smoke in the street or ye'll hev the air raid wardens after ye." His eyes were getting used to the dark. "How auld are ye?"

"I'm auld enough," Freddie replied. "We're training as police messengers."

"Aye well you'd better ask one of the polis' to give you training on how to smoke in the blackoot." He made to walk off.

"Couldn't ye tell us, Mister?" Freddie asked.

The man paused, and then said, "Why not? Ye lot gather roond and tyek your caps off." When we were all huddled together he made us hold wor caps ower his hands. "Noo give me a tab," he said. He put the tab in his mouth and holding his hands as near as he could to the caps he struck a match and quickly lit the cigarette. He then held it with his left hand while he moved his right hand ower, palm downwards, fingers bent at the knuckle, and said, "Noo, watch this." He put the tab between the fingers of his right hand with the lit end pointing to his wrist. "Ye can't see the tab end at all," he said as he lifted his hand to his lips and had a drag. "Thanks for the fag," he said as he turned on his heel and walked off laughing.

"Hey ye can't de that," shouted Freddie. "Ye can at least give me a light."

The chap just laughed. "Bugger off yem, you're too young to smoke anyway."

Then Jackie Hansen jumped on his bike, quickly overtook the fella, and pulled his bike in front of him. "You better give him a light."

"And what are ye ganna de?"

Me and Matty pulled in behind Jackie – Matty got off his bike, gave me the handlebars, and went towards the man – Matty was as tall as him and a lot broader. I'd put the bikes against the wall, stood beside Matty, and pulled me knife oot.

"Hey it's all reet, I was only joking."

Freddie got his light, and as we cycled up Ocean Road he puffed away with his tab in one hand like the man had showed him, while he steered with the other. "We're all marras noo," he shouted out to us, ower his shoulder, just as he drove his bike into the trolley bus pole.

An air raid warden came running across the road – we thought he was gan' to help Freddie, but he ran past him and stamped oot the tab that lay in the gutter. "Ye useless nowt," was all he said as he walked off. We got Freddie back to his feet – his front wheel was a bit wonky, but he said he knew someone who could fix it.

Freddie and Matty lived up the Lawe Top so me and Jackie headed off up Fowler Street. As we stopped at the corner of Winchester Street, he asked me if I always carried a knife.

"Naw, but I was a bit worried being oot on me own in the dark on the way back. Me Da' gave it to me when I was fourteen. He said noo I was a man I should have me own knife."

"Can I have a look?"

"You won't see owt in the dark - I'll bring it in next Sunda'. Get there a bit early."

That Sunda' I'd shown Jackie the knife before the others arrived. I kept it behind me back in a cloth sheath me Mam had made for me, and which I pinned to the inside of my trousers. "With me jacket on naebody kna's it's there."

I showed Jackie the blade which I sharpened with a whetstone at least once a week. "You could shave with it," I boasted. "I haven't tried, like. I cut mesel' enough as it is. D'ye shave?" I asked, and when he said nowt I rubbed me hand on his chin. "Wye it's as smooth as a lass's." Jackie pushed me hand away – I thought he blushed a bit, but the others started coming in so I didn't say owt more. I'd started growing hair on me chin, and somewhere else as well, when I was thirteen, but then that was probably me Arab blood.

We were gan' doonstairs to the basement when we heard Sergeant Cummings' voice booming along the corridor. "I want ye in here for a minute, me bonny lads. Constable Douthwaite reckons you've been terrorising passers-by – and with a knife an' all."

We were nearly at the top of the stairs and I knew I wouldn't be able to get away when Jackie Hansen, who was just behind, pushed right into me. "Hey, watch where you're gannen'," I shouted, then I felt his hands inside me jacket and doon me trousers, so I pushed forward into Freddie, and telt him he was a clumsy nowt. He bumped into Matty, and there was a lot of pushing and shouting. Davey Corbett looked roond and pulled Matty and Freddie apart. Jackie had disappeared – he'd managed to slip oot to the yard. Sergeant Cummings told Davey that he should learn to keep order, and we trooped into the Charge Office where Douthwaite was standing, with a smug grin on his chops. Sergeant Cummings lined us up and told us that an acquaintance of Constable Douthwaite's had been set upon by a group of lads on bikes – they'd said they were police messengers – he'd given one of them a light and taken a tab in exchange, and they'd come after him – one of them had pulled a knife. It was pitch black, but he'd seen their faces when he'd lit the tab as they all had their caps off covering the light.

Freddie then told Sergeant Cummings what had happened. "Well if ye let him take the tab in the first place ye can't really complain."

"Aye I kna' but he wasn't even gan' to give me a light."

"Well, I dain't think they'd make a tale like that up, Constable Douthwaite, but I think we'd better find oot aboot the knife. Is any one of ye carrying a knife?"

We all said naw. "Aye well, we'd better give them a quick frisking."

"There's nae need to search them all, Sergeant," Douthwaite said with a malicious smile on his face, "he said the one who had the knife was the dark skinned one with wavy black hair. It's the Arab lad. They all carry knives and they'll slit your throat as soon as look at ye. I knew we shouldn't have taken him on."

"Gan on then, if you're so keen," the Sergeant replied. "Undo your jacket, lad," he said to me. Auld Douthwaite felt in me pockets and round me belt. When he found nowt he had another go and discovered the cloth sheath. "Here, see this Sarge," he said as he pulled it oot.

"What's that then, Mossie lad?"

"I dain't like to say, Sergeant," I mumbled.

"Well if ye dain't, I'd say it was a sheath for a cunningly concealed knife – mind ye'd be mad to put a knife doon there – if ye fell backwards ye could cut your bollocks off." He roared with laughter.

That miserable auld sod Douthwaite didn't see the funny side. "I don't think you're taking this seriously, Sergeant."

It was Freddie who came to me rescue. He'd worked oot what all the pushing and shoving was aboot, and why Jackie Hansen was missing.

"I kna' what he keeps doon there, Sergeant; he telt me the other day."

"Grass," Matty whispered – everybody heard it.

"Well, are ye gan' to tell us?" Jack Cummings asked.

I was wondering mesel' – I should have realised that he'd come oot with something dirty.

"When he gans to the barber, he asks for something for the weekend, like, and he can hardly gan oot with it in his hand noo, can he, so he made a little pouch in his troosers for his French

letters." He looked at auld Douthwaite who was still holding
the sheath out. "He puts them back in there when he's used
them, until he can find somewhere to hoy them, Constable
Douthwaite."

The auld fella pulled his hand away so fast he nearly fell ower.
Sergeant Cummings burst oot laughing, and he was nearly in
tears as auld Douthwaite left the Charge Room muttering "dirty
little sod".

After he'd recovered, Sergeant Cummings told us to bugger
off to the yard. As we were gan' oot he said to me in a quiet voice
that wouldn't carry, "And tell Jackie Hansen that if he pulls a stunt
like that again, he'll be oot on his ear, and ye alang with him,
Mossie-lad."

Jack Cummings was a canny fella. He had one of those deep
nasal Shields voices that you can hear a long way off. He was all
reet so long as you could put up with his little jokes – whenever
I came into the nick he'd always ask if I'd come to sign the
Coloured Seamen's Register. I'd told him that I was born in
Shields, and that the furthest I'd been on a boat was across the
Tyne on the Dodger, but he still kept on.

When I got oot in the yard Jackie had arrived back – he'd taken
the knife and hidden it in the wash house in his back yard. "I'll get
it for you when we've finished this morning."

"So you did have a knife after all?" asked Jimmy Clay.

"You're lucky, Mossie," said Davey. "If it had only been
Sergeant Cummings then he might have just given you a telling
off, but old Douthwaite's got it in for you, and he would have told
Inspector MacTomney." I'd heard stories about MacTomney – he
was a scouser who'd retired to Shields and had been called up as a
pensioner reservist. He was one of the old school and could come
doon on ye like a ton of bricks.

"So, if you did have a knife then you don't put your johnnies in
the sheath," continued Jimmy.

Jackie looked blank and asked, "What does he put in his sheath?"

Freddie Skee started laughing. "Wye he puts his cock in it, dain't ye, Mossie. Ye never heard of a johnnie, Jackie?"

Jackie started blushing.

"Dain't take any notice of him," I said. "When auld Douthwaite found the sheath for the knife Freddie said I used it to keep me blobs in."

Poor Jackie was none the wiser. "He means contraceptives, Jackie," Davey said. "Have you never seen one?" Jackie shook his head.

"Well I haven't either," I said, "and I've certainly never used one - and noo with Sergeant Cummings' big gob it'll be all roond the nick."

Matty Lightfoot said that he'd seen one. After his cousin Billy's ship had been blown up Billy's older brother had taken him doon to Tyne Dock to a house in South Eldon Street where lasses let ye de it to them for three bob - it was in case he wasn't saved next time his ship hit a mine. "Billy says they made him put one on before he had it – so after he'd finished he asked if he could have one to take yem to show his mates. They charged him thre'pence extra for it, even though they get them free from the American sailors."

"Right that's enough of that sort of talk." Davey was a bit straight laced, but I noticed that later that morning Jimmy, Matty and Freddie were having a quiet natter aboot somethin'.

After that Freddie was always making cracks aboot Jackie not knowing much aboot lasses, and particularly about having it off with lasses. I wasn't one to talk myself, but I would sometimes join in. What made it worse was that Jackie didn't like it, and would get annoyed which was, of course, just what Freddie wanted.

On the last Sunday of wor training Freddie and Jackie won the

team contest easily – Jackie was very quick, and Freddie knew
all the back lanes and short cuts. We were in the Police yard
afterwards, and Davey said to leave wor bikes there and we'd
walk to DiBresci's Café. "Do ye think there'll be any lasses there?"
Jimmy asked.

"There usually is. Wally Duncan's a nice lookin' lad and he
gives them an extra squeeze of red sauce," said Davey.

Freddie couldn't resist joining in. "I could give a lass extra
sauce, if she wanted it, and at least I'd kna' where to put it – not
like wor Jackie."

I'd had enough of Freddie getting on to Jackie so I went to
punch him between the legs, not too hard. He laughed and tried
to de the same to me, but I put my hand doon to stop him.

"D'ye want a knacker twisting contest?" he shouted out as he
made a sudden grab between Jackie's legs. Matty did the same
to Jimmy, and then Freddie shouted out, "He hasn't got any."
We all stopped and looked. Jackie took a swing at Freddie's head
that would have knocked him into the middle of next week if he
hadn't ducked. "Let's take his pants doon and have a look." Jimmy
Clay didn't need any encouraging, and soon him and Freddie
had Jackie on the ground, and then Matty joined in. Jackie
started screeching like a girl, and then he shouts out, "Stoppit, ye
bastards, I'm a lass."

"We'll soon see," said Jimmy as he started untying Jackie's belt.
He screamed again and this time he definitely sounded like a lass.
Davey pulled Jimmy off and shouted to the others to stop. There
was an awkward silence as Jackie got to his feet.

"Are you really a lass?" I asked. Jackie just nodded.

"He might be just saying it so we won't see his tiny cock," said
Freddie. "And he hasn't got any tits."

"I put a bandage round them to make them flat."

"You could just be saying that."

"One of us could feel them," said Davey.

Jackie looked down at his feet and then Jimmy Clay chipped in, "It's either that or your drawers off." He took Jackie's silence as agreement, and then moved towards him with a dirty grin on his face.

"Naw, not you. I'll only let Mossie do it."

Jackie unbuttoned his jacket top and then put his hands up his shirt and pulled things aboot a bit. I could see that he had a bulge on the right of his chest where he'd pulled the bandage doon. I moved close to Jackie and looked in his eyes, and asked if he was sure. He nodded so I put my hand up his shirt and onto his chest – it was a tit all reet, not that I'd ever touched one before. Then I had a sudden pain in me crotch that made me move back and bend forward – something had stiffened reet up of its own accord and had caught in me underpants. I turned roond and put me hands down me troosers to sort mesel' oot. Jackie was nearly in tears saying she thought I was different, and the others were killing themselves. I ran off a bit shouting over my shoulder that he was a lass all reet.

"Right, quiet down the lot of you." Davey tried to take charge. Jackie pushed her bandages back into place, and I managed to stand upright without the bulge in me troosers being too obvious.

"Well if you're a lass we're going to have to tell the Sergeant."

"We don't have to," I said. "Jackie is as fast on the bike as any of us, and she and Freddie beat me and Matty easy."

"Aye Jackie's all reet," said Matty.

"We're all marras," Freddie joined in, "and now we kna' he's a lass it makes no difference that he hasn't got a cock."

Davey looked a bit unsure of himself for the first time since I'd known him. "Yes, but he, I mean she, must have lied to the Sergeant when she signed up, and I'd have to report that."

"I didn't lie," Jackie muttered half to hersel'. Then she looked up. "I came along in my normal clothes to ask if they'd take a girl, but old Douthwaite was standing at the top of the steps, and he said that he'd just had to turn an Arab away" – nae prizes for guessing who that was – "so they certainly weren't taking lasses, and I should gan yem and knit some stockings for our lads at sea. I went home and asked me Mam to cut me hair very short. I told her that they would take me, but that I had to have short hair to get my helmet on, and that I'd have to wear trousers and ride a lad's bike. I took some of my brother Chrissie's clothes and his bike. He joined up in the RAF as soon as War broke out - he's a rear gunner and overseas somewhere. I'm going to join the WAAF as soon as I'm eighteen, but I want to do something for the War in the meantime, and I can ride a bike as well as a lad. When I went back Douthwaite was just leaving, muttering under his breath about Arabs, and he didn't look twice at me as I walked up the steps. Sergeant Duncan asked me my name and my age. I told him – Jackie Hansen, sixteen. My name is Jackie – short for Jacqueline and he never asked me if I was a lass."

Matty punched Freddie on the shoulder. "Did Jock ask ye if ye were a lass, ye scrawny nowt." We all laughed. Of course he hadn't asked any of us if we were lasses.

So that was how Jackie Hansen stayed part of the PAMs at Keppel Street nick. We all went along to DiBresci's and me and Matty had to put wor hands in wor pockets for six tupenny ice-creams – that was half of me pocket money from me wages gone.

As we were walking back to the nick, wor faces all smeared with monkey's blood – that's what we called the red sauce that Wally Duncan had squeezed all ower wor cornets – I managed to get next to Jackie and whispered that I was sorry for what had happened before. "I couldn't help it – I've never felt a lass's tit before."

She turned her head. "And you won't feel one again either, at least not mine, so just forget it, Mossie."

But I couldn't.

CHAPTER 2
OCTOBER/NOVEMBER 1940

Whenever the sirens went I'd be oot of bed, uniform on, and into the back yard for me bike. Me Mam always got up as well – after the raid in August she'd talked to the Rutherfords and they'd gone to the Council for a brick shelter for the back yard – they had a special metal frame which was then covered in bricks – three courses deep. Jimmy Rutherford got some mates to help him dig the foundations and then the Council workmen finished the job – it still cost over £100 which was a lot of money but the Council let us pay for it weekly. We were told what to keep in the shelter: blankets, a paraffin lamp, candles, wor gasmasks, a stirrup pump and a bucket - which Mr. Rutherford would de his best to fill up if he'd been oot at the booza. Me Mam would get into the habit of filling a thermos flask with tea in the evening just in case, but then after a week with no raids she'd forget to de it, and the next neet off would gan the sirens.

We were sometimes asked to come in of an evening even if there were no sirens or raids, just to help the Sergeant on duty. We would make tea, answer the phone and generally make worselves useful. Me and Jackie were in one neet when one of the Special Constables came in with a young fella in an RAF uniform who was definitely the worse for wear.

"He was working his way from the north foreshore back to *Pinckney's*, Sarge; he'd got as far as the *Catherine House* – they threw him oot for being a nuisance, and he can hardly walk. He's all reet if you had on to him - his name's Johnny Wallis."

The young lad focussed his bleary eyes on Sergeant Duncan, and broke into a chorus of *Kiss Me Goodnight Sergeant Major*.

'Jock' Duncan groaned. "I can't put up with that all night, Lenny," he said to the Special, Lenny Cummings – he was a blacksmith at Harton Colliery, which was a reserved occupation, but had joined the Police Special Volunteers. He had lived in Percy Street but had been bombed oot, and now him and his lass lived back with his Mam and Da' and his brother Alan in Adelaide Street. I knew his wife from the fruit and veg shop.

I was thinking to mesel' that the young fella was deein' a good impression of Arthur Askey when he slurs his words, but the Sergeant didn't appreciate it. "Can ye no shut your trap, laddie," he half shouted, half laughed. The young lad stopped singing and politely enquired in a very posh voice if the Sergeant hailed from fair Caledonia – I was surprised when Jock nodded an 'Aye', as I had always thought he came from Scotland, and then the useless nowt hanging onto Lenny's arm broke oot with, *"I belong to Glasgie".*

Jock shook his head. "Can ye no' take him back to *Pinckney's*, Lenny – he'll be mair trouble than he's worth if we lock him up - particularly if there's a raid."

Pinckney's was what we called the *Volunteer Arms* in Cambridge Street, where the RAF officers who looked after the barrage balloons were billeted. It was just round the corner from Maxwell Street.

"It's off me beat but I'll tyek him if ye want – could one of the lads come with me in case something else comes up and I've got to leave him for a minute."

"Aye, you go, Mossie – and Jackie, you go along on your bike and you can bring Mossie back. It's mainly downhill so you shouldn't have any trouble."

Johnny Wallis was nae bother but kept babbling on – mainly

aboot women, and he started using one or two words that he shouldn't have – Lenny said nowt, after all we were all lads, or so he thought, but I noticed that Jackie cycled on ahead after a bit. As we were walking doon Maxwell Street Johnny looked roond, and realising where he was, said to Lenny, "I say, old chep, could you point me in the direction of Peel Street, number 22. I have a lady friend there who will look after me. If I'm lucky she might give me something hot."

Lenny seemed to grab his arm even harder and quickened his pace, pulling him along. "I'm taking ye back to *Pinckney's*," was all Lenny said.

When we arrived at the *Volunteer* we took him straight upstairs – young Johnny found going up the steps a bit tricky, and it needed both of us to steer him up. A Sergeant met us and shouted for Johnny's mates to come and get him – they had arrived back half an hour ago, and were in a slightly better condition than Johnny was - they'd lost him outside the *Pier*. The Sergeant thanked us and asked if he could buy us a drink – Lenny declined but asked the Sergeant if he could do him a favour.

"When the little sod wakes up in the morning can ye tell him that if he gans roond to 22 Peel Street again to see Myra Wade, then there's a few lads who know her husband Harry who'll give him the hiding of his life – Harry's a mate of mine and he's away at sea."

The Sergeant shook his head. "I'll tell him but they don't always listen to what we say where women are concerned. There's a strict order that married women whose men are away are off limits, but they're a randy lot of buggers, and if it's offered to them they won't say no."

Lenny was about to say something but then the Sergeant put out his hand and they shook. "I'll do my best."

I knew Mrs. Wade and I could see the Sergeant's point – she was a bonny lass – she came to the fruit and veg shop and was always laughing and joking. Her Harry had been away for a good six months and she had no idea of when he was likely to be back.

"Right ye two," said Lenny, "bugger off back to the nick, I'm gan' to look in at the *Prince Albert* to see if there's any trouble there." Unlikely, but he'd get his pint.

"Do ye want me to ride, and ye get on the saddle?" I asked Jackie.

She said nowt - just moved forward along the cross bar and then muttered, "Hop on, if you're coming."

I managed to put me bum on the seat by holding on to her shoulders, and then she pushed off. She was a bit wobbly at first till she got the balance reet - I had my legs wide apart to help, and she started gannen' a bit faster. Although it was dark and I couldn't see much, I was very close to her, and it didn't need me to move very much forward on the saddle to feel her bum as it moved up and doon on the pedals. Well you can guess what effect it had on me - so I slowly moved me hands from her shoulders, under her arms and was holding her roond the chest. I couldn't feel a lot with her jacket and the bandages, but my imagination made up for it and she couldn't do owt about it – or so I thought.

We were nearly at the end of Maxwell Street noo and she had to turn up Derby Terrace. As we took the corner I got even closer and managed to nuzzle her neck.

"Gerroff," she said.

"But I've got to had on," I replied.

"Well get back a bit." And she took one hand off the handlebars and tried to push me back, but all she got had of was the bulge in me pants. Well the bike swerved, we hit a trolley bus pole side on, and next thing I knew I was lying on the cobbles. Jackie had managed to stay on and was astride the bike. I didn't get any sympathy. "Come on, Mossie, if you lie there much longer you'll get run over by a bus." I got to me feet. Me right hand was all chafed where I'd landed on the cobbles and me knees felt a bit bruised, but I'd live. She told me that I would de the pedalling, as she wasn't being touched up again, so she got on the saddle behind me. We'd just started gan' doon Fowler Street when she moved her hands from me shoulders to roond me chest, and then started gan' doonwards. She shouted oot, "How do *you* like it, Mossie?" Well I did like it, so I just said nowt but moved me bum back so I was nearly sitting in her lap and then she kissed me on the neck. I must have lost concentration as I suddenly heard a horn gannen' off and just avoided being knocked ower by an Army lorry. We got back into the yard and neither of us said owt, but when we'd finished the shift and were gan' yem I rode up Winchester Street with her. We went up the back lane, and after we'd both got off wor bikes I gave her a proper kiss just inside the back door – well, I'd never kissed a lass before but it felt like a proper kiss.

We'd always worked the same shifts so nae one thought it funny when we would come in and gan yem together; and her Mam thought nowt of it when Jackie came oot at neet with me, as she would just say we were on duty. It wasn't too difficult to find somewhere where nae one could see us with the blackoot on, and noo it was winter and we had to wear an overcoat Jackie wouldn't always put the bandage roond her chest – it led Sergeant Cummings to say one evening that Jackie was starting to fill oot. "Ye doing exercises, Jackie lad?" he'd ask. "Ye dain't look such a skinny nowt noo."

None of the lads guessed there was owt gannen on, and to them Jackie was just a mate, or so I thought at the time. But they were all desperate to have it with a lass. It was even worse with the War on when ye never knew when a bomb might drop on your heed - I found oot what Jimmy Clay was planning with Matty and Freddie. Jimmy had never forgotten the story aboot Matty's Cousin Billy Duggan having it off with a prossy, and had asked Matty to find oot the address where Billy had gone. Freddie had asked me if I wanted to gan with them but I said I wouldn't pay for it. He just said that he'd rather have it that way than not have it at all, and then get blown to smithereens. Well I left them to it, and it proved a good thing too.

I found oot what happened afterwards – we all did, but I had it from Freddie with all the details. Matty Lightfoot's Cousin Billy was home on shore leave and wasn't only happy to tell Matty the address, but said that he'd gan along with them and show them the ropes. The lass he'd had last time was called Annie, and he was keen to have another go with her. She was the youngest of the three and would only de it with young fellas that she liked. It was three bob and you had to bring our own johnnie or pay thre'pence for one. The house was in South Eldon Street – they usually picked up their men in the Tyne Dock pubs and then took them yem, so it wasn't really a proper knocking shop, but if they were in when you called they'd let you have it. With all the ships coming in, they were doing a roaring trade. The three young lasses were just doing their bit for the war effort – well it beat doing twelve hour shifts in a factory. The lads didn't want to gan looking for the lasses roond the pubs so decided to gan early evening aboot seven o'clock.

I knew when they were off, and happened to be in the Charge Office that neet with Davey Corbett. I'd been asked to turn in as Jimmy Clay, who should have been in, had sent a message to say he wasn't feeling well. There wasn't much happening, and I was making a pot of tea for Sergeant Duncan when the Specials started coming in - there were aboot six of them, including Lenny Cummings. Inspector MacTomney arrived and told the Sergeant that he was taking them down to South Eldon Street where there'd been a report of a disorderly house. "One of the neighbours had their front door nearly stoved in by a group of Norwegian sailors who were looking for the house where the girls lived, but they'd got the wrong number. They'd been banging on the door but the householder was in bed and wasn't going to answer. We're going in early - if we make any arrests they can be bailed and not held in the cells overnight, just in case there's an air raid. We'll take them down to the Tyne Dock nick."

"They expecting you?" asked Sergeant Duncan.

MacTomney paused. "I thought it might be better to wait till we get there – you don't want idle gossip to spread and warn them off." He said no more, and took the Specials off to the yard where the Black Maria was waiting.

I heard Jock muttering to himself. He looked at me. "D'ye hear that, son? He's going on to their patch with a gang o' Specials and not telling them."

I was more worried about Freddie, Matty and Jimmy who might find MacTomney and half a dozen Specials looking up their bare arseholes in aboot twenty minutes' time.

"I was just thinking, Sarge, as we're not too busy the neet, whether I could try oot a new shortcut to the Dock – I reckon I could be there in aboot quarter of an hoor. It might come in handy if we ever need to get an urgent message doon there, like."

He looked at me with a smile on his normally dour face. "Weel, don't break your neck, laddie. If you should happen to see Acting Sergeant Alec Dorothy, the officer in charge, you could tell him to put the kettle on, he might have some visitors. Mind, don't let the Inspector see you, he might get the wrong idea...." and I was off.

They'd demolished most of Holborn where the boarding houses for seamen used to be, but you could still get doon there and past the docks – ye had to be careful as the Home Guard would sometimes set up watch points ootside the dock gates, and if they thowt ye looked suspicious they could let off a few bullets. It was pitch black but I didn't slow doon, slithering roond corners with me boots on the cobbles, and I only came off once. I skidded up to the door of the house in South Eldon Street and banged on the cast iron knocker. I could see how the Norwegian lads had got the wrong door – the houses were downstairs and upstairs flats so you had four doors all together just like Maxwell Street. It was a while before the door opened and a woman's voice said, "Gerrin quick, then, if you're coming, or I'll have the wardens roond again." I left my bike against the winda ledge and went in. She was a woman aboot twenty five or six in a nighty which was half open at the front. She took one look at me and said, "Not another bairn. I'm sorry, son, I've already had to turn one away the neet - we're not a bloody nursery skyeul."

"I didn't come for that," I replied. "I've got a lass of me own, but I think a couple of me mates are here, and you're gan' to be raided by the polis in aboot five minutes."

"Ye bugger a hell – are ye sure?"

"I'm just on me way to tell the Dock nick to put the kettle on for ye'se lot when they take ye doon there. I better be off."

I was oot the door like a shot as I heard her shouting to the other lasses in the hoose to get their claes on. I jumped on me bike and headed off towards the Tyne Dock nick in Napier Street.

I'd met Sergeant Dorothy a few times. He didn't like the PAMs as it meant that he had fewer opportunities to bring any paperwork up to the main nick at Keppel Street – he liked to chew the rag ower a cup of tea with his auld mate Jock Duncan. He would usually find a way and would arrive if possible at dinner time so that Jock would take him doon to DiBresci's Café in Ocean Road where his son Wally worked. Me Mam knew Alec Dorothy from way back, and one of his sisters still lived in Maxwell Street. As I came through the door of the nick, he was sitting behind the counter with his feet up on a desk. "Well, look what the wind's blawn in," he said to no-one in particular. "A little Pamsy Mamsy." We were always getting cracks aboot being like girls. "Did Jock hev enough of ye, Mossie?"

"Aye, we weren't that busy the neet but ye might be – auld

MacTomney's bringing a bunch of Specials doon to raid a hoose in South Eldon Street where some lasses are having too many fellas roond."

"The bugger he is, and nae-one's thowt to tell us."

"Well, it was the first that Jock, I mean Sergeant Duncan, had heard of it. The Inspector had said not to let ye kna' but the Sarge didn't think it reet."

"Whereaboots is it?"

"Just before the railway bridge."

"Aw, he's not coming doon all this way just for the Andrews sisters." The look on my face must have given me away. "It's what we call the three lasses you're on aboot. They gan roond together and all hev the same hairstyle – they like the yanks an' all. They're nae real bother, and if they stayed in the back lanes near the pubs there wouldn't be any complaints, but they like to take the lads yem. Word gets roond where they live and you hev Norwegian sailors gannen roond trying to break the neighbours' door doon."

"Ye kna' aboot that too?"

"Wye everybody doon the Dock kna's. I sent one of the lads roond to give them a warning.

"Thanks for coming doon, Mossie. I take it that we dain't want MacTomney to kna' you're here." I nodded.

"Had on a sec, then." He went ower to the phone and gave the switchboard a number. "Hello, is that Arthur? Aye it's Alec here." The fella on the other end said something that made Alec laugh. "Two tins this time, Arthur, the usual for us, and one for Jock Duncan at Keppel Street - broken biscuits'll de for him. I'm sending a young lad up, name of Pam." He laughed as they exchanged a few more words.

"Gan on up to Wrights Biscuits. Arthur Davis'll be expecting you at the factory gate. Bring wor tin doon here and tyek the other one back for Jock. If MacTomney's here just gan strite back and tell Jock to get someone to bring the tin doon the morra'. If you can't avoid him, Sergeant Duncan sent you doon for some biscuits for the lads."

Ten minutes later I was getting close to the Dock nick with the biscuit tins in an auld flour sack in the metal basket at the front, and I was gan' dead slow – there was no sign of the Black Maria so I rode up to the front entrance. I saw the motorbike and sidecar at the last minute, but it was too late.

"Who's that?"

I said nowt, and was wondering what my chances were of making a dash for it when the light of a torch shone in my eyes. It went oot straight away – you were only allowed to flash your torch quickly in the blackoot.

"Is that ye, Mossie? It's all reet, it's Lenny."

"Aye, it's me but I'm not supposed to be here, Lenny – ye won't tell the Inspector, will ye?"

"That's the second time tonight I've been asked that. I just caught your mate Jimmy Clay running doon the back lane trying to keep his troosers up – he said you tipped them off. I'll say nowt, but you'd better bugger off quick or ye'll be in for it all reet - and you better get back to Keppel Street before we do or MacTomney's ganna' put two and two together."

I didn't wait to be telt twice, and as I pushed the bike off I heard Lenny asking what the bugger did I have on the handlebars – I shouted 'biscuits' ower me shoulder and was away.

I got back five minutes before a very unhappy MacTomney arrived in the yard. He didn't drop in for a chat. It was left to Lenny to tell the Sergeant what had happened.

What Lenny told to us PAMs later on in the yard was a bit different from what he'd told the Sarge - and I'll also tell ye what really happened inside the hoose as I had it firsthand from Freddie and Matty. MacTomney had gone on ahead with Lenny in the motorbike and side car. When the Specials got there, they parked the Black Maria in Hudson Street and went on foot to the house.

Lenny had been sent doon the back lane with another lad in case anyone tried to hoof it. They had a problem because not all the back doors had their numbers painted on. Lenny didn't want to shine his torch too much so they worked oot roughly where the door would be and each one stood on opposite sides a few yards away. A fella came oot of one of the back doors, trying to pull his troosers up, and ran straight into Lenny – it was pitch black in the lane. When Lenny asked him where he'd come from the lad said he'd been visiting his Aunty. "Hey dain't I know ye?" Lenny enquired and shone his torch into the face. "It's Jimmy Clay, you dirty little bugger. I kna' your Aunty – she lives four doors down from us in Adelaide Street."

"Ye won't tell on us, will ye, Lenny. It was me forst time, and I'd only just got started when Mossie telt the lasses there was gan' to be a raid."

Lenny just laughed, told him to bugger off, and shouted after him that he owed him a pint.

When the lads had arrived at the house they'd been invited in sharpish because of the blackoot – it was an upstairs flat, and when they got upstairs, Lizzy, the lass who'd let them in, had one look at Freddie and said she wasn't having it with a bairn. She knew Billy, and the other two looked auld enough, but she wasn't gan to get a reputation for child snatching. "You've got to be eighteen or look like it – syem as the pubs."

"Well, I'm the same age as them," said Freddie, "and I'm eighteen. D'ye want me to bring me birth certificate next time I come?" Freddie was a cheeky little nowt.

"Naw, there's another way," said Lizzy. She pulled oot one of the drawers in the table and took out a ruler. "If you're eighteen ye'll have six inches – get it oot and I'll measure it." The others started cheering Freddie on, but he just went backwards as Lizzy came towards him with the ruler, and he then turned, ran doon the stairs and oot the front door. The lads then paid their money and two of the lasses took Billy and Matty into the front room where there were two beds - Lizzy was gan to see to Jimmy in her bedroom. They had just got started when she heard me banging on the knocker. "I'd better gan," she said. "The neighbours complain if there's fellas waiting on the doorstep." The next thing those upstairs knew was Lizzy shouting blue murder to get their claes on - there was ganna be a raid. By the time she got upstairs Jimmy was half oot the back door, his troosers still dangling by his ankles, and on the way doon the back stairs. Billy and Matty were a bit further on with the lasses, and Lizzy had to gan in and drag Billy off Annie – he didn't want to stop. They'd just aboot got dressed when they heard MacTomney banging on the door and shouting "polis, open up".

Matty and Billy were aboot to take off doon the back stairs when Lizzy stopped them. "They'll be waiting in the lane for ye." She opened the drawer again and pulled oot a set of dominoes. "Sit doon and hev a game."

"Are ye daft?" Billy said.

"Of course I'm not and ye'se two are me Cousins."

When MacTomney and the Specials arrived at the top of the stairs, and pushed into the kitchen they saw Matty Lightfoot and Billy Duggan sitting roond the table playing dominoes with the two lasses - everybody had all their claes on and Lizzy says to them, "The two lasses are me lodgers, and those two are me Cousins, Billy and Matty. They just looked in to see me." Lenny Cummings and his mate came up the back stairs two minutes later – they'd seen nae one come oot the back door, apart from a lad who'd been visiting his Aunty who lived next door. MacTomney looked daggers at them. "You two just come over?" But he couldn't de owt.

He sent the Specials back to Keppel Street and paid a call to the Tyne Dock nick – he didn't mince words with the officer in charge, Sergeant Dorothy, and had asked him point blank if any one of his men had tipped them off. Alec Dorothy was half expecting it. "I doubt if they'd been tipped off about the neet, because I sent an officer roond there only the other day to tell them to watch themselves as there'd been a complaint when a group of Norwegian sailors tried to get into another hoose by mistake. They know we're keeping an eye on them so I doubt if they'll be using the house for any male visitors. I could have tolt you if you'd rung doon about the neet." MacTomney said nowt for a while – he knew Alec was right of course.

"There were two lads in there, Cousins, name of Lightfoot and Duggan, playing dominoes with two of the lasses."

Alec Dorothy who later told the tale said he could hardly control himself. "The Andrews sisters playing dominoes?" was all he could reply. "You sure there weren't any bugle boys waiting ootside as well!"

After everything had quietened doon Sergeant Duncan sent Davey oot to the Home Guard HQ down at the *Alum House* with a message. He then asked me to bring the biscuits in, and to make sure no one saw me with them. We went to the desk in the corner of the Charge Office and Jock opened one. "Broken biscuits – those will be the ones we're meant to have." He then opened the other tin – it was an assortment of their best makes: ginger snaps, bourbons, rich tea, Marie, custard creams and a few others. Jock whistled. "Alec does all right for himsel' – look at those. We'll just tell him that you got the tins mixed up." He paused for a minute. "If I leave this box lying about then it will either disappear, or we'll be up on a charge of black marketeering." He opened a drawer and took out two paper bags. "I'll take half, and you can have the other half. Your Mam and your young sister'll like them."

I thought for a minute. "Have you got another bag, Sarge?" He looked up. "It's just that Lenny Cummings could have tolt on me to the Inspector when he saw me ootside the Dock nick."

Jock picked up a bourbon, bit off a good half and started chewing. "Aye, and I bet he recognised the young lad coming out of the back door who said he was visiting his Aunty. And somebody who knew his mates were going to be there must have tipped them off, and I suspect Lenny would have worked that one out - he's not stupid, oor Lenny."

I said nowt. "You're pleading the fifth?" he asked. I'd seen enough gangster films to know exactly what he meant. He chuckled. "It's all right, Mossie, I can remember years ago when me and my very good friend Walter Heron saved one of oor fellow officers from being caught with his pants down. Here," he said, handing me a third paper bag, "you fill that one up and pass it on to Lenny."

"I'll drop it off on me way yem," I said, relieved.

We would often meet at DiBresci's in the evening and, so long as there were not many customers in, Wally Duncan was happy for us to sit there for an hour or two, even if we just had one ice-cream or a cup of coffee.

Mrs. DiBresci was not an Italian – she was called Little Audrey and was Big Audrey Waite's daughter. She was just like her Mam, tall and blonde, but she didn't have the same gob on her as Big Audrey. The Waites of Agnes Street were known throughout Shields. Big Audrey had a fish and chip shop in Dale Street and Harry Waite, who was away in Durham Jail, specialised in breaking into pubs. The three oldest lads were trawler men and hard as nails – and they looked oot for the two youngsters, Audrey and Dekka. When she was a lass Little Audrey had fallen for Tony DiBresci, the son of the DiBrescis who ran a café in Ocean Road and had a little ice-cream kiosk on the sea front just doon from the Casino before it was burnt doon. Tony was a couple of years older than Audrey and he was warned off more than once, but they eventually got married – they had to. Little Audrey now helped run the café and managed the fish and chip counter. When War broke oot Tony and Dekka joined up and that's when Wally started working there. He lived above the café and was treated like one of the family. His mother, Jock's first wife, had died when he was a bairn and he'd gone to live with his Grandmother for a while – he never got on with Jock's second wife and was more than happy to move into the café when the chance came up. The DiBrescis were interned when Italy joined the War but unlike the other Italian families weren't released. Mr. DiBresci was put on that boat to Canada which the Germans sunk and he went doon with the ship. Mrs. DiBresci came yem to Shields but died a few weeks later so Little Audrey ran the café with Wally.

That evening we heard all aboot the lads' visit to South Eldon Street in every detail – Matty was just beginning to tell us how far he'd got when Davey said to watch his tongue, looking at Jackie. Before she could say owt, Jimmy Clay jumped in. "Jackie's a lad so far as we're concerned, Davey. If we start watching how we behave, and what we say, someone's ganna twig." He looked at Jackie. "That's reet, isn't it, Jackie?" Jackie nodded and Matty continued. Jackie didn't usually blush anymore when we used rough language or talked aboot lasses, but I noticed her going a lovely shade of pink once or twice, particularly when Matty started telling us what happened after MacTomney had gone and Billy had asked for his money's worth from Annie. Lizzy said that she wasn't having anyone gan' into the bedrooms in case the polis came back, so Billy just grabbed Annie, pushed her under the table and... This isn't a dirty book so you're just ganna have to use your imagination.

CHAPTER 3
DECEMBER 1940 -
FEBRUARY 1941

There were mair ships coming into the Tyne than ever, and with all the mines in the North Sea some didn't make it. We still met up on a Sunda' morning even if we weren't wanted at the nick. One Sunda' in December it was just me and Jackie. I was hoping I could persuade her to come back to wor hoose, and we could sneak in the back yard and spend a few minutes in the air raid shelter. We'd done it a couple of times at neet, but you had to be quiet if someone came oot to the yard to use the netty. We did kissing and cuddling and such like, but Jackie wouldn't gan any further. It was a bright day but freezing cad with a north wind coming straight off the sea. You could still get on the pier then but the north foreshore was all blocked off with barricades, and if you got too close you might get shot. We stood for a while watching a tanker coming in. It wasn't too far oot when we heard a geet big explosion, and a huge spout of watter shot up in the air at the stern of the ship. It didn't gan under but lost all head way and was floundering in the swell. "It's hit a mine, Mossie, we'd better tell the Sergeant," shouted Jackie, and without waiting for a reply she sped off towards the Ocean Road police box. There was phone on the outside for emergencies, and Jackie told Sergeant Cummings aboot the ship – he said he'd contact the Naval HQ but unless the wireless had been put oot of action they would already have called for assistance. We headed back to the pier and went along as far as we could. Not long after, we saw five tugs heading oot. There were quite a few people watching. The tugs got lines on her and started towing her into the harbour. There was an auld fella besides us with binoculars who said that the ship was called the *British Officer* – he couldn't see the names of all the tugs but the *Joffre* and the *Langton* were there. They had towed her across the bar and were just past the entrance when there was a terrible grating sound as she grounded on a sandbank. The tugs couldn't shift her but managed to push the bows inwards so that she wouldn't block the channel - lines were tied to the pier to keep her from drifting oot. The tugs started taking off the crew – the dead and injured came first - we found oot later that fifteen had been killed. Two tugs had to stay oot to keep her stable.

"We'd better be getting back, Mossie." Jackie said, and off we pedalled. We would both be late for wor dinners so there was nae question of a quick cuddle in the air raid shelter. We stopped at the corner of Winchester Street, and just as we were about to part Jackie looked at me in a queer way, and said that Davey Corbett had asked her if she wanted to gan to the flicks with him, one neet. "They're showing *My Little Chickadee* at the *Palace* in Frederick Street." She looked at me. "He's asked me if I can go as a lass."

"Tell him naw then."

"Just like that."

"Naw, explain to him that if anyone sees you with him they'll say Jacquie Hansen, the lass, is gan' oot with Davey Corbett - and someone else who kna's there's a Jackie Hansen, the lad, who's a PAM like Davey, is ganna put two and two together. Tell Davey you'll gan as a lad and you'll ask the others. Ye can sit beside him if ye want, and let him run his hands up and doon yer legs." She gave me a thump and rode off laughing.

As I was pedalling ower the cobbles in Maxwell Street I saw

the Pastor from the Mission for Seamen on his bike just ahead
of me. It wasn't a good sign. When they saw him coming doon
the street people used to cross themsel's - well not us Muslims,
like. He was the one who called on families when a seaman had
been lost at sea. He was oot most days, and had started to look
more miserable each time you saw him. My heart sank when he
stopped at wor door. He took a piece of paper oot of his pocket
to check the address and was just gan to knock when I caught
up with him, and said I'd let him in. Me Mam was at the range
keeping the dinner warm, and was just ganna shout at me for
being late when she saw him. She slumped into her chair by the
grate. "It's Ali, isn't it, Pastor?"

He was as upset as she was. "Aye, I'm sorry, Mrs. Hamed. I had
the news in from the Federation Offices yesterday but couldn't
get round any earlier. You're my first call the day, but you'll not
be the last. *The Empire Wind* was sunk earlier in the month – it
was 250 miles off Ireland. A German plane attacked it and scored
a direct hit. Some of the crew managed to get away in lifeboats
and were picked up by other ships in the convoy, but most of the
engine and stokehold crew are missing presumed dead."

"Aye, it was me husband's ship."

The Pastor stayed for a cup of tea and me Mam even let him
have a spoonful of sugar. He asked her how she would manage
– the Mission had a hardship fund. The Pastor said a short
prayer and then asked me if I went to the Mosque – when I said
I did sometimes he suggested I should see the Imam to find out
whether they would be having any sort of ceremony. My Dad was
one of five Shields Arabs who'd gone doon with the ship. Their
bodies would never be found. My Mam asked who they were –
we knew two of them who were married to Shields lasses but the
others were single men who lived in seamen's lodging houses.

It wasn't long before word spread – most of Maxwell Street
knew that the Pastor had called at wor hoose before he'd left.

Bella Rutherford came in not long after, and she wasn't the only one.

There was a knock on the door aboot half past seven that evening – me Mam asked me to answer it. "Dain't let anyone in unless it's a friend of your Da's, Mossie. I can't put up with much more." I opened the door and there was Sergeant Cummings. "Can I come in, Mossie-lad?" I just moved back and he stepped into the room.

"It's Sergeant Cummings, Mam."

"I'm sorry to bother you, Mrs. Hamed, but we heard doon the nick that Mossie had lost his Da'." He looked at me. "Alec Dorothy was roond at his sister's this afternoon. I just called in to say how sorry we all were and to see if Mossie was all reet, and to tell him that he needn't come in for a bit if he doesn't feel up to it." It was a serious side to the Sergeant that I'd not seen before. I asked him if he wanted a cup of tea, but he said he wouldn't impose.

It was difficult for me Mam, and it became worse when she received a letter two days later from the shipping company expressing condolences for me Da's death, and that his wages would be stopped from the date of the sinking. Me mutha' then found oot that as me Da' was in the Merchant Marine, and not the Royal Navy, that she wouldn't be getting a war widow's pension either. She had Mary and me to look after and it would not be easy for her to work.

I was back at the shop on the Tuesda'. I couldn't just stop at home – there was nowt to de and me Mam was always talking aboot how we were ganna' manage. I also went into the nick that evening just to thank Sergeant Cummmings. I bumped into Freddie. "Ye comin' to the flicks on Thursda'? Davey and Jackie are gannen so I thowt I would as well – half past seven at the *Palace* in Frederick Street. Can I leave me helmet at your hoose in case the sirens gan off?" And he was away.

Freddie had a point – he'd probably asked the other lads as well, and if we were all in the flicks in Frederick Street when the sirens went off it would take us hoors to get back to Keppel Street all kitted up. I went doon the steps and along the corridor. Sergeant Cummings was in the Charge Office, and for the first time since I'd started he didn't ask me if I'd come in to sign the Coloured Seamen's book. I thanked him for coming to the house and asked him aboot gannen to the flicks.

"We've not had a raid for a while but that doesn't mean we won't get one – tyek your bikes with ye, and leave them in the sub-station at Frederick Street with your tin hats and your gas masks – if the siren gans off just pelt doon here – ye should de it in ten minutes. If any bombs start flying aboot take shelter where ye can."

When I asked me Mam if I could gan she wanted to kna' if I had enough money. She said it might be the last time – she was ganna have to take all me wages noo with nae money coming in. Me Da' had put some away behind the skirting in a tin box but it wouldn't last long. He had some rings and a watch that she could pawn or sell, but things were ganna be difficult even if she got a job. We'd just heard that women between eighteen and thirty who weren't married would be called up for war work, so there should be jobs aboot.

When I came back from work the next day me Mam had had a visitor - Said Hussain. He was Geordie Hussain's – that's Alice's man - brother and belonged to the same tribe as me Da'. When his Da' had died he'd taken ower the boarding hoose – the auld one in Holborn had been knocked doon, but he now ran one in Commercial Road. He'd come to give his condolences, but he also handed ower an envelope with £150 in. Me Da' had always lodged with the Hussains before he got married, and they had acted as his banker ever since. Me Mam knew nowt aboot the money. Arab men like to keep their finances to themselves, so

39

it wasn't too much of a surprise. When me Mam tolt me about it she said that she had decided that she wasn't gan to spend it unless she had to - she'd rather keep it for a rainy day. She'd taken £25 of the money to tide us ower until she could get a part-time job, but she gave the rest back to Said to keep for us. "Ye never kna' when you or Mary might need something," she muttered.

Said's boarding hoose was nearly always full noo with the War on, and some of the men staying there had regular work on the colliers that took coal to Lowestoft and London. Some of these men were looking for lodgings where they could settle doon a bit and Said had said that if me Mam was interested he could find her a lodger. Me Mam would have regular money coming in - it would also help Said as he had more than enough trade as it was. He went on to say that, if me Mam was thinking of looking for a job, he could take her on in the lodging house or the café that he ran next door. The lasses who worked there noo were likely to be called up for war work. He said that me Mam could gan part-time. I think that clinched it. Me Mam said she'd happily work in the café, but would have to talk to me and Mary aboot wor dinners and such like. She wasn't keen on taking a lodger though, but would think aboot it.

I wasn't really thinking too much aboot that mesel' at the time, to be honest – I was more worried in case Jackie might take a fancy to Davey Corbett – the problem was that because she was supposed to be a lad I couldn't very well ask Davey oot for a fight to settle it. Things didn't start very well on the Thursda' neet – auld Douthwaite was in the Frederick Street nick and wasn't ganna let us leave wor bikes till I telt him to ring Jack Cummings - he kept us waiting ootside while he did. He then said that if he had still been working at the *Palace* he wouldn't have let us lot of troublemakers in. I asked aboot afterwards, and he used to be a commissionaire there before the War – walking up and doon the pavement in a fancy uniform keeping order – it was all he was good for.

Davey Corbett was the only one who hadn't brought his bike – I hadn't tolt him. He was reet at the front and asked Jackie to stand beside him. The others in the queue didn't mind just one pushing in, but the rest of us had to gan to the back. When we got inside Davey and Jackie were sitting together in the back row, and we were split up all ower the shop. I was beside Freddie and after he'd lit up he spread his legs oot wide and they were rubbing up against mine – I wondered whether Davey Corbett was deeing the syem. But it was a good film and at least Davey couldn't walk Jackie yem – she came back on her bike with me. I managed to persuade her to come into the back yard and we had a cuddle in the air raid shelter – she had heard aboot me Da' and let me get me hands a bit further than normal. When I rode back with her to Winchester Street, she said Davey had asked her on the way oot of the *Palace* to gan again sometime without the others, but she had said naw as folk might get suspicious. "But if the others go I couldn't really refuse."

It was a cad winter that year and we were lucky that we had the Rutherfords next door. They got free coal so we bought ours from them for thre'pence a bucket – others charged a tanner, but we'd known the Rutherfords for years. Me Mam was working by then at Said's café as a waitress. She worked from nine to three so she had time to make wor breakfasts and see Mary off to school. She'd make us something for dinner – it was either sandwiches, or she might cook something the night before and put it in a billy can. Mary came ower to the shop for dinner and we had it upstairs with Alice Hussain and her three kids, Jasmin, Ali and Little Geordie. Jasmin was aboot fourteen noo, had just left school and was working in the shop. She had light broon hair, blue eyes, soft broon skin the same colour as mine, and at fourteen she was well built. Once or twice when I'd got close to her in the back shop I'd been tempted to try something, but if her mutha' found oot she'd kill us, so I kept me hands to mesel'.

Me Mam's wages weren't great but she had her own meals at the café, and would sometimes bring some left-owers yem – with that, and whatever spare fruit and veg I could pick up from the shop, we were not as badly off as some. I was still always hungry, but most folk were as well. We had heavy snow in February and it was freezing – try riding a bike in the dark ower cobbles covered in ice and snow, and ye find oot what us PAMs were up against. There were so many patches on me uniform troosers that me Mam said I looked like I was wearing a quilt.

It was a Saturda' neet when things started getting serious – the fifteenth of February 1941 – not a date I'll forget in a hurry. The sirens went off just after eleven o'clock – I'd not long been in bed and had just started to warm up so I didn't fancy the idea of getting oot into the cad, but it's what ye had to de. I put on one of me Da's thick jumpers under me uniform, grabbed me helmet and me gas mask, and was oot the door and on me bike just as me Mam and the Rutherfords were piling into the shelter. Me Mam had a flask, and a stone hot water bottle that she'd left in the oven to keep warm. Mr. Rutherford and Jimmy had both been doon the *Auld Mill* and they'd need the bucket. I was happier to be oot in the open air. There was still some sna' and ice on the groond and I went steady. By the time I got to the nick I could hear the sound of planes, and the ack-ack guns were blazing away. It was a pitch black neet with nae moon and I thought to mesel' that we might still be lucky, but it turned oot to be a big raid. We learned later that there were about 130 enemy planes in the skies from Berwick to Hull - bombers and minelayers coming ower in waves. We were all together in the basement. Sergeant Ernie Leadbitter was on duty - he was a real auldun' and only worked neets. He would deal with any calls to the nick with help from us, if he needed it. Sergeant Cummings came in muttering aboot the Germans not letting you have any rest – Ernie told us later that Jack had just returned from a session in the *Douglas*. "I'll gan doon to the pier and see what's gannen on, Ernie. I'll ring in from the Ocean Road box – if you hear nowt send a couple of the lads doon." The guns were still blazing away, but there had been no bombs, and no calls for assistance. Jack Cummings didn't call, and at about quarter past twelve Ernie asked Freddie and Wally Duncan to bike doon to the front. "Dain't hang aboot – see if you can find the Sergeant and then come back – if any bombs start coming down, head straight for the nearest shelter."

Aboot ten minutes later we heard the sound of an enemy plane, as though it was owerheed, and then there was a loud crash. The phones started ringing, and it needed Ernie with Davey and Jimmy to handle the switchboard – an enemy plane had come doon in Bents Park and all officers on duty were tolt to get to the sea front. Three fire tenders at Keppel Street were sent oot, and the auxiliary fire service was alerted. Aboot ten minutes later Freddie and Wally came tearing in from the yard. Freddie was babbling on so quick that we had a job to catch what he was saying. "We've got one. We saw it all - the ack-ack gunners hit a Henkel. It started to lose height then it flew strite into a balloon cable – its wing broke off and it came doon like a rocket reet in Bents Park, just off Beach Road. It's blazing away. The crew'll be bornt to a crisp, but the pilot bailed oot – he landed on the trolley bus wires at Sea Road by the pier, and he's frizzling away dangling heed first. They're trying to get a ladder to him, but they'll have to be careful in case he's live."

"Will he try to shoot them?" Jackie asked.

"Naw, ye stupid nowt. I dain't mean *a* live – I mean live from the wires. They said he was jerking aboot as though he had St. Vitus's Dance."

Just then we heard the sound of bombs gan' off. It came from the seafront. The other German planes were using the blaze to guide them in. We had some more calls and then Ernie took a breather. "Reet," he said to Wally and Freddie, "you two have had enough excitement for one neet. Ye can stay here and help with the phones – Davey, you go down to the seafront with Mossie and Jackie – they may need messages passed along down there. But be careful, and if any more planes come in dropping bombs you take cover."

We couldn't wait to get there and dashed oot into the yard for wor bikes. We started off tearing along Keppel Street, but Davey skidded on the ice and went flying. After that we had to slow doon. We went straight into Denmark Street, and I shouted to Davey to ask if we could cut up to Ocean Road to see the dangling pilot. He said we should gan straight to the wrecked plane where most people would be. Jackie then piped up and said, "Please Davey – if we went to the plane first we could be sent anywhere for messages and not see the pilot." Had it been just me then I'm sure that Davey would have insisted, but I dain't think he wanted to say naw to Jackie, so he said we'd need to be sharp about it. We turned up Shortridge Street to get to Ocean Road instead of going straight on. We'd just turned into Ocean Road and could see a fire tender with a ladder oot and an ambulance on the corner of Sea Road - then there was a blast like I've never heard since – not even when they bombed the Market Place. There was a sheet of light, and then we were all hoyed off wor bikes onto the cobbles. The windas that hadn't been boarded or taped up were all blown oot and when I came to, as well as being bruised, I could feel something in me foreheed just ower me right eye. Davey came ower. "Are you all right?" Then Jackie appeared. "There's blood all down your face, Mossie."

I put my hand up to my foreheed. "Aaa." I felt a pain as my finger touched a piece of glass. "Can one of ye pull this oot." Davey sat on his hunkas in front of me. The blaze from the plane had lit up the sky, but he needed his torch to see properly. He pushed me helmet reet back and carefully took had of the glass

spelk which was just ower me eyebrow and very gently pulled
it oot. "We'll have to stop the bleeding and you might need
stitches." Jackie pulled oot her handkerchief and held it tight to
my heed. There'd been a dead silence for aboot five minutes after
the blast, and then we heard the sirens coming from all ower.
Davey said he was gannen off to where the plane was, and asked
Jackie to try to get me to the ambulance just doon the road.

"Aw, it's only a scratch." I hated fussing. I was all reet once I
got to me feet, but we decided to walk on with Jackie pushing the
two bikes as I kept dabbing me foreheed with the hanky. They
were just putting the pilot into the ambulance – it was one of
the auxiliary ambulances with a woman driver and a first aider. It
wasn't like a proper ambulance, but was a saloon car that had had
the back roof cut away and replaced with metal plates so it looked
like a van and had more room inside. They were in a hurry to
get off but the first aid lass had a look. "You should really have
it cleaned and stitched, but if we take you to the clinic you'll be
lucky to be seen tonight – there'll be a lot of casualties over there.
There must have been an unexploded bomb on the plane the way
it went up, and there were policemen and firemen all round it."
She was a nice lass, only aboot twenty, and very well spoken. "I'll
do what I can now, and if you think it'll need stitches, you can
go to the clinic at Chichester tomorrow or you can see your own
doctor." That wasn't gan to happen – me Mam hadn't been able
to keep up the doctor's panel payments after me Da' died, so it
was the clinic or nowt.

"Hurry along, Glenda," shouted the driver, a big lass. "The
sooner we get shot of this one the sooner we can get back."

Glenda dabbed the cut with a cotton wool ball soaked in
something that stung like blue murder, then put a lint dressing on
and tied a bandage reet tight all roond me heed. Jackie laughed.
"You look like a wounded soldier now, Mossie."

"Aye and he'll likely have a scar for a bit, so don't frighten any lasses!" Glenda laughed, got into the ambulance and off it went. As we rode up Seaview Terrace we could see the scene, and as we got closer it got worse. We heard more planes coming in, and more bombs were dropped on the Lawe.

There was nowt left of the plane, and the three fire engines that had been close to it were on fire and completely wrecked. There were bodies all roond and we could hear the groans. A few were standing, and Davey was talking to a big fella with what had been a police uniform hanging off him in rags. Davey came ower when he saw us. He was as pale as death but still in control of himself. "Jackie, get back to the nick and tell Ernie to call out all the ambulances he can, and we need doctors here as well; there must be about twenty injured. Officer Milburn says they were putting out the fire when it went up. He reckons there was a mine in the plane that they hadn't dropped, and the heat from the flames must have set it off. We'll also need a couple more fire engines to douse the remains. One of the survivors tried to ring from the Marine Park box but it must have taken some of the blast, and the phone's out of action."

Just then, one of the bobbies who had been going roond the bodies shouted ower. "If you're off to the nick you'd better tell them that the dead officer's called Cummings."

Constable Milburn, who was standing close by in a state of shock, said that he'd been talking to the Sergeant just a few minutes before the explosion.

As Jackie pedalled off, Davey turned to me. "Mossie, you get down to the Ocean Road box, and try ringing in from there. See if they have any orders for us but tell them we'll almost certainly need more messengers." He paused. He was obviously thinking as he talked. "Then go to where the other bombs have dropped, see who's in charge there and tell them what's going on down here." He then looked twice at me. "I'm sorry, Mossie, are you all right?"

"Wye aye," was all I shouted as I pedalled off.

The outside phone in the Ocean Road box was working, but one of the firemen was on the line to ARP headquarters in Chapter Row and I had to wait a while. When I was given the phone I managed to speak to Jimmy Clay who was on the switchboard. Jackie had just arrived and was giving all the details to Ernie Leadbitter. Jimmy said they'd had a call from the *Lord Nelson* in Woodbine Street and they needed the rescue team, and anyone else who could help, at Brodrick Street. Several houses had been demolished and there were people in them. "Ernie's ganna' put Freddie on the switchboard and me, Matty and Wally are coming doon as soon as we can. It was terrible news aboot Sergeant Cummings. Ernie's gan to have to break the news to Jack's wife, poor soul - she's in the shelter with the other wives."

When I got to Brodrick Street there were only a couple of air raid wardens in the ruins. There had been a direct hit and a couple of houses were completely demolished. "They're sending oot the rescue teams," I shouted as I jumped off me bike and went ower to them. They were clearing bricks with their bare hands. One of the wardens looked up. "There's an auld couple in here. They wouldn't gan to the shelter when I telt them to. We think there's someone else next door as well, a young couple with a bairn - they had a Morrison shelter in the kitchen." He looked at me and saw the bandage. "Here, lad, ye stay with Geordie – he'll hand you the bricks and ye hoy 'em ower there. I'll have a look further on," and he scrambled ower the debris to the hoose next door. We were making slow progress, and Geordie shouted to me to tell him strite away if I smelt any gas. Broken mains were one of the hazards of rescue work – if there was a gas leak everything could blow up. I saw two figures half running half walking doon the street toward us. They were polis – they had on their greatcoats and tin hats.

Bomb damage in Brodrick Street

"There's help on the way – young Douggie here got to a phone at the *Lord Nelson*."

The voice sounded familiar, but me ears were still ringing from the blast. As he approached he saw me and shouted, "Is that ye, Mossie-lad? Ye look as though ye've been in the wars."

I thowt I was seeing a ghost. It was Jack Cummings all reet – you'd recognise his voice anywhere. "You're not deed then, Sergeant Cummings?"

"Not yet, Mossie-lad. I was lucky - I decided to come ower here when I heard the bombs dropping, and then I was blawn off me feet with the blast from the plane."

"It's just that they said that the deed polis was called Cummings and we thowt it must be ye."

"Oh bugger and sh**e," he said angrily, "it'll be young Lenny Cummings – he was helping the auxiliary firemen."

"I kna' Lenny," I said.

The fella next to Sergeant Cummings asked was I sure – his voice sounded on the verge of breaking into sobs. "He was a good mate, was Lenny – he can't be deed. I was just oot for a drink with him and his lass a couple of neets ago."

"I dain't kna' for sure," I said, "but there was one deed polis, and someone said his name was Cummings. Henry Millburn thowt it was ye, Sergeant, because he'd been talking to ye just before."

Jack put his hand on the other lad's shoulder. "Let's wait till we get back to the nick before we're certain. There's more than enough to de here, and we need to keep alert."

Just then a lorry came slowly doon the road – it was the rescue squad. A fella jumped oot and ran ower. "We'll take charge noo, lads." He looked at Geordie. "Do ye kna' if anyone's missing?"

"Aye, Mr. Scott. There's an auld couple in here and we think there might be a couple with a bairn in a Morrison next door."

Mr. Scott was a small, stocky man who seemed to kna' what he was deein' and he looked roond for a minute. "We'll have to double check when it's light but we'll have to close off all this block. Can ye find oot the street numbers, and then warn the people in the shelters that they may have to go an emergency rest centre unless they've got friends or relatives who can put them up. Ye'll need to alert the billeting officer."

He looked at Jack Cummings. "The other crew's been sent to St. Aidan's Road. All the ambulances are doon at the plane crash." He paused and glanced at me. "Is the lad a messenger?"

"Aye, it's Mossie Hamed. I was thinking of sending him back to the nick anyway as he's injured."

"Ye gan back as quick as ye can Mossie," said Mr. Scott. "Tell them we need at least one ambulance here and another at the Lawe, and a couple of fire crews in case we have a gas explosion or a water main bursts."

"Three fire engines were blown up doon at the Bents," I chipped in.

"They can ask for help from other forces – it depends where the Germans have dropped their bombs. If there are any more of you lads who could help us here send them doon – any pair of hands will de."

"There's some messengers on the way."

"Good, off ye gan, lad."

As Mr. Scott went ower to the ruins and started organising two teams to get rid of the rubble, I turned to Jack Cummings. "I'll get back as quick as I can. Jimmy Clay said that Sergeant Leadbitter was gan to tell your wife that you're deed."

"Aw, the poor hinny. She'll be having a brandy for the shock, and she'll need another when she hears I'm still alive. Aye, ye get back." He shone a light on my forehead. "Ye stay at the nick, Mossie, or gan to the Chi clinic. I dain't want to see ye oot here again the neet - your mutha's got enough on her plate as it is." He patted me on the shoulder and off I went.

I didn't get yem until after five, when the sirens sounded the all clear. It was not a neet I'll forget in a hurry. I had to gan with Sergeant Leadbitter to see Mrs. Cummings so I could tell her that I'd seen Jack with me own eyes. She grabbed ahold of me and was slobbering and crying, and saying "bless you, son". It was busy at the nick – Lenny Cummings was the only officer killed but six others had been injured and three of those were serious. Superintendent Lamont had come in, and he decided to wait until the all clear before telling the relatives. He went doon to the Bents with Inspector MacTomney. When they got there everything was well organised. There were no senior officers there, but

Davey Corbett had seen to things for himself – the deed and the wounded had all been moved away from the wreckage, and Davey had insisted that the first doctors and nurses that arrived checked everyone quickly to see who needed taking to the Ingham first. He'd asked the fire crews that arrived to help to carry the injured to the ambulances before they started dousing the flames.

The Super was impressed and Davey got a commendation from the Chief the next day. MacTomney took ower and Davey was sent back to the nick to write up a report on what he'd seen and done.

News had spread of the casualties and a lot of officers came back to the nick to find oot who'd been injured. The firemen had it worst – two had been killed outright and two who were in the Ingham had been given the last rites. More than seventeen were injured that neet - the 'more than' was me – I was included in the official report even though I tolt them it was only a scratch.

When I got yem I found the hoose in a state – most of the front windas on wor side of the street had been blown oot when the mine had gone off, so we weren't the only ones with empty panes. The shops and big houses on Fowler Street had boarded their windas up or put tape on them, but naebody had bothered in the side streets. And I wasn't the only PAM to arrive yem with a puncture. That was soon mended, but it was weeks before we had any glass in the windas – we'd used what we could to board them up and keep the cad oot.

When I'd left the nick Matty, Wally and Jimmy had not returned, and I only found oot what they'd been up to a couple of days later. Mr. Scott had set them to work with the men searching the ruins for survivors. They were shifting bricks and lifting the roof tiles and beams when Wally suddenly shouted oot. He'd put his hand into something bloody and soft – he'd found a deed body. Mr. Scott took ower. The auld couple had been in bed when

the house had blown up and they'd been badly cut up by the blast
– Wally had to gan and be sick, but Matty took ower from him
and helped Mr. Scott to lift a heavy beam off the bodies while
they were pulled oot and laid in the road. The young couple in
the Morrison were much better off – it took nearly an hoor to dig
them oot but they were all reet – they were badly shaken and the
bairn was crying but they had survived. Mr. Scott wanted them
taken to the Ingham to be checked ower, but no ambulances had
arrived so he sent Jimmy Clay to gan up to St. Aidan's where the
other bombs had dropped to see if there were any there. Jimmy
was lucky and he found the ambulance team that had looked
after me. He'd ridden back in front to show them the way, and
helped them get the family into the ambulance. He took a real
shine to Glenda, who had put me bandage on, and it was all he
could talk aboot. Matty had stayed with the rescue team until
daylight, and would have stayed on longer, but Mr. Scott sent him
back to the nick and told him to gan yem – he'd done more than
enough. A couple of days later Mr. Scott called into the nick to
see Sergeant Duncan. He'd been so impressed with Matty that he
wanted to see if he would be willing to work permanently with
the rescue team. They did more than just rescue people, they had
to make the buildings safe, and they also demolished buildings
and helped the Council oot with repair work. Some of the men
were volunteers who turned out if there was a raid, but there
were others who worked permanently and Mr. Scott wanted to
offer Matty a job. Jock was not too keen but he said that he would
not stand in Matty's way if that was what he wanted, and he gave
Mr. Scott Matty's address. Matty didn't take long to decide – he'd
not stopped talking aboot Mr. Scott and the work he'd done the
neet of the bombing, so we lost a PAM. We still kept in touch and
Matty would meet up with us when we went to DiBresci's Café.

CHAPTER 4
FEBRUARY/MARCH 1941

It was only a few days after the raid that there was a knock on wor door. It was Mr. Henderson, who lived a couple of doors doon. He was just gannen to the gasworks for the ten o'clock shift. He'd found a fella in uniform beaten half to death crawling oot of the back lane between Peel Street and George Street. "I cut through that way and I nearly fell ower him. At forst I thowt he was drunk, but I struck a match and there's blood all ower him. I haven't got time to stand roond. I kna' ye work for the polis so I thowt ye wouldn't mind stayin' with him. I'll call the polis and an ambulance from the Derby Street box. It's near enough on me way."

I put me overcoat on, got me bike, and followed him to where the lad was. He was starting to groan a bit. I shone the bike's front light on him and bent doon to have a look. His nose was flattened, he had a couple of teeth missing, and one of his eyes was shut but I still recognised him. It was that Johnny Wallis who Lenny Cummings had brought in a few weeks back. He was starting to come roond and I tolt him that an ambulance would be along in a minute. Just then I saw a bike's lamp coming towards me. "Mossie?" a voice called oot. It sounded like Jimmy Clay. "Aye, ower here."

Jimmy pedalled up to me. "An ambulance is on its way – it's one of the auxiliaries. There's just been an accident at the junction of King Street with Mile End Road – a lorry drove smack

into a cart. The Sarge said I better come up and look oot for
the ambulance to make sure it found its way – the drivers dain't
always kna' their way doon the back lanes. Jock has had to call oot
all the beat bobbies to the scene to keep the traffic flowing. He
said one of us should gan to the hospital with the victim and see
if he's got owt to say."

He was off away before I could tell him who the lad lying on
the cobbles was. He came back in five minutes with an ambulance
following up. He jumped off his bike and ran ower to me quick.
"It's Glenda," he said. "She recognised me from the other neet. I'll
gan up to the Ingham with them."

Glenda and the driver both got oot and gave the fella a good
looking ower. "He's been given a hiding all right. He's hit his head
on the cobbles and is badly concussed." Glenda looked at us. "I
think his ribs are either broken or bruised, and he might have
internal bleeding. We'll have to lift him on the stretcher. You two
strong lads can give us a hand."

The driver was a big lass called Gertie, and she got us organised
so that the fella only groaned a bit when we lifted him into the
back of the ambulance. When we'd finished Glenda asked me if I
was the lad who'd had the glass in his foreheed the neet the plane
crashed. When I nodded she shone her torch in me face. "You
didn't get it stitched then?"

"Naw, we had enough to de when I got yem with all the windas
oot."

"Well you'll be all right so long as you take your girlfriend out
in the blackout; she won't see the difference."

Jimmy started laughing, and then so did Gertie.

"Aw, shurrup, man. Anyway, I haven't got a lass."

"You should get yourself down to the hostel for the women
auxiliaries," says Glenda. "We're cooped up in there with nothing
to do, and we don't like going out on our own."

I didn't like the way the conversation was going, and neither did Jimmy for that matter. "I could take ye oot, Glenda, if ye'd like, and I haven't got any scars."

Gertie didn't give Glenda the chance to answer. "You can do your courting some other time. We need to get this fellow to hospital. Can you lead the way again, Jimmy, till we get out on to the street."

"I'll come up to the Ingham with you," said Jimmy, "then I can report back to the Sergeant."

I spoke up. "I kna' who he is. He's Johnny Wallis. Me and Lenny Cummings had to take him back drunk to *Pinckney's* the other week."

Glenda and Gertie looked blank.

"It's the *Volunteer Arms* in Cambridge Street where the RAF officers are billeted."

"They'll want to know as soon as poss," said Gertie. "Could you ride round and tell them? They'll send someone up to the Ingham to see how he is."

"Aye, I will. Jimmy, when you get to the hospital can you ring doon to the nick and tell Sergeant Duncan. He'll want to kna'."

When I got to *Pinckney's*, the Sergeant was in the bar and seemed as though he'd had a few. He recognised me from the last time. "Is young Johnny Liszt again?" He asked, laughing. My face must have given me away. "Brahms and Liszt, pissed." He was a cockney and doon Sooth they speak in rhymes apparently.

"Naw. We found him half kicked to death in a back lane off Peel Street. They've taken him to the Ingham."

"Well, he had it coming, the dirty little sod, having it off with a married woman, and her husband away at sea. I warned him off after your china called last time but he couldn't leave it alone. Mind, he's not the only one who calls roond Peel Street to see Mrs. Wade."

He didn't seem too bothered about doing anything else, so I asked him if someone would gan roond to the Ingham.

"I suppose it'll be me. I'll have to tell the Squadron Leader. He's down at the foreshore. I'll give him a call and then pop over to the Hospital to see how Johnny's faring."

"The first aider said he had concussion and broken ribs."

He was only half listening as he drained his pint down. "He won't be so pretty either with a broken nose and teeth knocked out." He looked at me and moved a bit closer, breathing sour beer all ower me. "Although some ladies like a lad with a scar on his face." He chuckled away to himself, and I left him to it.

I went back yem, and didn't hear what had happened at the nick till the next day, when Jimmy Clay came roond to wor hoose. Me Mam was just putting oot the tea. I'd brought home a couple of onions from the shop the day before. Mrs. Hussain knew someone with an allotment and got a few noo and again, but only sold them to her regular customers at thre'pence each. She had hoyed them at me as I was leaving, and said they were gan' rotten. Well the ootside layer was a bit mouldy but they were fine inside – and she knew it – she did what she could to help. Me Mam had managed to get hold of some corned beef. Jimmy Rutherford had a mate who worked doon the dock, and he'd been selling it to his mates for a shilling a tin. Jimmy hadn't charged us as me Mam often let Bella have a few spuds or some veg that I'd brought back from the shop. We were having panacklety made with the corned beef – it smelt tasty and me Mam could see Jimmy Clay's mouth watering. "Ye'll have had your tea, Jimmy."

"Aye," he said, his face dropping, "it was pea and ham soup without the ham. It's the third time this week we've had it. I'm still hungry though."

"Si'doon then, I'll give ye a small bowl of this." He didn't even try to say naw for politeness sake, and when it came he wolfed it doon. That's the way it was in those days, even if ye had next to nowt, ye'd still share it with your friends and neighbours. We'd made a space for him and he sat next to Mary – I noticed that she kept looking at him with her big broon eyes. Wor Mary was nearly fourteen and was starting to grow into a bonny lass. She'd started her rags already, and had been gan' on aboot getting a bra', but me Mam said she wasn't auld enough.

Jimmy had asked Glenda to gan oot with him and she'd said all reet, so long as he brought a friend for big Gertie. He asked if I would come with him - I said naw straight away. I had nowt against Gertie, but I knew how I'd felt when Davey had sat beside Jackie at the flicks, and she would find oot soon enough that I was gannen' oot with someone else. "I've got nae money to gan oot with. All me wages gan' to me Mam, and then we just aboot manage." Jimmy said nowt – his mooth was full of biscuit. Me Mam had put oot a plateful of the ones I'd got from Wrights and Jimmy was trying to eat them all himsel'.

"Why dain't ye ask Davey – he's your mate, and would be happy to de you a favour."

Jimmy swilled the biscuit crumbs doon with a mouthful of tea – milk but nae sugar. "I already have and he said naw. I said it would de him nae harm and he blushed a bit, so I asked him if he had a lass - he said he might have but he was keeping it to himself."

Well I was starting to get worried then because I knew exactly who Davey had in mind. Jimmy didn't notice the funny look on my face, and said he'd have to ask Freddie.

"Ye should de," I said, "he's always gannen' on aboot lasses, but dain't tell him how big she is."

Jimmy laughed. "He'll be all reet. His eyes'll be level with her belly button." Mary burst oot laughin'. Me Mam said not to be cruel, but she was deein' her best not to crack her face with a smile.

There was a tap on the back windas. "It'll be Jackie," I said as I got up to open the back door. "We thought we'd gan for a bike ride." And that was probably all we'd de. Jimmy Rutherford had got hold of some chicks from a mate of his. Me Mam had agreed to go halvers, and we were rearing them in the air raid shelter, so it was off limits for a quiet cuddle.

When Jackie came in me Mam made another pot of tea. I told Jackie quickly how Johnny Wallis had been given a reet hiding and was in the Ingham. Jimmy then asked, "Did ye hear what happened last neet at the nick?"

Me and Jackie both shook wor heeds.

"I'd rung Sergeant Duncan from the Ingham and he said to get back as soon as I could. The doctor said that Johnny couldn't remember owt, but that he wouldn't be in a fit state to be interviewed until the next day. So I had a word with Glenda, and then shot doon to Keppel Street. I've got a date with Glenda, Jackie, but Mossie here won't come with me and gan oot with her friend Gertie."

Mary straight away asked Jackie if 'he' wanted to gan oot with Jimmy and Glenda – she said Gertie was a lovely little lass. She was trying not to laugh but Jackie still started blushing and said that his Mam didn't like him gannen oot with lasses. Jimmy didn't say owt but went on with his story.

"When I got back there was a lot of people aboot and the Super was in the Charge Office with Jock. Then the Black Maria arrived, and they started unloading boxes and tins: corned beef, sugar, tins of tabs, bottles of whisky and there was even some oranges. The Super came oot. 'I've asked Sergeant Duncan to make a list of everything that comes in, and if one tin goes missing then someone will be sacked. There's a war on, and I'm not having any of my men acting like black marketeers.'

"It turned oot that a Home Guard lorry had been gan' along King Street, and had driven reet into the side of a cart that was crossing the junction with Mile End Road. The driver of the lorry had had a skinful in the bar of the *Alum Hoose*. It was pitch black and he hadn't seen the cart. The horse had to be put doon, and

Jack Simcox the driver's got a broken leg and was taken up to the Ingham. The trolley buses couldn't get through and the fire brigade was called oot to clear the road. It was when they started picking up the tins and boxes from the cart that they realised it was all black market."

"Like wor corned beef," I said smirking.

"Shurrup, Mossie," said me Mam.

"CID were gan to investigate where it had come from, and the Super had sent one of the detectives to formally arrest Jack Simcox and see if he was well enough to talk to us. He'll say nowt though.

"Jock was trying to do the list, but he also had to organise the relief to deal with the traffic control, and to allocate some bobbies to help CID. He was not in the best of moods when this Squadron Leader from the barrage balloon squad walked in and tapped on the counter. Jock went ower and asked, 'Is it about Johnny Wallis?' 'It is as a matter of fact.' He spoke in a real la-di-dah voice, just like they de on the radio."

Jimmy tried to imitate him and he had us in stitches – he was a good mimic. "'I've just heard from my Sergeant. He's been to the Ingham Infirmary and Johnny is in an awful state. He'll be out of action for weeks and I need every man that I've got. And to cap it all, my Sergeant says that he thinks he knows who did it. Some spat over a woman who's been throwing herself at my young officers, and Sergeant Hines says it's one of your Special Constables. What are you going to do about it?'

"'Did your Sergeant give a name?'" Jimmy was deein' Jock's voice noo.

"'Yes he did. The fella brought Johnny home drunk a few weeks ago - said that if he saw him seeing a certain Mrs. Wade of Peel Street he'd get a good hiding. Apparently a young Arab lad was a witness – not that you can rely on the word of an Arab.' I'm only repeating what he said, Mossie. Then the Squadron Leader twirls his tash and says the assailant was Special Constable Lenny Cummings.

"There was a dead silence. Then Jock started talking – you kna' that voice he puts on when there's bother coming. 'We were all sorry to hear about your young officer, and two of my lads here helped to get him to hospital and warn your Sergeant. But I can tell you here and noo,'" (Jimmy had Jock's accent off pat) "'that Lenny Cummings had nothing to do with what happened to Johnny Wallis, and before you say anything else you ought to know that Special Constable Cummings was killed whilst on duty two days ago when the German Henkel blew up. So unless he's come back from the deed, I canna' see how he could have assaulted young Johnny.'

"Jock was standing reet close to the Squadron Leader. If he'd said owt funny I'm sure Jock would have gone for him. But he just mumbled that he was awfully sorry; two of the balloons had been damaged by the blast and he'd been working non-stop with his men to get them up and ready. He knew there'd been casualties but hadn't known their names. He'd speak to Sergeant Hines. He put out his hand – Jock hesitated but then shook it. As the Squadron Leader walked off he saw the pile of tins and bags - he stopped and looked. 'You've caught our thieves then, Sergeant,' he says to Jock. It turns oot that they've been having quite a lot of thieving from the depot where they keep their stores. 'When I asked Sergeant Hines to report it to the police he was reluctant to do so - he said it was probably just the lads taking a few things to give to the local girls, and that you probably wouldn't put yourself out over a few bags of sugar and some corned beef; but I gave him a direct order to report it – we can't have our men involved with the black market.'

"Jock then says that no report of stolen goods had been made, and explained how we'd found them on Jack Simcox's cart when the Home Guard lorry had run into them. They're ganna look into it together."

Me Mam had been listening. "Is that the Mrs. Wade that lives in Peel Street, Mossie?"

"Aye, she comes to the shop noo and then."

"Peggy Whiteheed was on her front step talkin' aboot her the other day, telling anyone who wanted to listen. She was running her doon something terrible. Peggy said Myra Wade has a young RAF lad who comes roond at neet. She thinks nae one kna's because he comes doon the back lane and in the back door, but Mrs. Snaith who lives in the doonstairs flat turns her lights off and looks through the curtains if she hears anything. And then the other day another fella from the RAF knocked on Mrs. Snaith's door – he'd got the wrong number in the dark. This one was a bit older and wasn't an officer – he spoke like a cockney. Well, Mrs. Snaith told him to knock next door, but she only half closed the door and heard the fella saying he wanted what Johnny was getting and then he pushed himsel' in. So she reckons she's got at least two fancy men - and her husband Harry's away at sea. Mrs. Snaith doesn't think that they're giving her money but Myra has been letting her have a few biscuits, and the other day she gave her a couple of slices of corned beef. She said she got them from a friend."

I knew who Mrs. Wade's other visitor was. "The cockney fella's Sergeant Hines. De ye think he could have been the one to give Johnny a hiding?"

There was a silence then Jackie said, "I think Myra Wade knows. I think she's in trouble and she won't tell the polis."

"Aye," said Jimmy, "and I bet Johnny will say he saw nowt and heard nowt."

"I think someone ought to talk to her," said me Mam. "Someone she kna's. And there's not many in Peel Street she'd trust - they all knew her Harry and some won't talk to her noo."

"Mrs. Hussain kna's her quite well," I said, "and always has a natter with her when she comes to the shop."

"I think her Mam and Da' used to live doon Holborn where the Bates had their shop," me Mam said. "She was a Sibson before she married Harry. Alice Hussain went oot with Billy Sibson for a bit until Billy and his brother found her in the straw with her Geordie. And I'm not tellin' ye lads anything else aboot that – I dain't want to give ye ideas."

Mary, who'd been sitting quietly looking at Jimmy every chance she got, decided she'd had enough of wor talk, and asked if anyone wanted a game of dominoes. "Wye aye," said Jimmy; "ye in, Jackie?" Jackie nodded. I think she felt it would be odd to insist on gannen oot on the bike with me. It was bitter cad anyway so I wasn't too put oot. Me Mam got the used matches oot as she wouldn't let us play for money. She sat by the fire knitting me some bed-socks, and the four of us had a good game. Jimmy lost nearly all his and Mary had a lucky run. When he was oot of matches she even lent him some sticks to keep him in the game. She couldn't stop talking aboot him after that. Mind, Jimmy was a nice looking lad, if you like sandy haired half wits with a stupid smile and a front tooth missing.

The next morning I told Alice Hussain the story while we went on the rounds. "I'm not surprised that Myra took a boyfriend. She was always one for the lads, and when she became pregnant it was Harry who was stupid enough to marry her. He wasn't the only one who'd taken her for a walk up Wilson's Stairs but he'd been away at sea for a nine month, and hadn't heard of her reputation. Mind she didn't kna' much aboot him either – he was never oot of the boozas when he was ashore. We'll gan roond the neet. De ye think she likes this Johnny whatyecallit?"

"It's Wallis – and I dain't see why I have to gan. I dain't even kna' her."

"But ye kna' him, and I let ye ride me bike when the bombs are flying aboot so you're coming."

Mrs. Hussain picked me up in the van at half past eight that neet. Myra's bairn would be abed by then. When we pulled up ootside the door there was a fella on the pavement hammering on the knocker – no prizes for guessing who – Sergeant Hines. When he saw me and Alice getting oot the van he scarpered, but poor Myra was nearly in tears. It didn't take long for her to tell us everything aboot her and Johnny, but after she'd tolt us aboot the Sergeant coming roond and threatening to tell the Squadron Leader, she clammed up. Alice got a shilling oot of her purse and told me to fetch two bottles of milk stout and a bottle of lemonade for mesel'. She went with me to the door and said not to hurry. I went doon Adelaide Street to the *Benton*. When I got back Alice and Myra were talking aboot the price of fruit - that is if you could even get any. We had the drink and it perked Myra up. She started asking me aboot me work as a PAM, and when I tolt her aboot the bomb and getting cut, she put her hand on me knee and said poor soul, and could she have a close look, at the scar she meant, and gave oot a real dirty laugh. Alice then said we should gan.

She came in to wor hoose, and then told me and me Mam what Myra had said. Well not everything, but enough to spare me blushes. She liked Johnny and he was starting to get serious. Auld Hines wanted to put a stop to it so that he could have what Johnny was getting. When Myra had told Johnny he'd been furious. He couldn't tell the Squadron Leader aboot Myra or he would end up in the glass hoose - RAF officers were under strict instructions not to gan oot with married women in toons where they were billeted - but he could tell him aboot the black market racket that Hines had organised. He must have threatened Hinesy with that, which was why Hines had given him a kicking. But Myra wouldn't tell the polis, and she didn't kna' how long she could hold oot against Hines.

I kept me ears to the ground the next day or two but it looked as though all CID's efforts were coming to nowt. Johnny, who was on the mend, and about to be discharged, was keeping stumm, and no one else was saying owt. Then I overheard Jock talking to the Super and saying that it might be worth keeping an eye on the other carters as whoever was organising the racket would need someone to ferry the stuff around. I made the Sergeant a cup of tea, and said, "If ye had an idea who was running the racket, and got someone to offer to take the goods and sell them for him, could ye nick the fella who was behind it all?"

Jock looked at me. "Do you know something, Mossie?" "Naw – I was just thinking - I'm sorry, Sarge, I shouldn't have listened to what ye were saying."

"Well, the trouble with what you're suggesting, Mossie, is that if we put someone up to approach the villain, and then we nicked him, he would say that we entrapped him." The look on my face must have given me away. "Entrapment's a term they use in courts. And he'd likely get off." He paused a second. "But if we knew nowt about it, but then a polis happened to bump into a fella walking down the street with a kit bag full of tins of tabs and bottles of whisky then that would be all right."

"And he'd be sent doon?"

"Twelve months minimum. The Magistrates have been ordered to make an example of black marketeers, especially those who are pilfering from the military."

We were all having an ice-cream in DiBresci's later that evening – it took a while to bring the conversation roond to Sergeant Hines as Jimmy couldn't shut up aboot his date with Glenda. "It's this Frida' but I've not decided where to take her."

"We should gan somewhere on the trolley bus," said Freddie.

"Ye gannen as well, Freddie?" I couldn't believe he'd fallen for it.

"Well Jimmy says Gertie's nice looking, and he reckons all these lasses deeing war work are desperate for it."

"Why would you want to go somewhere on the trolley bus?" Jackie asked. "They go dead slow at night, and they only have the emergency light on inside." Trolley buses ran until ten o'clock at neet, but because of the blackoot they had covered headlights - you could hardly see owt with them, and all the inside lights were turned oot apart from the little blue light at the top of the stairs.

"He doesn't want Gertie to get a good look at him, the scrawny nowt," said Matty Lightfoot, thumping Freddie on the shoulder.

"Dain't talk wet, man. There won't be many on the bus at neet. We'll sit in the back seat on the upper deck, and it'll be so dark nae one will see what we're up to."

Jimmy Clay was looking thoughtful. "He's right, ye kna'. We'll say we're gannen to the Marsden Inn."

"Which one?" Jackie asked. The old Marsden Inn and the new Marsden Inn hotel were on opposite sides of Redwell Lane. They had been gan' to close the auld pub when the new one was built, but when the Army camp at Marsden started filling up they kept both open.

"I doubt they'd let Freddie in the new one so we'll try the auld one."

I changed the subject and told them aboot Myra Wade, and how she reckoned that it was Sergeant Hines who'd flattened Johnny Wallis. "Your Da' doesn't think the polis will be able to nab him, Wally. Couldn't ye offer to buy some bags of sugar off him and we could lay a trap?"

"He kna's ye, Mossie, and anyway we dain't need any sugar. Mr. DiBresci had started stockpiling it before the War, and with what the Government lets us have we've got enough for your ice-cream at least for noo."

Ice-cream wasn't rationed – the powers that be thought that we should have one little pleasure, but sugar was still hard to come by and most ice-cream parlours only let ye have one a week.

"What he needs is a good belting," said Matty, "by someone who kna's what they're deein' so there's nae marks showing."

"Or the threat of one," Jackie added.

It set me thinking and the next morning when me and Mrs. Hussain were oot in the van I had a word with her.

"You thinking of wor Nobby?"

I nodded. Her brother Nobby had served in the First World War and although he was a useless nowt so far as the shop went, he was a big fella and could handle himsel'. He would tell me stories of how he'd once lasted three roonds with a gypsy who was taking on all comers at the Hoppings on the Toon Moor at Newcastle.

The next neet me and Nobby were standing ootside *Pinckney's*. "I'll gan in and ask him to come oot."

"Well, dain't be ower long, it's freezing oot here."

Sergeant Hines was standing at the bar, his foot on the rail, talking to a couple of blokes. I managed to push my way to him, and got a few funny looks. When he saw me, he asked me if I'd come to see Johnny. "He's upstairs in bed. He's on the mend. He's seen your lot – he's doing the Chinese monkey." My face gave me away. "He's heard nuffin', seen nuffin', and he's saying nuffin'."

"I'll gan up in a minute, but there's a bloke ootside wants to have a word with ye."

"Well, he'll have to stay outside. I'm staying put – I've been down on the foreshore all day and I'm not going out in the cold again today."

Just then Nobby came in and made his way ower. "This is a friend of Myra Wade," I said, "and he wants a word."

"Any friend of Myra is a friend of mine. Will you have a pint? And how about you, lad?"

Well Nobby said yes please, rubbing his hands - I had a lemonade. It wasn't how I expected things to gan. Then when Nobby said that he didn't want the Sergeant to gan roond to Myra's any more, auld Hinesy said he didn't kna' what folks were saying aboot him, but he'd only been roond the once to tell her that Johnny wouldn't be showing his face, and he certainly wouldn't be gan' to see her again. "Loverly lady though she is. Have another pint, Nobby."

Nobby drained his glass and put it doon on the counter. "I'll gan up and see Johnny, then."

"All right, son. His door's the one on the right on the end. Here, you can take one up for him, on me." And he asked the barmaid for a whisky and soda.

Johnny was sitting up in bed with a thick jumper on. There was a fire going in the grate, but it was still on the cad side. He was pleased to see me, but said that he would not have a drink with Sergeant Hines, and said I was to give it back to him when I went downstairs. "You can throw it in his face, so far as I'm concerned." He started to laugh and then grimaced in pain. "Sorry, it only hurts when I larff." And that set him off again.

I wasn't sure whether or not to say owt aboot Myra, but after he'd thanked me for helping oot after he'd been attacked, he asked if I would mind popping roond to her hoose on me way yem to see how she was. I said that I'd already been roond with Mrs. Hussain and that she was all right. I said nowt about Hinesy.

"Well if you bump into her can you tell her that I was asking after her?"

I went back doon to the bar. Nobby collared the whisky and when I said I was gannen, he just replied all reet, he'd stay for another pint and then get the trolley bus from the Chi back to the Nook.

Me and Mrs. Hussain got the full story from Nobby the next morning when we were delivering the produce to the Nook shop – Edie was giving him the cold shoulder. He'd caught the last trolley bus at ten o'clock from the Chi and still had time for a last pint, or kna'ing Nobby, two pints, in the *Winter Gardens* before closing time or possibly after. The polis in the Nook sub-station used to drink in there, and weren't bothered aboot licensing laws. He'd been well away. But Nobby knew Edie would get ower it, and he was in a good mood. "He's a canny fella, Hinesy." He looked roond and put his hand up to the side of his gob. "He reckons he can get had of all sorts of stuff from the Forces stores that you can sell for double the price you'd have to pay, if you could get it at all – but he needs someone with a cart or a van that the polis wouldn't suspect, and who could sell it for him. Jack Simcox was helping him until a drunken nowt from the Home Guard drove into him and the polis collared him."

"So ye want to go in with him?" asked Alice.

"Aye, well, I thought that when ye de the early morning deliveries ye could just mention that you'd got had of a bag of sugar or some corned beef and you'd get rid of it in nae time – and wor customers wouldn't grass us up."

"Well, if ye think I'm ganna risk the good name wor Da' built up you've got another thought coming – and dain't bother aboot trying to de it on your own or I'll grass *yee* up."

I waited until Alice had gone quiet. Nobby was just standing there getting a tab oot of a little paper bag – sometimes ye could only buy them in fives.

"Have ye agreed to de it?" I asked.

"Naw, I said I'd have to ask Alice, and I wasn't certain she'd agree. He said to call in at *Pinckney's* tomorrow neet if I was interested. He'd have a bottle of whisky and some tabs for me whether I agreed or not."

I looked at Alice. "Well, I think ye should gan and say ye'll de it. Tell him Alice hadn't wanted to be involved, what with me working for the polis, but that ye'll de it on your own, and ye can use the van anytime ye want anyway – he won't kna' that ye find driving too much of an effort." I jumped back as Nobby threw a punch, muttering, "Ye cheeky nowt."

I didn't like the way Alice was looking at me, so I said very quickly, "And when he turns up with half the Forces' rations for the month in his auld kit bag the polis will nab him. He'll spend a year in the glass hoose and Johnny and Myra can keep each other company again."

Alice was happy enough but Nobby needed a bit of persuasion. "He'll come roond," said Alice as we were driving back up Prince Edward Road. "He wants the whisky and the tabs, and it's less trouble for him to agree with me than to have an argument. You'll have to have a word with Jock Duncan – on the QT mind. If there's any hint of entrapment he won't want to kna'."

Nobby came roond. He saw Hinesy and got his whisky and tabs – *Lucky Strike*. Hinesy said they were better than English tabs as the Yanks put all tobacco in them – not the sh**e that you got in British cigarettes these days. Nobby let me have a packet – I dain't smoke, but I thought I could give some to Freddie. Nobby was gan' to meet up with Hines the following week on Tuesda' aboot half past seven in the evening. Nobby would pick him up on the corner of Cambridge Street and they'd park up near the depot. Hines had his own key. He'd take a kit bag, fill it up, walk back, just like any other serviceman, to where Nobby was parked – he'd give the bag to Nobby and then gan back for another load. Once he'd handed that ower, Nobby would drive off to the Nook and Hines would walk back to *Pinckney's*.

The next evening I popped into the café and asked Wally if I could have a quiet word with his old man. Wally said to look in on me dinner break on Frida' as Jock always came in for his fish and chips. "Ye can have dinna' here if you want."

"I'm sorry, Wally, all me money gans to me Mam since me Da' died. Will it be all reet to have me sandwiches here?"

I could see that Wally wasn't too happy aboot that, but he was such a nice lad that he didn't want to say owt. Then I had an idea. I had Nobby's packet of *Lucky Strike* in my pocket. I pulled it oot. "Dain't ask me where I got these from, but would that cover a plate of fish and chips." Wally whistled. "Wye aye it would, and afters. Me Da's been smoking *Senior Service* recently, and even they're making him cough something chronic. He says ye dain't kna what they put in English cigarettes these days." He took the tabs. "I'll see you the morra' then. He's normally in just after twelve."

There was no haddock on the menu but we had cod – Wally had kept back two big pieces for me and his Da'. The chips had a funny taste, but Sergeant Duncan explained that fish and chip shops could only use vegetable oil, and they couldn't change it too often either. The cod ran oot at half past twelve and there was a lot of muttering as people had to make de with fish that they would normally give to the cat, or fishcakes, which were mainly tatoe. Little Audrey then said that she'd de spam fritters for those who weren't Catholics, so some went home happy enough.

Jock heard me oot in between mouthfuls of geet big flakes of white fish covered in crispy batter, light as a feather. "The best thing you can do, Mossie, is to set things up so that when Sergeant Hines is on his way from the depot to the van with his kit bag on his shoulder, he walks round a corner and bumps into a bobby on his beat. The polis naturally asks what the Sergeant's got in his kit bag, and your problems are over. No entrapment – Nobby Bates just drives off and makes sure he's got a water-tight alibi in case Hines grasses him up. And if you've got any sense you'll make sure that the Sergeant has dropped off one kit bag before he's nicked."

"What'll we de with it?" I asked, shovelling in a forkful of chips – they didn't taste too bad smothered in salt and vinegar, and brown sauce.

"I'm sure you'll think of something, laddie."

That Sunda' morning we were all sitting roond a table at DiBresci's having wor ice-cream with red sauce, and Jimmy and Freddie were telling us aboot their date with Glenda and Gertie. "How'd ye get on with Big Gertie, Freddie?" I asked.

Freddie was smirking all ower his face and Jimmy said, "There's no need to gloat, you dirty little twat."

"There's nae need for bad language, just because I had it and ye didn't, Jimmy Clay." Freddie was smirking even more as he licked the red sauce off roond the top of his cornet.

"Ye had your ho..." Matty started to shout oot and Davey Corbett punched him in the arm. "Keep your voice down, Matty, there's other customers in."

"Wye aye, I did."

"Aye," said Jimmy, "on the back seat upstairs on the trolley bus."

"How'd you manage that?" Matty asked, and Freddie told us the story.

"When I first saw wor Gertie, I thought ye'se bastards had set me up, but she was nice enough and when Jimmy and Glenda started holding hands I did the same and she didn't seem to mind. We got the trolley bus from the Chi, and we went upstairs so I could have a smoke. It was pitch black with just a little blue light in the ceiling at the top of the stairs so you dain't break your neck when you're getting off. Me and Gertie were reet at the back and Jimmy and Glenda just in front. The bus was gannen dead slow and we had plenty of time. I could hear Glenda telling Jimmy to be careful where he put his hands, so I pushed up reet close to Gertie and kissed her on the cheek. Well she did nowt so I put me hand under her skirt. She had no nylons on and I managed to rest me hand on her thigh. She didn't say owt, but when I moved it up a bit she put her own hand on it and it stayed put. She's a strong lass.

"I could hear Jimmy and Glenda kissing but I was comfortable enough as it was with me head on her tit and me hand on her thigh. We got off at Marsden and went into the auld Inn. There's a little room at the side for women. I kna' I look a bit young so I sat doon in the corner with Gertie and Glenda, while Jimmy got the drinks. They only had a petrol light on so it was very cosy. Me and Jimmy had pints, Glenda had a port and lemon, and Gertie said she didn't drink much hersel' but her Nan always had a bottle of Guinness with a port in, so she had one of those. After

a couple of drinks Gertie was quite giggly, and didn't mind me
hand on her thigh, on top of her skirt though. We got the bus
back and sat in the same seats as before. We were the only ones
upstairs. Well this time Jimmy and Glenda got straight doon to
the kissing, so I pushed up again against Gertie and she let me de
whatever I wanted. I managed to undo her uniform buttons and
get me hand reet in to feel her tits, and I got me other hand up
her skirt, and this time she didn't stop me. Then I heard Glenda
tell Jimmy he'd better stop what he was deein' or she'd get off
the bus, and Jimmy saying all reet and then starting again, but I
was sure he wasn't getting as far as I was. We'd passed the Nook,
and then the bus slowed reet doon to get roond the turn into
King George Road. Well the conductor was a lass who'd only just
started, and she thowt the driver was at the junction so she gets
off, but when she found the pole she couldn't find the lever to
switch the frogs ower because there wasn't one – she'd got off too
early - and the next minute we heard the trolleys coming loose
and the bus stopped deed. The driver got oot and wasn't very
happy. They tried using the pole to put the trolleys back on but it
was pitch black and they couldn't see what they were deeing so
the driver comes upstairs, and says he's gan to climb on the roof,
could one of us follow him up to keep him steady while he puts
the trolleys on the wires. Jimmy got up and the driver opened the
hatch and climbed up with Jimmy behind. Well I knew it would
take yonks so I pulled Gertie's knickers doon, spread her legs
wide and got between them. She just lay back with her hands
roond me shoulders saying, 'Oh Freddie'.

   "I knew I would have to be quick, and when I mumbled that
I was gan' to shoot me bolt, she got had of me shoulders and
pushed me oot of her. We were just getting worselves straight
when I saw Jimmy's legs coming doon from the roof trap."

   "You shouldn't talk about girls like that, Freddie." Davey
Corbett was a bit strait-laced. He knew the rule aboot Jackie, and

I dain't think he liked it when Freddie talked dirty in front of her. But Jackie had been as interested as the rest of us and said quietly, "You shouldn't tell anyone else about Gertie, Freddie. If she hears that you've been talking about her she won't be very happy, and she might not go out with you again."

"Aye I kna'," said Freddie a bit sheepishly, "but ye'se lot are always making fun of me aboot not having had it with a lass.

"I dinna' whether we're gannen oot again. She's not the sort of lass I'd take oot on me own. So it depends on Jimmy. He asked Glenda if she wanted to gan' to the flicks next week and she said she'd think aboot it."

"She'll say yes," said Jimmy. "When we were walking back to the hostel I asked her if she'd let me have it. She didn't answer but she said that she'd been surprised at Gertie, and that if she did give in it wasn't ganna' be on the back seat of a trolley bus or in the back row of the pictures. She'd want to have it in bed and I'd have to wear a contra-whatycallit..."

"Ye mean a johnnie," said Freddie. "If I de it with Gertie again I'm ganna de the same – I'm not sure that I came oot quick enough last time."

"I dinna' where I'd get one from."

"Wor Billy would get you one," said Matty. "He's been doon to see that Annie three times since we went last time but he's away at sea noo, and I dain't kna' when he's coming back."

I would be the only one not to have had it. While Freddie had been talking I'd been pressing me leg hard against Jackie's, while holding me hand ower me troosers so she'd not see the bulge. I changed the subject, and tolt them all aboot the plan to get auld Hinesey. I was gan to need their help.

The Depot was doon West Holborn not far from the Middle Docks – the beat bobby was under orders to walk past every hour to watch oot for pilferers. That Tuesda' me and Jackie followed Nobby's van from *Pinckney's* doon to the riverside. He hadn't driven for years and was gannen' dead slow so it wasn't a problem. They drove reet past the depot then Nobby turned right up Hill Street and pulled in near the top. Hines got oot and walked back doon the hill. It was quiet and there was nae one aboot. Jackie rode off to Laygate nick - I followed on behind Hines – I couldn't see much but I could hear his segs on the pavement. He didn't gan straight in but waited in a doorway by the corner – I then heard the heavy step of a polis who was coming along the road. I pulled back mesel'. Once his footsteps faded away I saw Hines move quickly and open the depot door – he had a key and shone a torch just for a minute so that he could see the lock. Aboot ten minutes later he was on his way back with a kit bag ower his shoulder. I followed him to Nobby's van. He tapped on the winda – Nobby got oot and opened the back doors. Hines jumped in, and a few ticks afterwards he was oot again with an empty kit bag, and on the way back to the depot.

I rode off quickly up to the top of the hill where Sergeant Cummings and Douggie Errington were waiting with Jackie. Douggie was the mate of Lenny Cummings I'd met doon Brodrick Street, and he reckoned he had a score to settle with Sergeant Hines. He'd heard how Hinesy had tried to lay the blame on Lenny for beating up Johnny Wallis. They headed doon Hill Street and me and Jackie followed. I banged on Nobby's van to warn him to be ready. When they were in position aboot ten yards from the corner I pedalled on ahead. No sign of Hinesy. Matty Lightfoot came pedalling up – it was so dark he nearly ran into me. "He's gan' a different way," he shouted, "he's off up Laygate Street."

"Tell Jack Cummings," I replied, "he'd better get up Hill Street as quick as he can. They'll have to stop him before he gets to Nobby's van."

I was worried sh**less that it would all gan' wrong – but it turned oot canny. Jack and Douggie were half running, half walking and feeling it – they turned the corner at the top of Hill Street into Commercial Road and walked reet into Hinesy. I was just behind and saw it all.

Jack shone his torch for just a second. "It's a funny time of neet to be walking roond with a kit bag?"

"I'm changing billets."

"Well, whether ye are or not we're under orders to check all servicemen with kit bags within a mile of the depot – there's been a lot of pilfering. Can you put your kit bag on the groond and we'll have a look."

There was a silence for a minute, then I heard Hinesy's voice. "Look I might have a few fings I shouldn't – you seem nice enough fellas – if you'd like a few fags and a bottle of whisky then we could forget about all this, and no 'arm done."

"Ye miserable little bastard." Douggie stepped in and gave Hinesy a clout in the chops.

"Dain't de that, Douggie, ye daft bugger." Jack's deep voice chipped in. "If you've got to hit him, thump him in the kidneys where it won't leave a mark." A groan from Hines told me that Douggie had taken Jack's advice. They opened the kit bag and Jack let oot a whistle. "Reet, you're coming back to the nick with us and we're arresting you for theft from a military establishment."

Jack then said in a loud voice so that I could hear, "We'll take him to the Laygate Lane box and ring for the Maria from there. Keep your eyes peeled, Douggie, for any carts – I reckon this fella must have been Jack Simcox's supplier and I bet he's got someone else in tow." This was for Nobby's benefit. We didn't want Hines to think for a minute that he'd been grassed up. They walked him off up towards Laygate Lane. I was quick off to tell Nobby to stay put for five minutes and then to scarper as fast as he could. We'd agreed that he would drop the stuff off at my hoose, and then get back to the Nook to sort oot his alibi in case Hinesy shopped him.

That was the last I saw of Sergeant Hines. He was taken to Keppel Street. Jock Duncan had been adamant on that – he was worried that if they took him to the Laygate nick some of the evidence might disappear. I read the entry in the charge book the next day. "Sergeant Hines had an unfortunate accident when he was being taken into HQ. He lost his balance and fell down the five stone steps. Constable Errington who tried to stop his fall stumbled himself, and as he was carrying a heavy kit bag could not prevent himself from falling with all his weight on top of the Sergeant." Hinesy spent the night at the Ingham. Two front teeth knocked out, broken nose, bruised kidneys and cracked ribs. Nearly as bad as what he'd done to Johnny. There were no complaints from the Squadron Leader.

We went back to Maxwell Street. Me Mam and Mrs. Hussain were sitting roond the kitchen table eating chocolate with Mary and Jasmin, and trying to sort oot all the things that were on the table. You'd nivver guess hoo much you could cram into a kit bag. Nobby had already taken a bottle of whisky for himsel' and some tabs for the polis at the Nook. If anyone asked they would have been drinking with Nobby in the *Winter Gardens* from seven onwards that evening.

We divvied it all up – Jock was to get a bottle of whisky and some *Lucky Strike*. There were a dozen oranges. We were all licking wor lips ower them, but I said that I knew someone who'd lost some teeth, and who would welcome a nice juicy orange that he could suck on, so Johnny got three.

Mary couldn't keep her eyes off Jimmy, and Freddie was getting a bit too close to Jasmin for my liking so I tolt him to go and play noughts and crosses with Mary – she was always playing it. It wasn't long before she was laughing and joking with him but when I was sitting next to Jasmin I noticed that Jackie was looking very hard at us. There were a couple of bottles of egg flip on the table and me Mam opened one of them and gave everyone a glass except me and the lasses. Mary wanted to play dominoes but there were too many of us, so me Mam cleared the table and got the cards oot and we had a game of Newmarket for matchsticks. We had a good neet and everybody went yem happy. I had begun to realise that Mary and Jasmin were growing up and were getting interested in lads. Mary was pretty keen on Jimmy and didn't mind showing it, and Jasmin was giving me looks all neet as well.

Sergeant Hines was sent doon for eighteen months with hard labour. They made an example of him. Nae one shed any tears. I heard from Johnny Wallis that when they heard the news in *Pinckney's* they all started singing *Roll Out the Barrel*.

The Volunteer Arms

CHAPTER 5
MARCH/APRIL 1941

I went roond to *Pinckey's* the next day in me dinner break to give Johnny his oranges. He was in the doonstairs bar and looked a bit better than when I'd last seen him. He was having a cup of tea and reading the paper. I didn't want to show everybody the oranges so I said could I talk to him upstairs. I felt a bit sorry afterwards as he was clearly still in pain as he went up the steps, but he said that he hoped to be back on the balloon placements next week. I tolt him that we'd nabbed Hinesy, and gave him the oranges. He said thank you very much and started peeling one straight away with his penknife. The smell was making me slaver – he looked up at me, and then gave me the one he was peeling and started on another. I didn't say naw – I loved oranges. We both stood there sucking the fruit with the juice running doon wor chops. Johnny finished his first and asked if we could have a chinwag. I didn't kna' what he meant, but I'd heard stories aboot some of these la-di-dah types, who were as keen on lads as lasses, so I stepped back a bit, and was wondering what to de when he laughed. "Do you know what a chinwag is, Mossie?"

"Naw, I dain't, and I'm not sure I want to."

"It's all right, you've nothing to worry about – it just means a talk."

I felt stupid but I was relieved that that's all it was, and I had wanted to ask Johnny something anyway. I reckoned that he might be able to get hold of some French letters for Jimmy and

Freddie.

"I wondered whether you could go round to Myra Wade's for me. Tell her that I'd really like to see her again, but I daren't go to Peel Street – the Squadron Leader would get wind of it and I'd be finished here."

"Me Mam reckons the neighbours are all talking aboot her anyway, so I dain't think she'd want ye coming to the hoose."

"That's what I thought. But ask her if she still feels the same way about me, and if she does then she might have a friend who might let us use their house to meet up now and again."

"I dain't think she's got any friends apart from Alice Hussain." I should have kept me gob shut.

"The woman who runs Bates' Fruit and Veg?" I nodded. "Of course, you work for her. That's a good idea, Mossie, and if she's willing I could come to some arrangement with her."

"I've not said I'd help yet."

"Oh please, Mossie – you probably don't understand what it feels like when you've got feelings for someone and can't even see them, let alone anything else."

"Aye mebbees not, but I've got two mates who have lasses, but they won't let them have it unless they put a johnnie on, and they can't get any. I was gan to ask you if you could help. If ye de, I'll gan and see Myra Wade."

He laughed. "Hold on a sec, Mossie." He went doonstairs and came back in aboot five minutes – I heard him groaning as he came up the stairs. He had two packets in his hand. "There's two packs of three. Will that be enough to be going on with? The Landlord of the pub keeps a stock in especially for us."

I took them. "Thanks, Johnny." I chuckled to mesel'. "I'll tell them they're johnnies from Johnny."

He picked up the orange that was left. "You can take this to Myra."

I went roond to Peel Street that neet, before gannen yem. Myra

Wade was glad to see me and her face lit up when I gave her the orange. When I tolt her it was from Johnny she laughed. "Aw I thought it was from ye, Mossie. I was trying to think what I could give ye in exchange," and she gave oot her dirty laugh.

"Johnny says he'd like to see you again but doesn't want to come to the hoose, like."

"Well I dain't kna' where else he could see me. Did he want to take me oot to the flicks or to Minchella's for an ice-cream?"

It was getting a bit embarrassing for me. "Naw, he said that he'd be in trouble with the Squadron Leader if he went oot with ye as you're married."

"So he's only after one thing then. Well he better give me more than an orange. He's a nice looking fella though, and I de get lonely with wor Harry away. Not that I see much of him when he's yem - he's always in the boozas. Tell him that I'll think it ower but he's probably gan' to have to come here."

"He was wondering whether Mrs. Hussain might help as she kna's ye and managed to help sort oot auld Hinesy."

"It's a lot to ask. I'll think aboot it."

The sirens went off later that evening and I was doon the nick with the rest of the lads. We heard some planes gan ower but there were nae bombs. I'd been thinking aboot Johnny and his wanting to have a chinwag, so I thought I might have a bit of a laugh. I waited until Davey was oot of the room because he would kna' what a chinwag was, and said to the others, "Ye kna' I went up to see Johnny Wallis the day. Well he took me up to his room, shut the door, and said that we should have a chinwag." Their blank faces gave them away. "I said I wasn't that sort, but he kept on so I gave in."

Freddie fell for it – of course he was a dirty little nowt so I wasn't surprised. "You let that Johnny give you a chinwag?"

"Aye well ye kna' what these upper class lads de to each other in their posh schools."

"What was it like then?" said Matty.

Jackie stood up. "I'm not sitting here and listening to this. You lot, you only think of one thing, and you, Mossie, should be ashamed of yourself leading them on. A chinwag is what southerners call a chat. Johnny had a chat with Mossie, that's all."

"Aye well I never said it was owt else; it was Freddie's dirty mind, not mine."

"Ye bastard," said Freddie as he charged across the the room at me followed by Matty, Jimmy and Wally.

We'd just got into the corridor when we heard 'Jock' Duncan's voice booming oot of the Charge Room. "If ye little beggars have got nowt else to do but fight I'll come and sort the lot of you oot. Don't ye know there's a war on?" That would have been the end of it had not Constable Douthwaite been loitering in the corridor. He preferred it inside – he came doon towards us. "Aye, ye lot should de what the Sergeant tells ye." His face was red and ye could smell the beer on his breath. Freddie Skee never lost a chance to rile up auld Douthwaite so he gans up to him, like and says, "We were just arguing aboot whether to tell anyone in authority aboot what happened to Mossie – he's too ashamed to talk aboot it himsel'."

"Aw shut it will ye, Freddie," I said. It only encouraged Douthwaite.

"Ye keep oot of this, Mossie Hamed. If young Skee thinks it's important then I'll listen." I left him to it. If people dain't' want to be helped that's up to them.

"Well," Freddie got reet close to Douthwaite – I expect he could see the little red hairs that poked oot of his nose and ears – "he went to see that la-di-dah Air Force Officer who got a hiding, and when he was in his room Johnny Wallis made him have a chinwag." Freddie was expecting a clout roond the ear but Douthwaite just stood there with his gob open. "Well Mossie didn't kna' what it was, but when Johnny started it was too late, and Mossie just had to let him de it. He daresn't tell his Mam."

Douthwaite looked at me with a sneer on his face. "Aye well ye kna' what they say aboot Arabs."

"But Mossie's only sixteen and that Johnny's a grown man."

It turned oot that Douthwaite hated la-di-dah officers more than Arabs. "It's not reet. Mind these officers think they'll get away with owt. I better tell the Sergeant."

If it had been anyone else on duty it would have ended there, but Jock never had a good word to say aboot the War Reserve Police, and when Douthwaite said that he'd like to investigate a serious complaint - Lieutenant Wallis had had a chinwag with one of the PAMs, Jock said he was pleased that the Constable was taking the matter seriously; but that Johnny Wallis had himself been the subject of a vicious physical attack. He suggested that the Constable ask for Johnny's side of the story before taking it further. "Who reported it, Constable?" he asked. "Young Freddie Skee – the Arab lad was too embarrassed."

"Aye, I should think he was."

Those of ye who've read so far will have guessed that I'm not ower clever, although I'm not as daft as some and I de kna' aboot sod's law. I shouldn't have had a laugh at the lads' expense, Freddie shouldn't have done the same with auld Douthwaite, and there should have been another Sergeant on duty. But naebody would have worked oot that at half past two the next day, when Douthwaite was on the pavement ootside *Pinckney's* trying to put the cuffs on Johnny Wallis, that the Chief would arrive in his car, with Major Todd, the Chief Air Raid Warden, by his side to pick up the Squadron Leader who was to take them on a tour of the balloon installations. I had it first hand from Johnny Wallis some time later.

The Chief got oot the car. The Squadron Leader, who was trying to stop Douthwaite, said "thank heavens", and asked the Chief to call Douthwaite off.

"What are you doing, Constable?" The Chief was a big tall fella and his voice boomed oot.

"I'm trying to arrest this man, Sir, to take him doon the station for questioning."

"For what offence?"

"Indecency with minors."

"That's a very serious charge, Officer."

"Aye, he's admitted it."

"Admitted what?"

"Having a chinwag with that Arab lad who's one of wor PAMs."

The Chief was silent. Johnny Wallis never knew whether he didn't kna' what a chinwag was as well, or whether he was just struck dumb. Major Todd had also got oot the car, had been listening, and helped them oot.

"Do you know exactly what a chinwag is, Constable?"

Auld Douthwaite looked a bit puzzled. "Well, I kna' it's not reet."

"And did the young lad complain to you?"

"It was his mate, young Freddie Skee; the Arab lad wouldn't say owt - he was too embarrassed."

"Hmmm - a chinwag, Constable, as we all know, is a south country slang expression for a chat. The Lieutenant was having a chat with the lad."

Johnny, who was trying to keep a straight face, just said that Constable Douthwaite had asked him if he had had a chinwag with Mossie Hamed, and he'd said yes and it had been very enjoyable.

"I think we've had enough enjoyable moments," the Chief replied. "Constable, return to HQ, go and see Superintendent Lamont and tell him exactly what happened and ask him to see me in the morning with a full report."

As Douthwaite walked away, muttering to himsel', the Chief,

who was the only one who wasn't trying not to laugh said, "Do you think they know there's a War on?"

I knew nowt of this at the time, but that neet just after six o'clock Jimmy Clay came knocking at the door. I was wanted doon the nick. Jimmy came in and had a couple of games of noughts and crosses with Mary, while I put me uniform on. When we were ootside I gave him one of the two packets of three. "They're from Johnny Wallis."

"Aw thanks, Mossie. I'll buy ye an ice-cream. I'm taking Glenda oot for a walk on Sunda' if the weather's all reet. I was ganna ask her oot to the flicks one neet. She might let me come back to the hostel. I've heard that there's a back winda where lads can climb in." Jimmy pedalled off yem.

I was gan' to give the other packet to Freddie but after his stunt the other day I thought I'd see what happened doon the nick.

Freddie was there as well. Davey Corbett had been sent to fetch him before gan' off shift. We had to see the Super. I think that he had more than enough on his plate without having to bother with us – he just asked us what had happened. "And you, Mossie, never made any complaint about Johnny Wallis."

"There was nowt to complain aboot."

"And you, Freddie, only said that Lieutenant Wallis and Mossie had had a chinwag."

"Aye. Well he's always getting on at us PAMs aboot something. I thought he'd kna' what a chinwag was, being a constable an' all."

"And you did nothing to stop him from making a fool of himself." We both just looked at wor boots.

"I'm giving you both a warning, and if you do anything stupid like this again I'll not only kick you out the door I'll get the old birch from the cupboard and give you both a couple of strokes as a parting present. Now get out and don't let me see you again."

As we got up to leave he looked up at us. "And you've got Jack

JOHN ORTON

Cummings to thank for me being so lenient. He says you both did well the other night when the German plane came down."

That was it. Sergeant Duncan was not so lucky. For some reason the Chief had never liked him and 'Jock' was fined a quid, and would have been reduced to the ranks if Superintendent Lamont had not stood up for him. I dain't kna' whether it's true or not, but Jack Cummings reckoned that after the Super had used up all his other arguments, he said that there was no one else who could do the job, and his only option would be to make Constable Douthwaite acting Sergeant. The Chief gave in.

On the way oot I gave Freddie his johnnies, but told him he wouldn't get any more if he got me in trouble again. "Aye, well ye shouldn't be having chinwags with la-di-dah officers. Ye ought to get yoursel' a lass. Come on, I'll buy ye an ice-cream at DiBrescis."

I hadn't been there for a while as money was always short, and I'd rather gan when I knew Jackie would be there. We had wor ice-cream with plenty of sauce and I listened to Freddie gannen on aboot what he'd de with the johnnies. Since he'd had it with Gertie, he'd tried asking other lasses oot but he was getting nae where. The trouble with Freddie was that he was a bit obvious, and most lasses didn't want to spend a neet oot just trying to fight him off. "I might see if Jimmy and Glenda want to gan oot again with me and Gertie. I doubt she'll say naw as we've already done it once."

"Glenda's tolt Jimmy that she's not gan on any trolley bus rides with him."

He just laughed. "We could try the flicks. If ye get into one of those corner seats reet at the back nae one can see what you're deein'. Ye have to be forst in the queue though."

We stayed there a good hoor. Wally Duncan wasn't very talkative that evening. I think he was worried aboot his Da'. We were pedalling up Ocean Road when Freddie pulled up. "Had on a sec." I braked and stopped beside him. "You see those two bikes ootside Minchella's?" Minchella's Ice-Cream Parlour was just doon from the junction with Mile End Road. It was all reet and the ice-cream was as good as DiBresci's, but we always went to DiBresci's because Wally worked there. It was not a full moon but there was a bit of light from the sky. We went ower and had a closer look. There was nae doot. You couldn't mistake Davey's bike, and I'd ridden on the back of Jackie's before so I knew it well.

"Ye dain't think Davey's after wor Jackie, do ye?"

Well I knew that he was, but I wasn't gan to tell Freddie so I just said nowt.

"Do ye fancy another ice-cream?" he asked.

"I've only got a tanner to last me the week, or I would. Why dain't ye gan in."

So he did, and I pedalled off in the pitch black ower the cobbles thinking aboot Jackie and Davey.

I didn't say owt to Jackie and she didn't say owt to me, but we still had wor kissing and cuddling sessions, and I was beginning to think that I might have to go and see Johnny for mesel' soon. Me worries aboot Davey and Jackie got worse a week later. Jimmy and Freddie had taken Glenda and Gertie oot to the *Palace* to see a Fu Manchu film. They'd agreed to meet a good twenty minutes before the programme started so that they could get a seat in the back row next to the wall, but auld Douthwaite who was in the Frederick Street sub-station wouldn't let them leave their bikes there. "I'm not deeing ye any favours," he'd shouted at Freddie. By the time Jimmy and Freddie had persuaded the auld hinny who was noo the commissionaire to let them leave their bikes and helmets in the foyer, all the back seats were full. Freddie said it was still worth it. He'd got his hand up Gertie's skirt and he'd pushed her hand doon his troosers. I wasn't too interested in that, but then he said that who did I think were sitting in the back row? Davey and Jackie.

That April we'd had a raid on the Munda' neet doon the riverside, and there'd been a good few fires. Some oil tanks had been set alight, and it had taken all the next day to put the flames oot. We weren't expecting what came on the Wednesda' though. The sirens went off at half-past nine and I was oot like a shot. I now wore my uniform troosers in the evening, and it didn't take long to put me jacket on, grab me tin hat and me gas mask, oot the back door and on me bike. Me mutha' was still getting wor Mary oot the bed, and Mrs. Rutherford was coming doon the back stairs with her coat on and a shawl roond her shoulders. Mr. Rutherford and Jimmy would be doon the *Auld Mill* most like.

Jackie was waiting on the corner of Winchester Street and we both tore doon Fowler Street. We could hear the sound of planes and the ack-ack guns were lighting up the sky. "It's ganna be a big'un," I shouted oot and the next minute we heard aboot twenty planes flying ower the Lawe Top and on the way to the docks. We didn't hear any explosions, and when we pulled into the nick yard we soon found out why. Davey Corbett came running oot and told us to follow him up to the Lawe.

"They're dropping incendiaries all over," he shouted as he jumped onto his saddle. "Henry Milburn's called in from the Mile End Road box and there are fires in Robertson Street and Fort Street. The fire watchers are doing their best, but they can only take on one house at a time. Most of the fire engines are being sent down to the docks – there's a timber yard ablaze and Redheads' been hit as well. The Sergeant wants us up the Lawe to help put the fires out before they take hold and guide more planes in. Henry Milburn's using the box as the incident post for the minute, but he needs us to keep him informed." With that he was off and we tried to keep up - not for long - he was standing on his pedals and with his gears he was soon oot of sight. Jackie was not too far behind him, but I was pulling up the rear as usual on me delivery bike. Once we were past the Railway Station you could see a few people in the street with buckets of watter and stirrup pumps ootside their own hooses, but there were flames coming oot of windas where the people had gone to the shelters. I got as far as Fawcett Street and left me bike in a shop doorway. Jackie came oot of a back yard in William's Terrace with a bucket of watter. "Davey's gone into the shop across the road," she shouted. "A bomb's gone straight through the roof and the upstairs's ablaze. I'm going to take him some more water."

The words were just oot her mooth when I heard a plane coming ower low and the whistle of a bomb. "Get doon," I shouted and pushed her ower to the wall of a hoose and onto the ground. I was lying on top of her when there was a geet big bang, and things started flying everywhere. Something hit me tin helmet and I lost me senses for a minute, but I soon came to when Jackie started pushing me off her. We looked roond. There was a crater in the middle of the road, half of Fawcett Street was doon, and there was just a big pile of rubble where the shop that Davey was in had been.

"Oh Davey." Jackie was nearly crying so I grabbed her by the hand and pulled her towards the ruins. "Come on, we'll find him all reet. I helped dig oot an auld couple at Brodrick Street so I kna' what to de until the rescue squads arrive." I didn't tell her that when they found the auld couple they were both deed. Then we heard more bombs coming doon and Jackie started crying.

"Lads don't cry, Jackie, and I can't dig him oot on me own."

The flames from the other buildings were giving off plenty of light so I could see where the roof of the shop was lying. I climbed ower the bricks and shouted oot as loud as I could. "Are ye there, Davey?" Nowt. I moved ower to the side a bit. "Are ye there, Davey?"

"Yes, I'm here Mossie." His voice was muffled but I could just hear it.

"Are ye all reet?"

"My legs are trapped but I can't see much."

"We'll get ye oot in a tick," I shouted but I doubted it. There were a lot of heavy timbers where the roof had come doon. I got as close to the sound of his voice as I could and started pulling oot tiles and bricks with me bare hands and giving them to Jackie. I was worried aboot her but I needed the help. After aboot ten minutes I'd managed to make a sort of tunnel just under a roof beam that was keeping the rubble up. I started making a bit more progress but I was crawling on me stomach - it was dusty and it was hot. I called oot to Davey every noo and again and I thowt his voice was getting weaker. After another ten minutes I was nearly all the way in and there was a bit of a space above me so I could kneel up. I then heard Sergeant Cummings' voice behind me. He was having a go at Jackie. "The ARP lads should be deeing that. The lines are doon and we need the rescue squads and ambulances. Ye messengers should be oot on your bikes."

There was then another geet big explosion and I felt the groond shake and a load of dust came on top of me. I thought I was gan to be buried alive but the roof beam held firm. I managed to pull a big lump of plaster away and then I heard Davey groaning. I shone me torch and could see his heed and shoulders sticking oot the rubble. There was blood all ower his face, one of his eye-balls was dangling oot the socket and his right arm was all bloody. "I've found him." I shouted. A minute later Jack Cummings was beside me.

"I didn't realise that it was Davey in here," he muttered. "I've sent young Jackie to the ARP HQ. They've got messengers there who'll take word that we need rescue squads and ambulances.

"Reet, let's get young Davey oot of here before it all comes doon."

We both used wor hands, and had cleared most of the rubble away from him, but there was a plank of wood that was pinning Davey's legs. We tried to lift it but the timbers above Davey's head started shifting. Just then we heard a lad's voice. "De ye'se need any help? I'm the street firewatcher."

"Can you crawl in, lad?" shouted the Sergeant.

"Aye but do I need me stirrup pump?"

"Naw, just bring yoursel', lad."

When he reached us we saw that he was only aboot my age but he looked a strapping lad. "What do ye want me to de?"

Jack had been shining his torch up at the rubble just ower wor heeds. "We need to get him oot but if we dislodge owt all that lot could come doon on top of us. What's your name, son?"

"Frank Foster."

"Reet, Frank. I'm ganna put me shoulders just under that timber to stop any bits falling on Davey. Mossie, ye hold Davey under the armpits. Frank, ye lift the plank that's pinning Davey's legs – do it slowly mind and as soon as it's up a bit ye pull Davey oot, Mossie."

The Sergeant bent his knees and supported the rubble ower Davey's heed, then Frank put his hands under the plank and lifted – nothing happened - then he half stood and really put his back into it. I pulled backwards and Davey's legs came out. "He's oot!" I shouted.

"Thank Christ for that," said the Sergeant. "Reet lay him on his back. Frank, ye gan oot noo, and get an ambulance here as quick as ye like. I'm gan next. Mossie, ye pull Davey backwards – when you get to the tunnel, lay flat yoursel' and come back as far as you can. I'll pull ye oot by the ankles." He then shone his torch on Davey. "Oh ye bugger a-shite. Quick take your belt off, Mossie." I just did as I was tolt. I was looking at where the Sergeant's torch was shining. Davey's right arm was all mangled and he was missing his hand. I'd not noticed it before as it had been covered by the rubble. I gave the Sergeant the belt and he tied it roond the bottom of Davey's arm. He just nodded at me. "Quick as ye like, Mossie-lad," he said, as he went oot backwards.

I'd got Davey a fair way oot but I didn't kna' if I had the strength to gan any further when I felt a pair of strong hands roond me ankles. I was pulled oot backwards and as I was dragged along so was Davey. We were lucky. Jackie had seen an ambulance coming doon Fowler Street and had sent it along. They took one look at Davey and had him on the stretcher. Just then another plane came ower low, we all hit the ground and there was another couple of explosions. Once the dust had settled we stood up – there was a geet big cloud of smoke coming oot the roof of the *Queens Theatre*.

"We'll have to get going," said the woman ambulance driver. "I don't think he can hang on much longer," she said pointing at Davey, "he's lost a lot of blood."

"I'd gan along Ingham Street and on to Ocean Road – I wouldn't risk gan' past the *Queens* in case it all comes doon," shouted the Sarge.

They drove off gannen very slow – it was still pitch black in the streets where there were no houses on fire, and you never knew what debris you might drive into.

"D'ye think he'll be all reet, Sergeant?"

"He's a fit young lad so he should pull through, but if he does it'll be thanks to ye and Jackie. Now bugger off on your bike. Try to find oot where the rescue squads are and bring them up here where they're needed." As I ran across the cobbles me troosers fell doon to me ankles. "Come here, you stupid sod," said Jack. He undid his tie and gave it to me. "Put that roond your troosers and let me have it back the morra'." He patted me on the shoulder. He was a canny fella even though he had a gob as big as Tynemooth.

There were a couple of fire engines oot noo and one of them was in front of the *Queens* that had received a direct hit. Henry Milburn was there. He looked dazed and didn't have much of an idea of what I should de.

"There's hooses ablaze all ower the Lawe Top." He said it as though he couldn't believe it. "I can't use the phone in the box so I thought I'd head back to the nick."

"D'ye want me to have a look roond?" I asked.

"Aye, but ye won't get through up the road. There's a geet big crater between Fawcett Street and Ellesmere Street - you'd better cut through to Baring Street."

Mile End Road Crater

I was about to pedal off when we saw what looked like a convoy of fire engines and lorries coming up Mile End Road from Fowler Street. The first tender pulled up alongside and a fella stuck his heed oot the winda.

"We're from Sunderland to lend a hand. We were told to come here first and do what we could, then we're to get down the docks. There's oil tanks and timber yards ablaze." Now ye'll notice that I've put his words into English – I'm not even ganna attempt a Sunderland accent.

Henry just stood there so I suggested that half the tenders should go as far as they could up Mile End Road to where the bombs had landed, and that I could lead the others up to Robertson Street and Fort Street to deal with any hooses that were on fire. The fella looked at Henry who he had taken to be in charge. "Is that all right?"

"Aye, I think I'd better check that wor lass is all reet. I live in Moon Street. She'll not gan to the shelters." Henry wasn't coping well – he'd already suffered shock when the plane went up at Bents Park.

The Sunderland fella looked at me and just nodded. They left one tender to help with the fire at the Queens - two headed up Mile End Road followed by their rescue and first aid teams, and I led the last two along Bath Street and then up Baring Street. As we got to Fort Street I could see that there were hooses ablaze there and also in Robertson Street. I stopped the first engine and agreed that they'd each take one street, and that I would act as messenger between them. I went up to Robertson Street and we could see a good half dozen fires. The fire engine stopped ootside the first one we came to. The upstairs was well ablaze. The fella I'd been talking to said to me that they'd start on this one with the hose, but some of the crew would take their own stirrup pumps to deal with the smaller fires. "Can you pedal along and see if you can find out if there's anyone trapped inside any of the houses that are afire?"

There was a whistling sound and the next thing I knew I was blown off me bike and was rolling on the cobbles. I was a bit dopey but managed to get to me feet. One bomb had landed just up the road and demolished aboot six houses. Other bombs dropped by the same plane had landed on Fort Street and Mile End Road. The lads from Sunderland took ower. One of the ARP wardens and a couple of firewatchers teamed up with us. They knew that one family was in one of the hooses – they never went to the shelters. Then the ARP warden told us who had shelters in their back yards. The rescue team went to work, but the driver of the fire engine said that his men would put the fires oot first – they were leading the planes to us, and there was no sign of the raids finishing. We got a young lad oot of one of the hooses – he was lucky - he'd been sleeping in the front of the doonstairs flat and when the bombs had started gannen off he'd got under the bed. His mutha' and fatha' and their dog were in the kitchen when the bomb hit the hoose, and there was little hope for them. The youngster had been pulled oot of the rubble and there wasn't a scratch on him, but he was only in his nighty and he was crying, shivering and shaking. The first aid team were not sure what to de with him. With bombs still flying aboot it wasn't safe to keep him in their van, and they didn't want to leave the street until they'd seen how many more casualties there were. Just then a woman with a blanket on her shoulders came running ower from Cockburn Street. She had a lad aboot ten years old in her arms. He had blood all doon his face. "He was in bed with me mutha' – the windas were blawn in and me mutha's stone deed but little Ernie's all reet apart from the cut on his face." One of the first aiders took the lad and bandaged him up.

The woman saw the other lad who was sitting in the back of the van. "Eeh, is that ye, Tommy?" The lad nodded. She looked at me and speaking very quiet asked if there was any sign of his Mam and Da'. I just shook me head. "And wor Biddy," the lad said. There was nowt wrong with his hearing. The first aider handed young Ernie back to his Mam.

"It's not a deep cut and it should really be stitched, but he'll be safer staying indoors. Have ye got a shelter?"

"Naw, and the public one in Mile End Road is always full."

"Push a table against a wall and pull furniture in front to stop any shrapnel getting in."

"Wharraboot me Mam? She's deed in bed."

"If it's no bother it might be best to leave her there till the morning."

The woman looked at little Tommy. "Do ye want to come with us, Tommy, till they find your Mam and Da'?" He said nowt – just got oot the van, took little Ernie's hand and they all ran back across the road.

The fireman I'd been talking to looked across at me. "We've got our hands full here, but if I were you, son, I'd either go back to the Police Station or find a shelter. Until we put all the fires out the planes are not going to stop, and you can see the glow from the dockside from here. We can't get down there to help until we've done all we can here."

Just then we heard more planes flying ower and more explosions.

"I'll have to gan to see Sergeant Cummings. Last time I saw him he was heading up Mile End Road."

He put his hand oot and shook mine. "Glad to know you, I'm Ralph Thorburn; if you're ever in Sunderland look me up."

"Mossie Hamed."

The dust got thicker as I got nearer to Mile End Road. I nearly rode into a fella who was lying on the cobbles. I got doon and saw a stirrup pump just by him. It was Frank Foster. I shone my torch on him but couldn't see any blood or owt so I gave him a shake. He started coughing and then came to.

"Are ye all reet?" I asked him.

"I think so. I had to gan into a hoose that was ablaze to pull oot auld Mr. Voss. It was full of smoke so I put me muffler ower me mooth, but it took me ages to find him. I managed to drag him oot but I felt a bit funny, and when the last lot came doon with all the dust I must have blacked oot."

"There's an ambulance doon the street."

"Aye, but I'll be all reet. I live just along the road. Me Mam and Da' and wor Tommy'll be worried aboot me anyway." Me heart sank but I just said, "I'll walk along with ye."

"Naw, ye'd better get across the road. There's a shelter been hit."

"Frank, we just pulled a little lad called Tommy oot of a hoose, just opposite Cockburn Street. There's not much hope for your Mam and Da'."

Frank didn't say owt for a bit then he walked on. "Thanks for the warning, Mossie." He turned his heed. "Was wor Tommy all reet?"

"Aye. He was worried aboot his dog. A woman from Cockburn Street took him in. She had a bairn called Ernie."

"That'll be Mrs. Pells. I'll gan and see if she can put me up as well."

I was beginning to worry aboot Jackie when all of a sudden I got a punch on the shoulder, and three bikes pulled up beside me. It was Freddie who'd hit me, and Wally Duncan and Jimmy Clay were either side of him. "We've been looking all ower for ye. De ye kna' where Sergeant Cummings is?"

"I was after him mesel'. I'm thinking of gannen back to the nick, Freddie. I've nearly been blown up twice and I had to dig poor Davey oot, more deed than alive. Is Jackie all reet? I've not seen her for a bit."

"Jackie's up at the Ingham with Davey," Wally Duncan said. "She came back to report and didn't look too good hersel' so Ernie thought she might be better off oot of it. After she'd gone he said that Jackie was a sensitive lad."

"If ye'd seen Davey's eyeball running doon his cheek, ye might have felt a bit sensitive yersel'."

"There's nae point coming back to the nick, Mossie," Jimmy Clay spoke up. "A couple of HEs landed on Oliver Street and there's not much left of it. The back wall of the nick yard's doon and there's nae electricity. When he'd got ower the shock Inspector MacTomney sent us all oot. He wants us three to tell the Sunderland lads to get the rescue squads doon there as soon as they can. We think there's a lot of folk buried. There's not many shelters handy and most people there just stayed in their own hooses."

Wally Duncan spoke up as well. "Aye, and when we were coming roond the corner from Baring Street an air raid warden came running ower and tolt us that Pearson Street and Harper Street have been hit. With all the lines doon it's up to us to get messages through."

"The Sunderland lads have their hands full as it is up here, and they're under orders to get the fire engines doon the riverside as soon as they've put the fires oot. Ye and Freddie have a word with them, Jimmy. Wally, can ye come with me and we'll see if we can find Jack Cummings."

Me and Wally went roond the corner, and as we approached Fort Street we could see a geet big crater in the middle of the road and all the hooses on both sides were in ruins. A fireman saw us and waved us ower. He was holding an axe in one hand and a crow bar in the other. "After the first bombs came down the polis that was here and the wardens dashed for the surface shelter. I was going back to the tender to tell my lads to do the same, but I was too late and I took cover in a back yard." He pointed with his hand at a gap in the terrace where the houses used to be, and where there was now only smoking ruins. "That's where the shelter was. I'm putting together a rescue squad. If you ride to the fire engine in Fort Street they'll give you some shovels and pick-axes and then you can help me."

A few minutes later we were picking oor way ower the debris that was all that was left of what had been three or four hooses. We then heard shouting. A deep nasal voice was bellowing oot.

Surface Shelter Mile End Road

"That's Sergeant Cummings," I said and the fireman laughed.
"He's the quiet sort, is he?" We found the shelter. It was covered
in rubble but it was still standing. The houses that had been
on either side were just bricks and dust noo, but the shelter
had withstood the blast. There were some heavy roof timbers
blocking the doorway so we had to put wor backs into it, but
we managed to get to the door. That was the most difficult part
– the shelter had shifted a good foot and the door had buckled.
We had to smash it in which bought some interesting language
from inside. When we finally managed to break it doon, a billow
of dust blew oot, then came the Sarge. He saw me standing
there with me pick-axe in me hand, and he grabbed me by the
shoulders and gave me a bear hug. "I never thowt I'd be so glad
to see your ugly mug. Didn't I tell ye to get back to the nick." He
put his hand oot and shook with the fireman and Wally as the
twenty or so folk who'd been crammed in the shelter staggered

oot. There was some coughing and spluttering but no one was injured. "I thowt we were done for when the bomb landed. The whole shelter moved and some bricks came oot the wall but that was it. And then I thowt we'd suffocate if nae one found us." He looked around. "Jesus, we were lucky."

The fireman was looking roond as well. "What we going to do with those?" he asked, pointing to the folk who'd made it oot of the shelter and were wanderin' ower the bricks like lost souls.

"They won't want to gan into any more shelters, even if there are any with space left. We'll just have to start knocking on doors to see if any of the neighbours will take them in." He paused a minute. "Aye and dain't give them a choice." He turned and looked again at the shelter – there was a split in the right wall aboot six inches across that went from the ground to the roof but the rest was intact. "I'm ganna find oot who put that up and buy him a pint!"

For the rest of the neet until daybreak we were flying roond the cobbles in all directions. There was not really anyone in charge although Jack Cummings did his best, and we had to tell the firemen and the rescue squads where they were needed. If it was a team from Sunderland, we had to lead them, and that wasn't always easy as many roads were blocked. The planes that had been dropping bombs on the Lawe turned their attention to the riverside. The first incendiaries that had landed on the docks, the shipyards, and the timber yards had been put oot by the fire watchers, but they couldn't be everywhere, and once a few fires took had, the German planes had their beacons, and let loose with their high explosive bombs to de as much damage as they could. We had to take the Sunderland lads doon to the riverside – an emergency control centre had been set up in the Tyne Dock nick after the Anderson Street Fire Station was bombed and we had to pass messages between there, the Laygate ARP station and the *Alum House*, where the Home Guard were based. Everybody said that we owed a lot to the Sunderland fire fighters – they worked reet through the neet alongside wor lads with bombs landing and shrapnel flying but they didn't stop. Ralph Thorburn paid the price – he was in with a group trying to hose doon a blazing oil tank when it exploded. He was the lead man and took most of the blast. He wasn't killed outright and I was the PAM who had to sit in the front of the ambulance with the driver, who was also from Sunderland, to show him the way to the General Hospital. He was a mate of Ralph's and he kept the throttle on the floorboards all the way. Me hair was sticking reet up by the time we got there. It didn't de Ralph any good – he might have recovered from the blast but he'd inhaled too much smoke and his lungs packed up.

The all clear had gone at 4 o'clock and Jack Cummings called us back to the nick aboot an hour later. They'd managed to get the electric back on, and there was a mobile canteen in Keppel Street so we got a hot cup of tea. Every single bobby in the Shields force had turned oot, and they would stay oot until later that morning. Those that weren't helping the rescue teams or the billeting officer were directing traffic or putting up barriers where houses had been demolished. Once the barriers were up a bobby had to stay on duty. He'd help those who turned up wanting to find oot what had happened to relatives. They also had to stop looting. Ye got to see all sorts during the War – those like Frank Foster and Ralph Thorburn who were ready to give up their lives for others, and those who'd sneak roond to see what they could take from a ruined house.

The Chief Constable had sought help from neighbouring forces and we were to have an Inspector, three Sergeants and twenty one Constables to help oot. But it caused different problems – they all had to have billets and they had to be fed.

Before we went yem Sergeant Duncan called us together. He said we'd done well. Davey was still on the danger list, but if we all prayed for him he would pull through. The rescue teams needed as much help as they could get. We were to go home and get some sleep and if we wanted to volunteer we'd be welcome. "Those of you who have jobs will have to get permission from your boss."

There was a bit of pushing and shoving between Freddie Skee and Jimmy Clay. Jock looked up.

"Freddie'll be coming in, Sergeant," said Jimmy, "and I dain't think that Mr. Hertrich is ganna complain." Freddy worked as a butcher's boy at Hertrich's in Mile End Road.

"It's not funny, Sarge." Freddie was as near serious as I'd ever seen him. "The front of the shop was blown in last neet. I dinna' when Mr. Hertrich's ganna open again, and when we were closing last neet he said he'd put aside a nice bit of steak and kidney for me to give to me Mam today. She'll be lucky if she gets owt noo. We're registered with Hertrich's for meat."

"It's going to be hard for everyone, Freddie. There's some that have lost their homes, and everything in it, some have lost their lives, and young Davey's lost an eye and part of his arm." Jock looked worn oot. He'd been up all neet and he'd be on duty all day making sure that the new lads were shown the ropes.

We trooped off not saying much till Wally asked Jimmy why he and Freddie had been late coming in after the sirens had gone off. "We wouldn't have got here at all if that bastard Douthwaite had had his way, the little piece of sh**e." It wasn't like Jimmy to use that sort of language aboot someone – he was an easy going lad. "We'd been oot for a drink at the Westoe with Glenda and Gertie, and got back to the hostel aboot nine o'clock. Me and Freddie climbed ower the wall into the back yard and waited until we saw their light come on, and then clambered on top of the wash-house roof and up the drainpipe. One of the neighbours in the hoose ower the back lane must have seen us and thought we were borglars so they went oot to find a polis. Auld Douthwaite came roond knocking on the front door. The Matron wasn't gan to let him in as she had a fair idea that whoever was climbing in at nine o'clock in the evening wasn't after money or valuables, but Douthwaite insisted. She took him up the stairs and the first thing that we heard was a knocking on the door next to us, and the Matron asking the girls to open the door and that they should make themselves decent as there was a polis with her."

Freddie butted in. "Jimmy was still kissing and cuddling with Glenda, but I was having it off with Gertie under the sheets when we heard the Matron's voice. Well wor Gertie pushed me off so quick that I went rolling roond the floor bollock naked, and then the sirens went off. The Matron had just opened wor door, and could see Gertie with next to nowt on and me pulling me troosers up, so she slammed the door shut and shouted at the top of her voice to everybody to get their uniforms on and get on duty. We could hear auld Douthwaite demanding to arrest us – he said he'd seen us. The Matron said that she wasn't having a man in the hoose while the girls were getting into their uniforms and he'd have to arrest us ootside. Well me and Jimmy nearly broke wor necks getting oot the winda and slithering doon the drainpipe and me with only me troosers on – Gertie threw the rest of me claes oot the winda." He pulled up one of his trooser legs. "Nae sock – me mutha'll kill us."

"Ye'll have to tell her it was blown off by a bomb," Wally said. We were killing worselves laughing.

Me and Jackie rode back as far as Winchester Street. It was just getting light, and you could see the plumes of smoke still going up from the riverside. I went back with her and we had a few minutes in her back yard. I held her in me arms and put her head on me shoulders. "I'll never forget what you did for Davey, Mossie." I said nowt. "I had to go and tell his parents once the all clear had sounded. His brother Archie was shot down and killed two weeks ago."

"He never tolt us."

"He told me, but said he didn't want the others to know."

"Are you gannen back to de the rescue work?"

"I don't think so. I'm exhausted enough as it is and if there's another raid tonight then I'll need all my energy. What about you?"

"I'll have to see Mrs. Hussain. She'll be wondering where I am. I'd better be off."

I gave her a long kiss and then got back on me bike and was away to Frederick Street. Mrs. Hussain took one look at me and said that I should get back yem and go to bed. I said I would but that I'd help her with the early morning deliveries first. That didn't take long. All the roads to the riverside, where the warehouse was, were closed off. Alec Dorothy was on the barrier. "The fires are still blazing and Redheads' been hit bad. We've got orders to keep the roads clear for the fire services to get through. It's not safe anyhow at the minute. It should be all reet the morra' unless there's another raid." He looked at me.

"Ye all reet, Mossie? I heard that you saved your mate, Davey Corbett." News always travelled fast in Shields. I just nodded and told him that we were getting some more polis from neighbouring forces. "Thank Christ for that. I've been on since six o'clock yesterday morning – apart from a couple of hoors yesterday before the sirens went off."

Mrs. Hussain dropped me off at home. Before I got oot, she asked me if wor chickens were laying.

"Roosters dain't lay eggs," I replied. "Two of the chicks died and the other three started crowing at four o'clock in the morning so they ended up in the pot once they were big enough." She went roond to the back of the van and got oot half a dozen eggs in a paper bag. "Dain't ask me where I got them from, but get your Mam to cook you a couple of these for breakfast."

Me Mam was relieved to see me and soon had the skillet oot.
I had fried potatoes and two fried eggs. You couldn't always get
broon sauce any more but I had plenty of salt on it and some
bread and marge. Me Mam even let me have a spoonful of sugar
in me tea. "Could you wake me at ten o'clock, and I'll get back
to help them dig for survivors." I mustn't have sounded very
enthusiastic because the next thing I knew it was four o'clock
in the afternoon and me Mam was tapping on the door. I had a
cup of tea and some bread and jam and went off doon the nick. I
wanted to find oot how Davey was and see if they needed me to
do owt.

As I walked up to the Charge Office desk there was a new
fella there – an Inspector. "Have you come to sign the Coloured
Seamen's Register?" he enquired. Unlike Jack Cummings this one
was being serious. "No thanks," I said as politely as I could, while
Freddie and Matty, who were just coming along the corridor,
were sniggering behind the backs of their hands. "I'm Mossie
Hamed, one of the PAMs."

"The one who saved that Corbett lad's life?" He put his hand
out and shook mine. "I'm pleased to meet you, son. Herbert
Mullins – I used to be Inspector here until I retired. We moved
back to Durham and I was brought back into service with the
Durham Force. When the Chief here asked for aid I was the first
to volunteer."

"I was wondering how Davey Corbett was - he was in a bad
way last time I saw him."

"He had to have an emergency operation last night. He's lost
one of his eyes and they had to amputate his right arm below the
elbow. He's critical but the doctors say he's young and he's strong
so they're hoping he'll pull through. Your mate Hansen's been
going up to the Ingham for news. Is he a special friend of Davey's?
He seems very upset."

"We're all mates in the PAMs. Did you want me to come in to

help oot?" I asked.

"We're just about managing – Sergeant Leadbitter's coming on at eight. I think we'd rather have you fresh for tonight in case there's another raid."

My face must have dropped. "We're hoping they won't come again but we have to be prepared. You run along with your mates. Mr. Scott, the rescue foreman, just gave Freddie and Matty a shilling to spend on ice-cream. Seems they did good work." He raised his voice so that Freddie and Matty who were waiting for me by the five stone steps could hear. "Apparently they rescued a couple of budgies." Just as I was leaving he chuckled and said, "It was those two beggars who told me that an Arab seaman had come in last night to register, but had had to be turned away, and that he'd coming back tonight. They said he was a young lad with a scar on his face." I ran oot and Freddie and Matty had to shift up the steps or I would have murdered them.

We heard all aboot the rescue of the budgies while we were licking the monkey's blood off wor cornets. Jimmy Clay was there and so was Jackie.

Freddie had been put to work with the rescue teams at Oliver Street. Not many houses there had backyard shelters, and it was a long walk to the nearest public shelter so most of the homes had been occupied. A dozen or so survivors had been rescued the neet before together with as many deed bodies. Matty told us that the foreman, Mr. Scott, had made up a list of those who were missing, and the teams were slowly removing the rubble and debris. Every quarter of an hour Mr. Scott would blow his whistle and they'd all stop and listen in case anyone was shouting for help. The surest way of hearing owt was to lie on the ground and put your ear reet on top of the rubble.

"Me and Freddie were working together at a hoose where an auld couple lived. The firewatcher tolt us that they always stayed in bed – they never even bothered to get under a table or owt. We'd cleared most of the roof timbers away when Freddie suddenly shouts oot that he heard something from the hoose next door."

"Aye I did. And it sounded like a bairn crying," said Freddie.

"I shouted for quiet and then Mr. Scott came ower. We listened carefully and then we all heard it. It was a squeaky little voice and then it started chirruping. 'It's a budgie,' said Mr Scott and went to walk away."

"But the sound I heard was different," said Freddie, "and I tolt Mr Scott. I was sure it was a bairn."

Matty continued. "Mr. Scott got his list oot and had a good look. 'A couple lived here but they didn't have any bairns, and they were both brought oot last neet – deed, both of them.' Then Freddie said he was certain of what he'd heard and he was gan' to start digging towards where the sound had come from. Mr. Scott didn't look too pleased, but I said that I would help Freddie and that with the two of us it wouldn't take long. Mr. Scott just left us to it."

"Aye and half an hoor later we found two budgies in a cage on top of a small table reet up by the wall and underneath the table was a little bairn – he was covered in dust and had tears and snot running doon his face but he was alive. As soon as he saw me he held his hands up and I pulled him oot."

"Aye and he got shite all ower his hands. The little bairn's nappies had leaked oot."

"I crawled back through the tunnel we'd made, with the bairn while Matty brought the budgies. I was shouting me heed off for help and Mr. Scott and the rest of them came running ower. One of the first aid nurses took the lad. Mr. Scott patted me on the back. Aboot an hoor later the little bairn's mutha' turned up – her sister and brother-in-law had been looking after the bairn for the neet as she'd been working night shift that week. She'd only just got up and a neighbour had told her aboot the bombing at Oliver

Street."

"Aye, well that's all very well," said Jimmy, "but wharaboot the budgies?"

CHAPTER 6
APRIL/MAY 1941

There was no raid that neet and things started getting back to normal. We weren't very busy in the shop and Mrs. Hussain let me go early. As I stowed me bike up against the back wall me Mam came oot.

"Ye've got a visitor, Mossie. You're a bit of a dark horse," was all she said. When I walked into the kitchen I got the shock of me life. Jackie was sitting by the fire dressed as a lass. I kna' it sounds daft noo but I'd only ever seen her in lads' claes, and I dain't think I'd have recognised her if I hadn't known who it was. Jackie was dressed very smartly in a grey suit - her hair had been curled as well. Seeing her like a lass made me think of what we did when we were on wor own, and it felt as though I was blushing – I could feel me troosers starting to bulge at the groin so I sat doon sharpish. Looking at her again I began to realise that she was the sort of girl who would not have looked at me twice had we not been PAMs.

Mary couldn't keep her eyes off her. "Are ye really a lass then, Jackie?" she asked.

"Aye, she is," said me Mam, "and nae wonder your brother wanted to gan oot in the evening with her. When Jimmy Rutherford said he'd seen ye'se two coming oot of the air raid shelter one neet, I thought ye'd been smoking. I didn't think ye'd been canoodling." Mary let out a laugh. "Mossie canoodling with a lad!" Then she saw that Jackie had started to blush. "But ye were a lad then, weren't you?"

Me Mam looked at me and then back to Jackie. "I'm gan' next door to see Bella Rutherford to borrow half a cup of tea leaves, and ye can come with me, Mary. And keep your gob shut aboot Jackie." As they went oot the back door little Mary shouted oot, "And nae canoodling."

"I've never seen you dressed as a girl, before, Jackie."

"I know, Mossie, but I had to come round and tell you. I went and told Davey's parents that he was in hospital. I was just stood on the step, and I had my uniform and helmet on so I don't think they got a good look at me. They called round the house this afternoon. They asked if I was Jackie Hansen, and then said that they had some bad news. Well I thought Davey had died but of course they didn't know that I knew that Davey was injured. They said that they'd been able to have a quick word with him after he'd come round from his operation and he'd asked if I could visit him. He'd told them that he'd been going out with me for a while. I just couldn't say no, but I'm going to have to go as a girl. They said to meet them there at six o'clock, and they'll say I'm family."

"I kna' you'd been to the flicks with him but I didn't kna' you'd been gan' oot with him, Jackie."

"Well, it was only a couple of times, and I certainly wasn't going to get serious with him. You know how I feel about you, but I can't not go to see him."

"Course you can't. We'll all gan up I expect, when he's a bit better. Did they say how he is?"

"No more than we knew all ready. He's lost his right eye and part of his right arm - the doctors think that he should recover but it will take time."

"So he won't become a pilot like his brother."

"He won't even be able to be a PAM."

Me Mam came back and we told her aboot Davey. She asked

Jackie if she wanted to stay for tea but she had to get off.

After Jackie had gone me Mam looked at me and was just gan to open her mouth when I stopped her. "Dain't say owt," I said.

After me tea I went into the back yard and sat in the air raid shelter for a bit. It was cad but I didn't want any company. There was a shout from the door, "Ye've got another visitor."

I went in. It was Sergeant Duncan. "I was passing and thought I'd look in to see if you were all right. I'm proud of you, lad, and of the others. You're only supposed to be messengers, but you're saving lives and putting your own at risk - and young Freddie Skee's even rescuing budgies." He laughed. "I was up at the hospital just now to see young Davey. It's a terrible thing for the lad but it could have been worse if you and Jackie Hansen hadn't acted so quickly."

"Aye but it was Sergeant Cummings who put the tour-n-i-whatsit on. I couldn't have done that."

Me Mam handed him a cup of tea. She even offered him some sugar and he said just half a spoonful would be fine. She gave a cup to me as well, but I didn't get the offer of sugar.

"Davey's parents were there and they had a young lass with them. They said she was Davey's girlfriend." He paused and sipped his tea. "You and Jackie Hansen are best friends, aren't ye, Mossie?"

"Aye."

"And ye knew he was a lassie?"

"Aye. We all did."

"You all did and none of you thought to tell me or Sergeant Cummings."

"Davey wanted to but she's one of the quickest bike riders and we all liked her – I mean even when she was a lad."

"I'm surprised at Davey."

"Aye, well the thing is Jackie never told any lies when she applied."

Jock said nowt.

"When she had turned up in a dress auld Douthwaite had said she should gan yem and knit some socks for wor lads at sea. She went yem, got her Mam to cut her hair short, put on some of her brother's claes and went back. Douthwaite just sent her along to ye, and ye never asked her if she was a lass. She answered all your questions – her name's Jacqueline but everybody calls her Jackie."

A smile nearly broke oot on Jock's face.

"We're one short with Davey being injured so we can't afford to lose anyone else just now, but I'm going to have to take it upstairs. If anything were to happen to her, and it came out that we'd turned a blind eye to her being a lassie, it wouldn't look good."

I just nodded. He stayed on for a good while. He'd known me Mam and me Da' for years. He looked tired. One of his jobs was to liaise with the Army aboot unexploded bombs. He'd been doon at Templetoon most of the day. The ARP had called him oot as a geet big hole in the ground had appeared in the yard at Newton and Nicholson's, the packing factory, after the raid. They thought it might be a bomb hole. Jock's job was to have a look and work oot if it was worth calling the bomb disposal squad at Low Fell. He'd measured the hole and it was more than two feet across. He couldn't think what else it might be but the maximum width of a bomb hole he'd learned aboot at the briefing sessions was eighteen inches. He'd put oot a call to Tyne Dock nick and they'd sent someone oot to Harton House Road where the bomb squad were dealing with a UXB that had come down in someone's back garden. A Sergeant and a couple of sappers had turned up an hour and a half later. "The Sergeant was a Willie Leslie frae' Arbroath. I'd just shaken his hand when a voice I recognised says, 'Hello, Sergeant Duncan.' It was Dekka Waite, Little Audrey DiBresci's brother."

For those of ye who aren't from Shields someone who's got

the same first name as their fatha' or mutha's called 'little' and the parent's 'big'. Noo Audrey's Mam was called Big Audrey even before the lass was born – she was aboot six foot tall and five foot wide. She was married to Harry Waite, a villain who was noo in Durham Jail, and she ran a little fish and chip shop in Dale Street. Little Audrey DiBresci who ran DiBresci's Café was not so little either – she was tall, not as stout as her Mam and had lovely yella' hair and blue eyes. She'd married Tony DiDresci whose parents had started the ice-cream business before the last War. Her mutha' had taken against him from the start when Little Audrey used to gan into the DiBresci's kiosk next to the Casino for an extra squeeze of sauce from young Tony. People still tell the story of how Big Audrey came yem early one neet from the fish and chip shop and caught Tony in bed with Little Audrey who was supposed to be ill. Dekka, who was a mate of Tony's, was the look out, but he had his eye glued to the crack in the door to see what they were up to, and Tony had to jump oot the winda and ower the back yard wall with nowt on but his combs. Big Audrey had two of her sons with her, Bobby and Jack, both trawler men - they had their knives oot, and would have cut something off Tony had he not ran smack into Sergeant Duncan who was on his rounds. He knew the Waites and saved Tony's bacon by arresting him for indecency. Tony and Little Audrey got married a few months later, just before another Little Audrey was born.

Sergeant Duncan sipped his tea from his saucer. "I said to Dekka that I thought he'd still be in the glass house – the last I'd seen of him was when I arrested him for being AWOL - but he just smirked. 'With all the bombs coming doon and sappers getting blown up they were desperate for men, so I was offered three months off me sentence if I volunteered for bomb disposal.' 'They must have been desperate to take you, Dekka,' I told him and then Sergeant Leslie said that he was lucky to have been given Dekka and a couple of other rascals. 'Some other sections got conscies. Men, who are too scared to fight the enemy, digging up bombs that can go off any minute! They'd be jumping oot the shafts every time anyone farted.'"

The Sarge chuckled. "Dekka might be around for a bit because Willie Leslie reckoned it was a bomb all right, and a big one. He had a bit of equipment like a chimney cleaner's rod but without a brush on the end. He made us all step right back and he slowly put it down the hole, screwing on fresh lengths every six feet. He reckons it's twenty feet down at least and that it may have jinked off sideways. It could take a week to find it. He wanted to have the factory evacuated but Mr. Nicholson refused. He said he had important orders for the Navy to fill. He'd let people who were afraid stay at home but they wouldn't get paid."

Jock then asked me Mam aboot wor Mary. She'd been evacuated when the war broke oot, but had come back yem for Christmas and stayed like most of the little ones. "If we start having many more raids like the other night then we're going to have to think of evacuating those bairns who returned. I'd have a word with your lass's teacher. They might be organising something." Jock slurped the last drop of tea from his cup and then stood up to go. "Och, and Jack Cummings says that he's still waiting for his tie back, Mossie."

I pulled up me jumper - it was still there. "I've not got me belt back, and I'm not sure I will."

"Aye well you better find something else for your trousers – Jack's wearing a tie I lent him – it was my father-in-law's, and I'd like it back." Me Mam said she was sure that she still had a couple of auld belts of me Da's, so Jock left.

Me Mam found me a belt - we would have to punch another hole in it to fit roond me waist as me Da' was a stocky fella, but that could wait - it would de. I said that I might as well gan doon the nick to give Sergeant Cummmings his tie back. It didn't take five minutes and then I went up to Winchester Street. I guessed that Jackie would be back by noo. I tapped on her back winda with my special knock and she came oot. "It's Mossie," she shouted to her Mam.

I didn't say owt, I just pressed her against the yard wall and started kissing her. She put one hand roond me waist and one roond me neck. I took had of the hand that was roond me waist, and put it doon me troosers – the auld belt was loose enough – she tried to pull her hand back but I held it firmly.

I'm not gan' to tell you what happened because that's between me and Jackie, but when I pulled away, I told her that the next time I wanted to have it properly. I pushed her against the wall again and started nuzzling her neck.

"We could have been killed the other neet - or injured like Davey. All me mates have had it." I've never been good at words and just muttered, "Dain't ye want it, as well?"

She kissed me on the lips then said that I should come roond next Sunda' morning. "Me Mam has started going to the early morning communion at St. Mark's at eight o'clock. We'll have an hour."

I'd tried to see Johnny for a French letter but he was back on the balloons and they were working all hours. They were repairing the ones that had been damaged and putting more up.

She was good to her word and that Sunda' I was rippin' me claes off as she got back under the sheets with just her nighty on. That came off quick enough. She said did I have a johnnie - I tolt her that I couldn't get one, but that I'd pull oot before I shot me bolt. This is not a dirty book so I'm only telling ye what happened because ye need to kna', to understand things later on. It took a bit of patience for me to get it in as I'm quite big doon below, and it was wor first time. By the time I was reet up her I was so excited that I blew me dust nearly strite away. I didn't even have time to come oot, but I didn't groan or owt as I wanted it to last, and just kept moving backwards and forwards as though nowt had happened. Well by the time I was nearly there for the second time, Jackie was moaning, digging her nails into my back, and then I did pull oot and shot all ower her belly.

As you've probably gathered I'm not ower clever, and when I rode oot of their back lane I was ower the moon. Me and Jackie would keep gannen oot together and we could have it every Sunda' in bed, and if we were lucky, during the week in the air raid shelter in wor back yard. I'd track doon Johnny Wallis as well so I wouldn't have any more accidents.

I met up with the lads at DiBresci's later that morning. Jimmy wasn't there and Jackie didn't turn up either so it was just me, Matty, and Freddie. Wally was there of course. He said his Da' was coming in for dinner with that Inspector Mullins who was billeted with him. Wally said you should have seen his Da's face when Mullins turned up on the doorstep with his little canvas suitcase. "All me life I've had to put up with me Da's tales aboot auld Mullins and how he made me Da's life a misery when he was a constable, and noo he's putting him up." He laughed as he gave us another squeeze of monkey's blood on wor ice-creams.

Freddie put his hand in his pocket and pulled oot a pocket watch. "Where'd ye get that?" asked Wally. It was quiet in the café and he had joined us at the table. "I foond it in one of the hooses we were pulling doon."

"Ye'd best put it away, ye stupid nowt," said Matty. "Ye kna' we're not to take things. Mr. Scott would go mad if he knew ye had it."

"Ye can't keep it, Freddie." I said. "There'll be someone who's lost their hoose and has nowt left – you can't take that from them as well. It's stealing, isn't it?"

"Aw, I've seen others take things when Mr. Scott's back's turned, and besides we'd taken corpses oot of that hoose so it won't be claimed."

"That's even worse," I said. "Stealing from the deed. You

should hand it in."

Wally was looking a bit pale. "I heard me Da' talking to auld Mullins the other day, and they were saying that the bobbies on the barriers of the bomb sites had to be on the look oot for looters. They said that if there were any army lads on hand they would shoot them. They reckon that if they caught anyone they'd be sent doon for a long time."

"Ye bugger a-sh**e," said Freddie, "I'm not a bloody looter."

"That's what they all say," said Wally. "Me Da' reckons there was a volunteer fireman in London caught taking things – he had two cigarette lighters and a pipe – he got six months with hard labour."

"Aye and there was those two lads of ten somewhere doon sooth who got four strokes of the birch," said Matty.

Freddie got up. "I'm gan back to the nick to hand it in. I'll just say I found it in the street when I was walking past this morning." He caught up with us later on when we cycled down to the pier and along Sea Road. The sea front hadn't been sealed off then so ye could still watch the ships come in. Ye had to be careful, mind – if you noted doon what ye saw ye could be arrested. A woman and her daughter from George Scott Street had been sittin' on the rocks writing doon details of the ships they saw gannen oot and coming in. She'd been deein it for years apparently. Some lad saw them and told one of the war reserve police – they were up in Court and fined five pund each.

"Did ye hand it in all reet?" I asked Freddie.

"I was gan up the steps and auld Douthwaite was there. He asked what I wanted so I telt him. He said he'd give it to the Sergeant."

The sirens went off on Tuesda' aboot eleven o'clock and I was oot like a shot. Jackie wasn't at the corner of Winchester Street where we usually met. I waited five minutes and then went off on me own. The ack-ack guns were gan crazy and by the time I got to Keppel Street ye could hear the bombs gan' off but it all sounded a bit far away. Newcastle and Tynemouth were badly hit but only a couple of bombs landed doon by the docks in Shields so we just stayed in the nick and helped oot in the office. There wasn't a lot to de and then Jack Cummings came in. "I thought ye lot would be here. Ye'll have heard that they've found oot aboot Jackie." The blank look on the other's faces gave them away. "You haven't told them then Mossie?"

"They all knew."

"I'm not talking aboot that. I kna' they all knew that she was a lass, and I'd twigged months ago. I may look auld to ye'se lot but I can tell a lass when I see one, even if she is wearing troosers. But Jock didn't kna' till he saw her up at the Ingham visiting Davey, and his parents introduced her to him as Davey-lad's girlfriend. And Jock being Jock had to play it by the book."

"You mean she's oot," said Freddie.

"Aye. Sergeant Duncan had to tell the Chief, but he did suggest that they might consider taking lasses on as PAMs. The Chief wasn't having it and told Jock off for even suggesting it. Jock went roond to Jackie's Mam's today to tell her. Jackie had already guessed that she'd get the bullet. She wasn't too upset – apparently she's engaged to Davey noo. He put the question yesterday. He's ganna be oot in a week or two and they won't be having a long engagement. She reckons they'll be wed by the end of the month – his parents have a big hoose in Hepscott Terrace and they'll live there.

"That was a surprise, I tell ye. I thowt it was wor Mossie she was after. And if I'd thowt she was a lad I would have been worried aboot the way them two were always gannen roond together."

"Did ye think he was sticking a tail on Jackie, Sergeant Cummings?" It was Freddie – the dirty little twat.

Jack laughed. "Well noo, if Mossie had been a coloured seaman then Jack-the-lad might have had something to worry aboot." He started laughing then caught sight of me face.

"Reet, Freddie, less of the dirty talk and put the kettle on. I want a word with Mossie aboot something. Come on Mossie-lad," he said to me, "there's nae one in the CID room - we'll gan in there. Bring two cups along when you're ready, Fred."

Sergeant Cummings didn't say owt for a bit. "Were ye and Jackie gan' oot together, Mossie?"

"Naw, we couldn't because if anyone saw us they'd kna' that Jackie Hansen was a lass."

"But you and Jackie were more than just friends."

"Well, I thowt we were. I knew Davey fancied her and he'd asked her oot, but she'd only gan to the flicks with him dressed as a lad and with the others. Or that's what she telt me. I can't afford to gan to the flicks mesel' much. D'ye think she took pity on him?"

"Mebbes not pity, but how could she refuse him? We all knew he was gan to be a pilot, and noo he won't even be able to be a PAM. If she'd said naw, people would have thought it was because of his wounds."

"She came roond to wor hoose the other neet dressed as a lass. She seemed like someone different - the sort of lass who wouldn't look twice at someone like me."

Freddie brought the tea in. The Sarge said that I should just put it doon to experience – there were a lot of lasses in Shields deein' war work and it wouldn't be too difficult for me to get one of them to come oot with me. "But dain't gan climbing up any drainpipes to get into the women's hostel, mind." He let oot a dirty laugh. He didn't say much more after that and we took wor cups of tea back to the Charge Office.

"Did Constable Douthwaite give ye that watch I handed in, Sergeant Cummings?" Freddie asked. Jack knew nowt about any watch, and there wasn't any entry in the lost property register. "It should have gone to the ARP headquarters anyway - he probably took it there."

The next time Freddie was ower at the ARP offices in Chapter Row he asked them if a watch had been handed in. They kept a register of all valuables found on bomb sites – no watches on the day Freddie had handed it in, or any of the days afterwards – at least not from Oliver Street and nothing from Constable Douthwaite. We had a chinwag aboot it, but it would only be Freddie's word against Douthwaite's, and after the trouble we'd got into it wasn't worth it.

I was thinking aboot other things anyway. I'd not seen Jackie since she'd stopped coming in. We heard from Glenda that she had volunteered to become a first aider, and was also being given driving lessons. Davey was oot of hospital and he called in one evening with Jackie. After he'd shaken me hand and thanked me for rescuing him, I just went oot into the yard, got on me bike, and went off to have a quick ice-cream with Wally.

There weren't many in the café and then the door opened and in walked this soldier. Wally took one look at him and then shouted oot, "Hey Audrey, it's Dekka." Little Audrey came running oot from the other side of the café and the soldier lad gave her a big hug. "Si'doon and I'll get you a cup of tea," she said and pushed him into a chair on the table where I was sitting. "This is Mossie," she said, "he's a mate of Wally's in the PAMs." Dekka held his hand oot and we shook. "Any mate of Wally's a mate of mine." He had curly black hair, brown eyes and a shifty eyed sort of smile – nowt like the other Waites.

"Are ye the Dekka Waite that's working with the bomb disposal squad doon at Templetoon? Sergeant Duncan said he met ye there."

Little Audrey was just behind the counter. "He's deein' what!"

"I was gan to tell ye. I'm a sapper in the Engineers noo – I was let oot early from the glass hoose on condition that I volunteered

for the bomb disposal squad. It's canny work, mind. We dig doon
for the bombs and the Lieutenant gets in the hole and either takes
the fuse oot or is blown up. There's a big bastard in the groond
at Newton and Nicholson's. We're already ten foot doon and
we've got a good bit further to gan. Willy Leslie, the Sergeant,
reckons it's a Satan. There's only been two dropped in England so
far. They're 1000 killygrams." My face must have looked blanker
than usual. "That's two thousand punds to ye, Mossie. The
Lieutenant's had to gan doon to London for a couple of days so
Willie's in charge. He said I could have the neet off if I wanted. Is
wor Jack ashore?"

"Naw, ye've missed him by a couple of days. If he was he'd be
in here with Bobby or at the *Marine*. Wor Bobby only gans oot
when Jack's yem."

I knew Bobby and Jack Waite - they were the oldest of the
Waite brothers. They were both big lads - Bobby was fair haired
like his sister and Jack was a carrot heed.

They'd been trawler men before the war and had their own
boat. Once War broke oot the North Sea became like a minefield
and ships were being blown up all ower the place. The Navy
wanted more men for their Naval Patrol Boats – they were
trawlers that had been taken from their owners. They were
needed for minesweeping and for patrol work including search
and rescue. A lot of the Shields fishing boats and half the Hull
fleet of ocean going trawlers were put under the white ensign,
but they all needed crew. Bobby and Jack were called up onto the
Evalina, a former Hull trawler.

The *Evalina* was sweeping for mines aboot five miles oot from
the Tyne when a mine they were clearing went up and the *Evalina*
went doon. A few lucky ones managed to scramble into the one
lifeboat that wasn't blown to smithereens. There were about three
or four in the watter and they managed to fish them oot, but then
they saw Bobby and Jack holding on to a piece of timber aboot

fifty yards away. Bobby was unconscious and in a bad way – Jack shouted that one of Bobby's hands was blown off and he thought his legs were broken. They managed to get Jack into the boat, cramped as it was, but Bobby could not help himsel', and when they tried to pull him in, the boat nearly capsized. The Skipper swore, then called oot that he was not going to jeopardise the safety of the rest of the crew and he ordered the oarsmen to pull away. Jack didn't say owt – just stood up, dived ower the side and swam to Bobby who had just started to gan under. That was the last they saw of them. The survivors were picked up and Bobby and Jack were listed as missing presumed deed.

Two days later news came through from the Grimsby Police that two lads had been landed the day before from a Danish trawler – they were both in a bad way but one of them was a bit agitated. He wanted his Mam to know that they weren't deed. That was Jack.

One of the Danish trawlers that had come ower after the outbreak of war, and was fishing oot of Grimsby, had been half way through a trawl when they'd heard the explosion. One of the crew had spotted the two lads – they'd only just reached them in time. Jack had tight ahad of Bobby but was just gan' under as one of the Danes, who'd jumped in with a rope tied roond him, had got to them. By the time Jack had recovered enough to talk they had loaded the fish and were heading for their home port of Grimsby – none of the Danes spoke much English and they thought Jack was Norwegian as he kept on aboot gettin' yem. Their Skipper, who had been at sea for ower forty years and had picked up a fair amount of practical medical knowledge, kept Bobby alive until he was put ashore and sent to hospital. He lost a hand and a leg, but he was a fighter and pulled through. When the story spread roond Shields there were some who said that Jack should have a medal and others that he was daft but lucky. It took Bobby months before he got oot of hospital. Jack went straight back to the Navy Patrol but managed to get posted to a boat oot of Shields and would spend all his shore leave with Bobby.

Dekka finished his coffee, wolfed doon a plate of fish and chips, and then went off to see his Mam and Bobby. Before he went he asked Audrey if he could come back and kip doon at the café. She said it was all reet but Dekka was only there the one neet. When the Lieutenant got back he had insisted that Dekka stay with the rest of the men. They were in Shields nearly a week. They had to dig doon twenty feet and then found that the bomb had jinked across another seventeen feet so they had to dig another shaft. When they finally located it they saw that it was the biggest that they had had to deal with. It was a Satan. The Lieutenant ordered that the premises be cleared when he was defusing the bomb. He went doon the hole and unscrewed the fuse cover. It wasn't a time delayed fuse, but just in case it was booby trapped he fitted a tool they called a Crabtree to the side of the bomb and put a length of twine roond the fuse. He then climbed oot the hole and got behind a wall of sandbags before trying to pull the fuse oot. The twine snagged so he had to gan doon again but the next time it came oot all reet. Once the fuse was oot the sappers had to pull it oot of the shaft. They had what they called a sheerlegs, which according to Dekka was like a photographer's tripod but much bigger. It took them hoors to hoik it oot and when they weighed it, it was 1800 kilograms. Mr. Nicholson organised a whip roond for the sappers – they drank it all in the nearest pub as soon as they'd finished.

The next day me Mam had a visit from the billeting officer – he'd been informed that her husband had been lost at sea, and that she would have room to take in someone. The RAF were in need of accommodation for the new balloon crews. Me Mam said there wasn't room, but he had a look roond and said that all three of us could sleep in the one bedroom and if we didn't like that then me Mam could put a bed doon in the front room. As he was leaving he asked why the polis should have known that she had room for a lodger and me Mam explained that I worked as a PAM. "Aye, that will be it. We normally have to rely on neighbours with a grudge against someone to tell us." He looked at his notes. "It was a Constable Douthwaite who contacted us."

I knew then that I was gan' to have Douthwaite on me back, but there was nowt I could de aboot it for the present.

Me Mam wasn't having a stranger in the hoose, and the next neet when I got yem from work there was this Arab lad sitting by the fire. "This is Saleem, Mossie. I kna' him from the café." Saleem stood up and he gave me the nicest smile I'd seen in a while. He was in his twenties, and was a stocky lad with jet black hair and big broon eyes. "He lodges at Said's but has been looking to find somewhere regular. He's a fireman on the *Sheaf Crown* that takes coals doon to Lowestoft and London. He's away for a week or more and then has a few days yem. If you dain't have any objections I'm ganna' take him as a lodger, and bugger the billeting officer. We can put a bigger bed in your room." Saleem stayed for tea and moved in a couple of days later when we had got a three quarter bed. It took up all the space, and if the one who got in first had to get oot in the night, he had to climb ower the other one. It was strange sleeping with someone else in the bed and Saleem moved aboot a lot particularly on the first neets after he'd got yem from a voyage. I was complaining aboot it to the lads at DiBresci's one neet when Freddie comes oot with a chorus of *Keep Your Feet Still Geordie Hinny*.

Keep yor feet still! Geordie, hinny, let's be happy for the neet,
For aw mayn't be se happy throo the day.
So give us that bit cumfort, -keep yor feet still, Geordie lad,
An' dinnet send maw bonny dreams away!"

Things settled doon. When Saleem was yem he would sometimes take me oot to one of the cafés for a cup of coffee, and a game of cards or dominoes. I was the only one in wor hoose that spoke proper Arabic. We all tried to help him with his English – he could make himsel' understood but that was aboot it.

Every noo and again Mrs. Hussain and Jasmin would come ower of an evening and we'd all play dominoes or cards. She'd usually bring something ower for wor supper, like spam or corned beef or some cheese. I never asked but I worked it oot that Johnny Wallis and Myra Wade must be using her flat above the shop and keeping an eye oot for the two lads who'd be abed - Johnny would bring something with him to show his gratitude.

One neet I was in DiBresci's with Matty and Freddie when Frank Foster came in. He was the lad I'd met up the Lawe Top. He came and sat doon with us and Wally brought him ower a cornet. We all knew he'd lost his Mam and Da', and that him and little Tommy were living with the Pellses. Matty had dug oot their dog Biddy three days after the raid. She'd been covered in dust and could hardly stand but when he'd knocked on Mrs. Pells' door, with Biddy in his arms, Tommy had come running up and her little tail had started wagging.

After a bit he said that Constable Errington had told him where to find us. "I was looking for ye, Mossie. It's just that the other neet I was gan' yem from work with Jimmy Mothersdale, who lives in Reay Street, and I asked that auld bobby who's on the barriers if he knew whether they'd found a cigarette case and a lighter that belonged to me Da'. The polis asked me what number - I tolt him, and he said he'd ask roond. Well, I heard nowt the next day but then Jimmy asked me if I'd got anything. He'd seen the auld fella' poking aboot later that evening and he was sure that he'd put something in his gas mask bag. When I saw the bobby that neet he said it wasn't his job to search the ruins and I should ask someone in the rescue squads. Jimmy was adamant he'd taken something."

"What did he look like?" I asked.

"He's one of those war reserve lot with a little red badge on their shoulder. He's got a red face and gingery hair."

"Douthwaite," all three of us muttered.

Freddie then gave me a wink and said, "Hey Frank, would you want to have a chinwag with Mossie?" Frank didn't say owt but he moved his chair a bit away from me. We all burst oot laughing and tolt him the story.

"So if one of ye'se lot tell anyone they'll think you're picking on him again."

"Aye, and besides, if it comes to nowt then me and Freddie'll be reet in the sh**e."

"We've got to de something, though," said Freddie, and looking at Frank he continued, "I handed in an auld pocket watch to Douthwaite, but there's nae record of it in the registers. It's not reet."

"I dain't think Inspector MacTomney would help; he's a pal of Douthwaite's. Jock would have the same problem as us. Even Jack Cummings would think twice."

Wally Duncan had been standing listening. "I'll tell ye who might help." We all looked up. Wally usually didn't say owt – like his Da' – just listened. "Inspector Mullins."

"The new fella who thowt Mossie was a coloured seaman." Freddie ducked even before I'd thrown the punch.

"Aye. Me Da' and him are good mates noo but at one time me Da' was always running him doon. He used to say that Mullins always thought the worse of everybody, and wouldn't miss a chance to catch one of his own men at something or other."

We just sat there. "Well who's gan to speak to him?" said Freddie, looking at me. It was Matty who answered.

"Mr. Scott'll have a word. I kna' where he lives but he often gets in the *Woodbine* for a pint. I'll have a walk along noo. Do ye want to come, Frank?"

"I'll walk alang with ye but I dain't drink. Me Mam and me Da' were Methodists who'd taken the pledge, and I wouldn't want to let them doon."

"Nae bother," said Matty; "there's a back room where we can gan and ye can have a lemonade."

Mr. Scott was a quiet sort of bloke, and I dain't think he would have helped if Frank had not gone along, but he listened carefully, and said that he'd de what he could. He went to see Inspector Mullins that neet at Jock Duncan's hoose. Jock was there but said nowt.

It was all ower the papers so you'll probably kna' what happened.

"The Chief witness for the prosecution of War Reserve Policeman Algernon Douthwaite, who is accused of looting, was Inspector Herbert Mullins of the Durham Police, on secondment to the Shields Constabulary at the time of the alleged offence. He said that he was out inspecting the bomb sites late one afternoon when he thought one of the constables, who was manning the barriers in Robertson Street, was acting suspiciously. He approached the constable and searched him. He had twenty pounds in his pocket, and a cigarette lighter, two razors, and a china vase in his gas mask bag. They had all come from derelict houses that had not yet been demolished. The twenty pounds had come from a tin that had contained the life savings of the occupier who had been killed in the bombing raid. A search of Constable Douthwaite's home had resulted in many objects being recovered, some of which could be returned to their owners."

What the Gazette didn't say was that Mr. Scott had found the tin a couple of days before and it was at the ARP headquarters – there was £120 in it. He'd borrowed it back, marked all the notes and returned it to where he'd found it - in a pile of books amongst the wreckage of a bookcase. When he left the site that afternoon he'd had a chat with Douthwaite. He'd told him that the deed man's son had been to see him because he knew his Da' kept a lot of money in a tin behind some auld books. He'd said that he hadn't had time to do a search so could Douthwaite make sure that nae one got into the hoose. Inspector Mullins was waiting in Matty Lightfoot's front room in Fort Street having a cup of tea, nae sugar, and me, Freddie, and Matty were up a back lane doon the street where we could see what Douthwaite was up to. As soon as he'd come oot the hoose we'd been off to Fort Street and Mullins had gone into action. We'd got on wor bikes and found Douggie Errington who'd taken ower the beat from Henry Milburn who was off sick with the shell shock. Constable Errington took watch on the barrier until someone could be sent up to relieve him. When they'd searched Douthwaite's hoose they'd found all of Frank Foster's Da's valuables and a pawn ticket for the watch Freddie had handed in, together with quite a few other things.

Mullins made no mention of the part we'd played but a couple of neets later when we were in DiBresci's Wally didn't charge for wor ice-creams and said that they were on Inspector Mullins. He was off back to Durham soon and had wanted to show his appreciation.

Douthwaite was also sent to Durham – the jail, not the nick. He'd been held in the cells overnight and put up in Court the next morning. The Magistrates had remanded him to Durham Jail as they didn't have powers to send him doon for the stretch he deserved. We all thought he'd be oot in three months, but the Judge took a hard line aboot people in a position of trust, and he got eighteen months with hard labour. Naebody at the nick celebrated – nae one liked him, but we never thowt he was that stupid.

It wasn't much after that that the Pastor at the Mission called on Myra Wade to tell her that her Harry had been lost at sea in one of the Russian convoys. We all went roond to see her. She seemed more upset at losing Harry's wage than losing Harry. Then aboot four weeks later we found oot that the billeting officer had been roond. They needed accommodation for officers from the barrage balloon section as new personnel were being drafted in. She'd been allocated a certain Flight Lieutenant John Wallis who would be moving in as soon as they could send a bed roond. It was a relief for Alice Hussain as she'd heard the neighbours gossiping aboot her visitors and how it was giving the street a bad name. It did mean that she didn't come roond so often with Jasmin, who was nearly fifteen noo and was a real bonny lass - Alice had started to get worried aboot the attention Saleem paid to her. I didn't think there was owt in it. He was the same with Mary and me Mam – it was his way of being friendly.

CHAPTER 7
MAY - SEPTEMBER 1941

Noo that I wasn't gan oot with Jackie I was often tempted by Jasmin when we were in the back shop together even though she was a couple of years younger than me. She had light broon hair, lovely blue eyes, and she was well built for her age. Her Da' had been an Arab seaman who was Geordie Hussain's half brother, and her mother had been a fair haired lass who'd worked in the shop. She'd died in some sort of scandal that no one talked aboot, and Alice and Geordie had brought her up as their own. She'd sometimes look at me and smile, but I didn't really want to get involved with anyone else for the minute. I still spent most of my time thinking aboot the time I was in bed with Jackie, and I certainly couldn't de that with Jasmin or her mutha' would kill me, or worse.

Wor Mary was also growing up and was a nice looking lass, mind. She hadn't quite got ower her thing with Jimmy Clay, but Jimmy was gan' oot with Glenda whenever he could. He'd not asked me for any more johnnies, so I think he was going to try and wear her doon slowly. Freddie wasn't having any luck either. The Matron at the hostel had given Glenda and Gertie a final warning after she'd seen them with fellas in their room - and they wouldn't just be kicked oot of the hostel they would lose their jobs. Even though me Mam let me keep a bob pocket money, I wasn't seeing so much of the lads anyway - I just didn't fancy meeting up with the other PAMs noo Jackie was not aboot. I'd started gan roond to see Frank Foster and little Tommy and we'd gan for walks with their dog Biddy. Him and Tommy were still with the Pellses but the hoose was full, and Frank was looking for lodgings. He was an apprentice boilermaker and riveter at the Middle Docks and was earning aboot two pund a week - if Tommy came with him whoever took them in would get an allowance for him from the Council. I'd asked them roond to tea a couple of times when Saleem was away and Frank really fell for wor Mary, so the next time I went up to see them Mary came alang, and I was left with Tommy and the dog while Mary and Frank went off on their own.

May was nearly ower and the light nights had arrived. I would normally have been oot on me bike with the lads. Before the War I used to gan oot to Cleadon Park or the White Horse Hills with me mates, but I just didn't feel like it. There'd been no raids to speak of since the end of April and I didn't gan doon the nick unless the sirens went off – usually a false alarm – or if they asked me to come in, which wasn't very often. They'd appointed a new lad as a full time PAM in place of Davey Corbett. He was only sixteen but he seemed nice enough – Len Stonebanks, his Da' was a Chief Engineer – he had come straight from the Commercial School and could type and de shorthand. He could ride a bike as well, mind, but he spent most of his time in the Charge Room. There was another new lad who, like us, would only come oot if the sirens went off – Norman Proudlock. Norm worked on the counter at the Post Office, and was clever as well as being fat, but he was all reet. He lived in Grosvenor Road and I'd sometimes wait for him just opposite the Town Hall and we'd pedal doon to the nick together. His Mam was an air raid warden and knew Mrs. Corbett, Davey's Mam, so I'd sometimes hear news of Davey and Jackie – not that I was interested or owt.

Freddie Skee called roond one evening in early June aboot eight o'clock. He said he'd just come for a quick chinwag and I told him he was a cheeky nowt. We went oot into the yard and we sat in the air raid shelter with the door open.

"We've not seen ye for a bit and the lads were wondering
if ye were all reet." He took oot a paper bag with a couple of
Woodbines in and lit one up. "Ye didn't come to the wedding
then?"

"Ye kna' I didn't, and ye kna' why."

"Well you were oot with Jackie all the time so we all guessed
that you were keen on her."

He looked roond the shelter. "Did ye bring her in here?"

I said nowt but my face must have given me away. "Ye could de
almost owt with a lass in one of these?"

"Aye and what if the sirens went?"

"Well, I've only had it twice with Gertie and the second time
the sirens went off and I ended up rolling roond the floor with
nowt on but a johnnie."

He started laughing, and I couldn't stop mesel'.

"And before ye ask," I said, "ye can't bring Gertie roond here."
We had another laugh.

"I dain't see her much. Glenda's gone all prim and proper with
Jimmy, and she thinks that if we all gan oot me and Gertie will
start deein' something, and then Jimmy will get ideas."

"Ye could take her oot on your own."

He went silent for a bit. "I de like her but she's nearly twice me
size and six years older and ye'se lot will just laugh at me."

And then he started singing:

> "She's a big lass and a bonny lass,
> And she likes hor beer,
> And her name is Cushy Butterfield,
> And I wish she wez here."

"You're not that little, Freddie," I said. It was true - he had put
on a few inches and filled oot a bit since I'd first seen him. "Most

lads wor age are scrawny looking these days with the food we get. Apart from Fat Norm, that is. How auld are ye?"

"Seventeen and I'll be joining up in six months' time."

"Are there any other lasses interested in ye?"

He shook his heed.

"Well ask her oot somewhere on your own. Keep your uniform on – I dain't suppose anyone will give ye a second look, and if ye get a chance to be somewhere alone with her then ye'll probably get lucky. Once ye join up ye won't have any more chances."

He said nowt for a bit and then got up. "Haway then, we'll gan doon to see Wally, and I'm buying." He obviously wanted to change the subject. I couldn't really say naw so I went. Naebody mentioned Jackie or Davey and the next time I met up with them I asked Frank Foster along. Things were slowly getting back to normal. Frank and Matty Lightfoot already knew each other – they weren't mates or owt, but they'd both been to Baring Street School although Matty was a good year older. When Frank said that he was looking for lodgings for him and Tommy, Matty said he'd ask roond. It turned oot his Auntie Daisy had a spare room – her two oldest were married and the youngest, Billy, was away at sea noo – it was the Billy Duggan who I've mentioned before. He was on a ship in the Med and nae one knew when, or if, he'd get back. Her husband worked at the Middle Docks and knew Frank so it was fixed up in nae time. Frank and Tommy would share the bed in Billy's room, and when he came back they'd have to make up a bed in the front room. They had a hoose in Morton Street so it was handy for Frank, and Tommy could still gan and see the Pellses.

I'd mostly stopped thinking aboot Jackie noo, and thowt I was ower it, until Jimmy Clay came in one neet when the rest of us were having an ice-cream at DiBresci's. "Have ye heard the news? That Davey didn't take lang – Jackie's pregnant." I just got up and walked out. I'd always tried not to imagine what they might de together but noo I couldn't stop mesel', and if Jackie was pregnant already then Davey must have been having it away with her a lot. Well there was nowt I could de but that didn't stop me feeling miserable.

Wor Mary would leave school that summer and Mrs. Hussain had agreed to take her on in the shop at the Nook. The lass that worked there would be eighteen soon and would either join up in the WAAF or be called up to work in a factory or on a farm. Things didn't gan to plan. One morning in July me and Mrs. Hussain were doing the early morning deliveries – tetties, and what fruit and vegetables we could get had of. The Nook shop was wor last drop off before getting back to Frederick Street, and Edie usually had a pot of tea ready with some bread and jam. When we arrived that morning Edie ran oot to meet us with tears in her eyes. Nobbie had gone oot to the *Nook* pub as usual the neet before, but he hadn't come back. It was not unusual for him to stay late once in a while so Edie had just gone to bed. He still wasn't there when she woke up at six o'clock. She'd gone roond to the Police sub-station opposite the *Nook*. The officer in charge had said he was just coming roond to see her. A workman gan' to work at 4 o'clock had tripped ower Nobby lying on the pavement on the corner with Prince Edward Road. He'd taken a beating and was barely conscious – he smelt like a brewery as well. They'd called an ambulance and he was away at the General. He didn't have any money on him and his wallet was lying beside him empty apart from his identity card. Someone would gan up to see him when he was able to talk, to find oot what had happened.

Alice took ower. "Reet," she said to Edie, "you get yoursel' ready and give your Charlie his breakfast then get up to the General to see if you can visit him. Mossie, I'll leave ye here and I'll send wor Jasmin doon to help. You'll have to get fish and chips for your dinner. I'll get your Mam to take Mary oot of school and she can help in the shop with me. She's only got a few weeks to go anyway. Can Mary ride your bike?" I nodded. "Reet, she'll de your deliveries and ye can get the trolley bus back the neet."

I had already met the pensioner reservists who ran the small nick – if you could call it that. There had been a raid at the back end of April that hadn't lasted long but a dozen or so parachute mines had come doon all ower the place. One had landed in the South Marine Lake sending a geet shower of watter and mud into the air – others had fallen in King George Road and Lascelles Avenue just up from the Nook. A mine had also landed on Cleadon Hills by the Water Tower. Me, Freddie and Wally had been sent oot to the Nook to help. The auld fellas had not been very happy – they'd just been in the middle of a game of fives and threes when the bombs had gone off. Officer Beecroft, a big beefy fella, was manning the phone and Bill Spyles and John Burgess were oot at Lascelles Avenue – some hooses had been demolished. I was sent there to see if they needed any help and to run any messages. Freddie and Wally were sent up on Cleadon Hills to wait for the Navy and to take them up to where a parachute mine had landed. The army came oot for ordinary bombs but the Navy took ower when a parachute mine came doon and didn't gan off. Wally had to stay by the mine in the pitch black, and when Freddie came back leading the Navy truck he'd appeared oot of nowhere shrieking like a banshee and Wally had wet himsel'. He was a bit more sensitive than the rest of us. When we all met up at the Nook nick before gannen back yem, Constable Sam Beecroft made us a cup of tea, with sugar. He said there was a widow woman he knew up Quarry Lane who made jam and got as much sugar as she wanted, so she'd give Sam a bag every noo and again. Bill Spyles, who'd come back to report in, was sitting in the corner slurping his tea from a saucer. "Aye, and if he's lucky that's not all he gets," he muttered.

Sam blushed a bit. "He means jam, like. She sometimes lets me have a jar."

Sergeant Duncan would often tell us stories of when he was first on the beat, and when those three would get up to all sorts of things. When I saw him next I asked him why they were at the Nook as they all lived up around the Lawe area. They were all in their sixties and had been called up as pensioner reservists in 1939. They had all volunteered to go the Nook. Jock said they had never volunteered for anything in their life before. They wanted an easy posting and the Nook nick was the only one of the new sub-stations that was just opposite a pub.

Nobby wouldn't say what had happened - he did what auld Hinesy called the Chinese monkey trick – he'd heard nowt, he'd seen nowt, and he was saying nowt. The doctor reckoned he'd been struck by a blunt instrument – he'd lost a couple of teeth, had a few badly bruised ribs and a fractured wrist. The polis at the Nook didn't put themselves oot investigating who did it, and the culprit was never found.

I stayed at the Nook for a few months and would take a box of vegetables ower to the landlord of the *Nook* every week. I got to kna' him. He liked his beer and he liked a natter. He'd always pull me a pint as I came in and then, when I tolt him for the umpteenth time, that I didn't drink, he'd have to have it himsel' - he'd pour me a glass of lemonade. He was complaining one day that he never saw wor Nobby noo. "It's his own fault. Him and the three stooges" - that's what he called the three auld polis from ower the road – not to their faces, mind – "had a card school gannen. They used to play crib and then Nobby asked them one day if they fancied a game of rummy – he said he'd always fancied playing it but had never been any good. Well they fell for it - they'd play it all the time, and Nobby always won. They were playing for a penny a point and he would sometimes take five bob off one or other of them. Well Nobby's got a gob as big as Tynemooth. He'd told me years ago that he used to play rummy with his mates in the trenches – he always lost and the Sergeant

who they played against always won. When they were demobbed
the Sergeant told Nobby that he'd give him a tip to help him oot
in later life. 'Nobby,' he said, 'if you want to win at rummy, all
you have to de is to drop a card on the floor – it doesn't matter
which one, so long as ye kna' what it is – dain't let the others
see and ye put your foot on it.' Well, the neet he got hammered
Nobby was winning a packet, as usual. Bill Spyles was losing
heavily. Then at the end of a game Bill accidentally dropped a
couple of pennies on the floor, and when he bent doon to pick
them up he saw a card under Nobby's foot. It was the seven of
diamonds and Bill had been picking up card after card to find
that seven. Well Nobby played all innocent, but Bill went for him.
John and Sam had to haul him off and he stormed oot saying that
Nobby would regret it."

"Ye reckon it was him that did it?" I asked.

"Now do ye think that I would accuse a polis of deein'
something like that?"

Well I would, and I thought it was wrong. I was doon at the
nick at Keppel Street a couple of neets later and I had a quiet
word with Sergeant Duncan and asked if I should report what
I'd heard. He looked at me. "Mossie," he said, "someone who
cheats at cards deserves everything they get. Someone who cheats
Bill Spyles at cards might as well write out their last will and
testament at the same time."

I didn't de owt – I had other things to think aboot. Well, one
other thing – Jasmin - I was starting to like her more than I should
and she liked me. We were working together noo and we'd catch
the trolley bus back to Laygate each neet, and I'd walk her yem.
Nobby still had his arm in a sling, but he had a chair brought
doon from upstairs and sat just ootside the shop talking to
customers while me and Jasmin did all the work. One afternoon
me and Jasmin were in the back shop together – it was nearly
closing time and we were stacking the boxes. We were reet close

together, and I dain't kna' what came ower me but I just made a grab for her tits. "What ye deein', Mossie," she shouted, half laughing and I stood reet close to her, and put me hands roond her waist. She started struggling a bit, and then stood still and I nuzzled her neck and then kissed her. She put her hands roond me neck and started kissing back. So I started to gan oot with her. Mary would call roond of an evening to ask if Jasmin wanted to come oot, and I'd wait at Laygate for them with Frank Foster who'd ride his bike doon from the Lawe Top. Then Nobby caught us kissing in the back shop and of course he couldn't keep his gob shut and told Alice. She wasn't too unhappy as it turned oot, but she gave me a proper talking to aboot not getting too serious - so we started to gan to the flicks noo and again or for an ice-cream, and when the weather was fine we'd gan to Cleadon Park and try to find a quiet corner, but Jasmin had been warned by her Mam as well and me hands never got much further than her knees.

I was still a bit worried aboot wor Mary and Saleem. When he was yem he was always talking to her and even though she was nearly a woman he'd sit her on his lap and so on. But me Mam didn't seem to mind, and I knew Mary was keen on Frank so I said nowt.

Since I'd been doon at the Nook shop I'd not seen or heard owt aboot Myra Wade and Johnny Wallis. And then Mrs. Hussain tolt me that someone had got pregnant and it wasn't Myra – it was nae one we knew, but it was a WAAF working on the barrage balloons. Johnny Wallis was the father – he'd had a knee trembler with her one neet when they were supposed to be working, and he obviously hadn't had a French letter with him. The problem for Johnny Wallis was that she told the Squadron Leader who the man was, and Johnny had to marry her. He told Myra and said that it didn't make any difference - he'd still lodge with her and try and put the wedding off as long as possible, but when he came yem that neet his belongings were on the pavement.

It was dead quiet that summer, and apart from a raid in June when they had bombed the cemetery and did nowt but shake up a few ghosts, we'd not been bothered. Then on a Saturda' neet at the beginning of September I was woken up by a banging on the front door aboot five o'clock in the morning. I heard auld Mr. Rutherford shouting doon who was that in the middle of the neet. He'd thought it was his door. I then made oot Jimmy Clay's voice saying he was after me. I clambered ower Saleem and opened the door in me jamas. "Come on, Mossie, you're wanted." He came in while I got dressed, and tolt me all that had happened.

Some of wor planes were returning and a German raider had flown in behind them. Nae one noticed owt and the sirens hadn't gan off, but the plane had dropped two bombs in the Charlotte Street area. It wasn't too far away from Maxwell Street, but we had heard nowt because the bombs hadn't exploded. One of them landed on a bit of spare land at Mount Terrace, but the other one knocked doon a netty and a back wall before gannen reet into the ground in the back lane between Charlotte Street and Franklin Street. Jimmy said that Jock Duncan had had a look and was pretty sure that they were UXBs – unexploded bombs to ye. Because there were houses all roond and the gasometer was just ower the railway line, he'd rang the bomb disposal squad to see if they could come and take a look. Meanwhile they were starting to put the barriers up and began evacuating the houses next to where the bombs had come doon, but they wouldn't be sure how big the bomb was, and how far oot the cordon would be, until the bomb disposal squad arrived from Gateshead. Any emergency services coming in to the toon during the blackoot always went to the agreed meeting place in Dean Road where someone would meet them and take them to where they were needed. There were two blue lamps there so the drivers would kna' where to pull up. It was all part of the mutual aid plan - in the blackoot you

couldn't see where you were gannen and you couldn't read the
street signs, so newcomers to the toon needed all the help they
could get. That was gan' to be my job. Jimmy would take me up
there on the back of his bike, and I would bring them doon to
Charlotte Street.

They were coming from Low Fell and so it would be anything
up to an hoor before they arrived, depending on how well the
driver knew the road. I'd not been there much more than thirty
minutes when I saw a lorry coming along the road, and then
slowing doon. They'd seen the blue lamps and pulled up reet
close to me. It was them - there were three in the front seat
already, but one of them got oot and stood on the running board
so I could sit inside and guide the driver. The fella sitting beside
just said, "Lieutenant Brookes - Sergeant Hopkirk's driving and
my Subaltern Coxon's on the running board. Do you know what
we'll be dealing with?"

"Naw, not really. I was just sent up here to fetch ye. The
Sergeant thinks they're two bombs – both in the groond. They're
starting to evacuate the hooses nearby."

"Has the all clear sounded?"

"The sirens never went off – me mate Jimmy reckons it was a
single raider that sneaked in behind wor lot."

He just nodded. He didn't say owt else so I asked him if Dekka
Waite was still in his squad.

"Do you know him?"

"Aye, I met him last time you were here at Newton and
Nicholson's. His sister runs a café we gan to."

"Yes, Waite's still with us. He's sleeping it off back at our
quarters in the drill hall at Low Fell. We cleared a bomb from
a school yard this afternoon and the locals clubbed together
to give the lads some beer money. Some of them had one too
many – we don't mind on a Saturday night, and we had nothing
planned for today. Young Waite's been a bit nervy lately. He had

a narrow shave a month ago. We were digging down to a UXB at North Shields when the walls caved in – someone had stolen our wooden supports the week before and we were making do with what we could find. Waite was buried alive along with Sergeant Leslie – we managed to dig Waite out but the Sergeant was a goner."

I said nowt. From what I'd heard of him Dekka Waite had always been a bit nervy.

"We've only brought a couple of sappers with us in case we need to clear any rubble out the way - we're mainly here just to assess the situation."

When we got there we pulled in at Mount Terrace. You could see the gasometer on the other side of the railway line. Sergeant Duncan was standing together with Mr. Scott so I took the Lieutenant ower to them. It was light by noo so they all had a good look round. I just walked along with them and no one said owt. There was definitely a bomb hole in the bit of spare ground in Mount Terrace.

"It's a big un, all right. 1000 pounder or more I'd reckon," the Lieutenant said after he'd measured the hole and poked aboot a bit. "We'll have to sink a shaft down to get it, then we'll defuse it and pull it out." They then walked doon the back lane between Franklin Street and Charlotte Street. There were a lot of bricks strewn across the lane and it took a while to find where the bomb had gone in. It wasn't too deep as it had hit the netty first and had gone in sideways but it had made a mess of the mains as you could smell gas and see watter coming to the surface. The sappers cleared away some of the bricks and you could nearly see the bomb – it wasn't as big as the other one – the Lieutenant thought it was more likely to be a 500 pounder.

Mr. Scott asked what they should de aboot the watter and gas mains. The Lieutenant rubbed his chin.

"You'll have to get them fixed as soon as you can. The bombs are either duds or they've got delayed action fuses. We always work on the worst case. If they should go off and the gas main isn't sealed then you'll have an almighty explosion – it could take out the gasometer. The water main needs stopping as well – it makes life difficult for us if the shaft fills with water. They should try to close off the supplies from as far away as possible so as not to disturb the bombs.

"We're going to have to evacuate the whole area up to 200 yards, and close all the roads that lead up here. You'll need to open the emergency rest stations."

There were houses all round and it looked as though Thomas Street and Burrow Street would have to be cleared as well as Charlotte Street and Franklin Street.

"It's an awful lot of bother for a couple of bombs that didn't go off," said Mr. Scott.

"And that's exactly why the Germans fit delayed action fuses – a bomb that hasn't gone off on impact, but might do at any time, spreads panic, lowers morale and can cause as much if not more disruption to the local population than bombs that go off when they hit the ground. That's why Mr. Churchill has made bomb disposal a priority – the Generals sitting on their backsides in Whitehall saw us as non-combatants and didn't put themselves out to provide us with the tools and men we needed. It's getting better, but slowly." He paced around a bit and then looked at Jock.

"I'll leave it to you to decide on the precise extent of the evacuation – if there are any areas you're not sure about you always err on the side of precaution."

"How long should they expect to be away from their homes?" asked Jock Duncan.

"I'm going to classify them as category "B" bombs." I didn't kna' then, but I found oot by asking Jock afterwards that UXBs were always given a category letter. "A" was one that was in the most dangerous position and was causing major disruption – like

141

BLITZ PAMS - MAY - SEPTEMBER 1941

if these bombs had landed in the gasometer itself. If the bomb's a category "A" then the bomb squad had to deal with it straight away, whatever the risk to them. If a bomb has a delayed action fuse then it can gan off from three hours after hitting the ground, and up to aboot 80 hours after that. If the fuse hasn't gone off within that time then it won't gan off unless there's some sort of accident, or if the fuse is booby trapped. Category "B" bombs would be left where they were for four days and then work could start.

The Lieutenant said that they'd leave the evacuation and the repair of the mains to the civil defence. He was to be called if either of the bombs went off, otherwise he'd be on site on Wednesda' morning so long as there were no category "A" bombs to deal with that had landed somewhere else in the meantime. He was starting to put a shaft down to a category "B" bomb at Wallsend on Monda', and he'd deal with that one first.

"You'd better tell the people you're evacuating that they could be out of their homes for a week. It could take longer depending on how deep we have to go down for the bomb in Mount Terrace."

He looked at me. "Messenger, did you say that Waite's sister has a café here?"

"Aye, it's just five minutes away in Ocean Road."

"Do you think she might provide a bit of breakfast for us?"

"I'm sure she will. They're not usually open this early on a Sunda' but I'll gan ower on me bike and ask, if ye want."

He nodded. "We should be finished here in about half an hour."

When I got to the café Wally came doon to open the door in his jamas. He gave Audrey a shout and she said that they could rustle something up - I could stay and have some breakfast as well, so long as I helped Wally with the clearing away and the washing up. "Nae problem," I shouted as I was on me way oot to fetch them. They followed me in the lorry and we trooped into the café. Little Audrey had been working hard while we were gone. She'd put two tables together but the Lieutenant asked if he and his Subaltern could sit on a separate table. "We don't normally mess together," he said.

I usually just had bread for breakfast, with jam if we had any. This morning we had porridge, then bacon, just one rasher each, white pudding, scrambled eggs – made from dried egg, but Audrey had put extra butter in and they weren't too bad – beans, fried potatoes, fried bread and tea with sugar.

I sat with the Sergeant and the two sappers. They were Scottish and were both strapping lads. They looked a bit hung ower but it didn't stop their appetites. I didn't usually eat in the café and Wally gave me a plate with everything on, so I asked if anyone wanted me bacon. Big Jock – that's what they called him - just stuck his fork in the rasher before the others could say owt.

"Don't ye like bacon then, Mossie?" asked Sergeant Hopkirk.

"I dain't kna, I've never had any. I'm a Muslim."

"Ye don't sound like one," said Big Jock as he shovelled in a big forkful of bacon.

"I was born in Shields. Me Da's an Arab from Aden and was a fireman on the ships. There's a lot of Yemeni seafarers in Shields. Me Da's ship was sunk and he went doon with it. Me Mam won't let me gan to sea or I'd be away."

We got chatting then and I asked them if it was hard work digging the shafts. The sappers tolt me that when they were digging they split into three teams of two, and dug for fifteen minutes at a time.

"Wye I could de that," I said.

They laughed. "It's nowt to do with being hard work." Big Jock was looking a bit less like death warmed up noo he'd got his food doon. "If you only work a quarter of an hoor at a time, you've got less chance of being blown up if the bomb gangs off."

We'd all finished and I asked Wally if I could have an ice-cream. "For breakfast?"

"Aye, well I doubt if I'll gerrin later on with all the evacuation gannen on."

The others said nowt, but when he brought me cornet ower with lovely white ice-cream dripping with red sauce I could see by their faces that they were tempted. Audrey had seen it too. "Aren't ye ganna let Dekka's mates have one as well, Wally?" The Lieutenant politely declined but he did go across to have a word with Audrey. He offered to pay for the breakfast but Audrey said absolutely not. She did agree to provide them with sandwiches for their dinner when they started digging, and to fill up their billy cans with tea. He said that he'd send Dekka round for it so they could see each other – the Army would pay and they'd also bring doon cans of corned beef, ham and some cheese. I helped with the clearing up and then went back to Charlotte Street.

It took most of the morning to get the folk oot of their homes. Some went to relatives and friends. That's where me and the other messengers came in handy – we could ride ower to where the family wanted to gan and check that it was all reet. We also helped load what few belongings people wanted to bring on to the motor buses the council had provided to take them to the emergency rest centres. It was a big job for Jock as he had to ensure that there was enough polis to man the barriers - not only to keep people oot but to reassure those who were leaving that their homes wouldn't be robbed when they were away. The Landlord of the *Franklin Arms* came up to Sergeant Duncan with a set of keys in his hands. "There's beer in the barrels that needs drinking – but only by the polis and the bomb squad – and nae spirits." Then he looked at Jock. "Apart from your bottle that's on the back of the counter." Jock used to be the beat bobby round here years ago, and would still call in at the pubs he knew. Some publicans kept a bottle of scotch just for him. As me and Jimmy had been oot the longest Jock let us gan at aboot eleven o'clock so I did manage to get another ice-cream although I had to pay for that one.

That Sunda' neet the sirens went off at ten o'clock and I was on me bike tearing doon to Keppel Street. I held on a few minutes just by the Town Hall to wait for Norm. He wasn't long and as we pedalled doon Fowler Street, I tolt him aboot the bomb at Mount Terrace. It wasn't the first he'd heard aboot it. His mother was an ARP warden and she'd been asked if she knew anyone in the streets that she was responsible for, who had any spare rooms to take one of the families who'd been moved oot of their homes.

There was a raid that neet as well. A couple of bombs fell on the Bents Park and another one landed in a field in Marsden Lane. The one at Marsden didn't gan off and so they had to evacuate the auld *Marsden Inn*. I didn't have owt to de with it but I knew when the sappers arrived to dig it oot. Lieutenant Brookes and his men had started the shaft at Mount Street on the Wednesda'. I went roond after work. I was waved through the barrier and they let me have a quick look. The Lieutenant had worked oot, from the angle it had made when it went into the ground, and by poking doon with his chimney sweeps' rod, where the bomb would be – but he had to make a bit of a guess as to how deep it was. They'd sunk the shaft aboot 15 feet away from the hole. They'd been digging since first light and they were aboot twelve feet doon already. They had put wooden planks on the sides, and they had a sort of scaffolding inside so that they could lift the soil oot. Dekka was having a cigarette. None of them wore their tin hats. When I asked them why, Dekka just said had I ever tried digging oot a twenty foot shaft with a tin hat on. He said he might see me tomorrow as he was gan' to be sent ower to Marsden to start the shaft there. "With any luck the Lieutenant will stay here so I might get up to the Nook at dinner time."

He did as well. He parked the lorry ootside the shop and came ower for a natter. He'd been up to Ocean Road and picked up the sandwiches for the lads. "It's cheese today. Audrey said to pop in to see if you had any onions." He was making a joke as most people hadn't seen an onion since before the War but he was in luck. We'd managed to get two sackfuls the day before and I was giving them oot one at a time to regular customers only – sixpence each – the price had gone up since last year. They weren't on the ration books but you rarely saw any. One of wor auld customers had an allotment oot at Harton. He'd been a pitman during the lock oots in the twenties, and Alice and Geordie had let all pit families who shopped with her have tick for nearly nine months – he'd never forgotten. She paid for the onions, but would also let him have some eggs when she could, and had promised him an orange if we ever got one.

"Come in the back, will ye," I whispered to Dekka.

"What, are we ganna have a chinwag?" He must have heard the story from Wally.

"Aw, shurrup, man. Here, this one's a big un' – ye'll have to slice it up, mind. And dain't let anyone see you with it or they'll be queuing all the way doon to Freemantle Road." He couldn't believe his eyes. He put it up to his nose to smell and whistled. I nodded. He put the onion into his pocket. "I'm gan for a quick one in the *Nook* - I'll buy ye a pint."

"Naw, it's all reet, I dain't drink."

"Aye, I forgot." And off he went.

They defused the bomb at Mount Terrace that afternoon. They'd had to gan doon twenty foot, and then they had to dig a small tunnel to get to the bomb as it was a few feet off. I dropped in again after work and it was all ower.

When I got there the lads were standing by the bomb and this young fella was taking a photograph. I didn't kna' who he was – it was normally Miss Flagg, who worked in the library, who would take any photos. She was a keen photographer and had decided to make a record of all the bombings – you'd see her round all the bomb sites the day after. She was a tall, skinny woman, and very well spoken, but she didn't mind getting her shoes dirty to take her snaps.

Bomb disposal squad in Mount Terrace

"Is it safe to come ower?" I shouted.

"Aye, come on, laddie." It was Big Jock. When I got to where the bomb was lying, Jock said that once the fuses were oot then you could knock them aboot as much as you wanted. "Give it a kick, Mossie."

"I'm not daft, ye kna'."

He just laughed and gave it a geet big kick with his hobnailed boots. I jumped back aboot a yard and they were all killing themsel's.

"How did ye get the fuse oot?"

"We only dig the hole and pull the bomb oot; it's the Lieutenants who gang doon the pit and get the fuses oot. One shake of the hand and they're blawn to kingdom come. They have a drink to calm themselves doon, and they give the bomb a drink too."

I was drinking it in mesel' and the others were starting to snigger behind me back.

"The Lieutenant gives the bomb a good pint of beer – these Germans are awfu' thirsty." The others burst oot laughing and so did Big Jock.

"I'm sorry, Mossie. We can't tell anyone ootside the squad how the Lieutenant does it. If others knew and talked then one of these Quisling bastards could tell the Germans who'd change the fuses so we could all be blawn to bits."

I found oot later on that what Big Jock told me was not too far from the truth. As I was leaving I put me hand in me pocket and pulled oot an onion. "That's for your bait tomorrow – I gave one to Dekka this morning." Big Jock slapped me on the back. "I owe ye one, Mossie." He looked at the onion and decided he wasn't waiting - he took his knife oot and started cutting it thick slices. "We don't want it going rotten over neet, noo do we?" He handed the pieces oot to his mates and they ate them there and then. They'd no doubt wash it doon with a pint from the *Franklin*.

They all went to Marsden the next day and the bomb there was dug oot. It was a 500 pounder.

CHAPTER 8
SEPTEMBER/OCTOBER
1941

We needed the Bomb Squad again a few weeks later. It was a Tuesday neet – Saleem was yem and I'd gone doon with him to Said's Café for a cup of coffee. Most of the Arabs in Shields knew me because of me Da', and if I ever looked into the café I was never short of company. I'd been thinking lately that I'd have to decide whether I was gan' to go to sea as a fireman or trimmer, like all the Yemenis did, or whether I'd keep working with Alice and wait to be called up when I'd probably end up in the Navy as a stoker. Nearly every week noo we heard of someone who'd been lost at sea, and with the Arabs working as stokehold crew they were the ones who'd gan to the bottom if the ship was hit by a torpedo. Saleem was lucky he was in the coastal trade – your ship could still be hit by a mine or torpedoed, but you had a chance of being rescued. If you went doon in the Atlantic or the Med your chances of being picked up were nowt – sometimes the Germans even shot at the British lads in the watter.

The sirens went and we heard some explosions on the North side. It was aboot ten to nine. I'd put me uniform on and left me bike in the passage at the side of the café so I was off sharp doon to Keppel Street.

I'll never forget that neet. It was a wonder we all survived but we did. Lenny Stonebanks and Jimmy Clay were already there and me, Freddie, Wally and Norm had turned oot as well. The ack-ack guns were blazing away and we heard two big explosions. A bomb came doon behind the *Simonside Arms* – it turned oot later that it was a 1000 pounder but apart from leaving a geet big crater in the ground there were no casualties. Tyne Dock nick were on the phone to Ernie Leadbitter and were sending two of their men oot to report back. Another call came in from the Laygate Lane Police box – the Trinity Schools had received a direct hit, and another bomb had ended up in the bedroom of a hoose in Commercial Road but had not gone off.

Ernie Leadbitter looked round. "Lenny, you get down to Commercial Road and see what help you can be. They'll probably have to evacuate some of the houses."

Five minutes later there was another explosion that shook the building, and then a couple more.

"That was close, Sarge," Freddie said. "De ye want me to take a look?" The phone rang again – it was Jack Cummings from the Market. A stick of bombs had blown up half of Crofton's together with the café on the corner of Union Alley. Then all the lights went oot and the phone went deed. Ernie lit the oil lamp that was always kept handy. "Freddie, you go up to the Market – you Jimmy, go to the ARP offices and see what help they need and get back as soon as you can."

A couple of minutes afterwards the phone rang – they were back on. "Thank Christ for that," said Ernie. It was the ARP HQ. A bomb had landed in the electricity Power Station in West Holborn. It had stove the roof in, knocked through a wall, smashed up some steel girders, and landed on top of one of the boilers, but it had not gone off – yet. Electricity was off but the phones were back on as the exchange had an emergency generator which they'd got going. The bomb squad had been telephoned and they had asked that one of wor officers should

take a recce and let them know how things were. They were
unwilling to come oot anyway until the all clear had sounded.
Alec Dorothy, the officer in charge at Laygate had been asked to
gan doon there to report back, and keep an eye on things. "Can
you get there as soon as you can, Mossie? You might be needed if
the phones gan doon again – go to the Trinity Schools first. The
rescue squads were sent there but it sounds as if they might be
needed in the Market. Check in with Lenny and tell him what's
happening. Gan steady mind."

I was oot like a flash. I nearly ran into Jimmy who was coming
back. "Barrington Street's blocked," he shouted. "Chapter Row's
been hit as well – they just missed the ARP building but the rest
is in ruins." There's people trapped in the cellar of the café next
to Crofton's. A rescue squad was sent ower to Commercial Road,
but if there's nae bodies to be dug oot they need to get to the
Market quick."

"Reet," I shouted as I turned roond and then headed doon
Oyston Street past the gas works and then along Claypath Lane.
I had to slow up quick as I got near the Trinity Schools – there
was rubble all ower the road so I got off and started pushing me
bike carefully. A couple of ARP wardens were standing beside the
rescue squad lorry. "Is Mr. Scott there?" I shouted.

A figure came oot of the gloom.

"Aye, I've just got here."

"Was there anybody in the Schools?" I asked.

"No, there should have been, but the firewatcher had popped
over to the Church to have a cup of tea with the firewatcher on
the tower – she's a bonny lass, they say."

"A bomb's dropped on the Market and blown up Crofton's and
the café on the corner. They're people trapped in the cellars and
they need rescue squads. Can ye gan ower there?"

"Have you seen any fires yet?"

"Naw – but Barrington Street and Chapter Row have been

blown up."

Mr. Scott climbed up into the lorry, shouting, "Come on, lads, we're needed at the Market Place." He then asked the ARP wardens to get the fire brigade to come oot to the Schools to help clearing up, if they could.

The lorry reversed doon the road. I went up to one of the wardens. "I need to get to Commercial Road - can I come through?"

"Aye, we're closing the road to vehicles but you should be all reet. I'd carry the bike, mind."

I lifted me bike on me shoulder, and walked beside the warden whose torch lit up the ground. Even so I nearly went doon a couple of times but he grabbed me arm.

As soon as I was past the Schools I jumped onto the saddle. It only took me a couple of minutes to get to where the bomb had landed. I could see Douggie Errington and Sergeant Dorothy. There was an air raid warden and a family in their nightclothes just next to them. They'd been doonstairs in the house under a table when the bomb had landed. The ARP warden was putting a ladder against the house wall and Sergeant Dorothy started climbing up.

He shone his torch into the room and came doon the ladder twice as quick as he'd gone up. "It looks like a 500 pounder – undamaged. It's wedged between the bed and the wall. We're gan' to have evacuate everybody and close the road." He looked roond. "I want everybody away noo – it could gan off any minute."

I ran ower. The ARP warden tried to stop me and I shouted oot, "I've got a message for the Sergeant." Alec Dorothy turned round. "Not another bloody PAM. We've just sent your mate Lenny to Laygate nick to ring for more help here."

"Have ye not had the message aboot the Power Station?"

"I've been oot here for the last half an hoor, Mossie."

Commercial Road

"A bomb's come doon in the Power Station – it's landed on top of a boiler. Sergeant Leadbitter thought you were already doon there. It could gan off at any minute. The bomb squad want someone to have a look at it and report back to them before they set oot."

"That's all we bloody need." We were all walking and half running to get a few yards away from the bomb. "I'll get doon there strite away. Ye can give me a lift on your bike." He turned to Douggie. "Ye'll have to take ower. I want everyone including yoursel' away from here, and if anyone's still in any of the houses they're to be evacuated to the nearest shelter. The road will have to be closed, and nae one's to return until we've cleared the bomb – that may be a while. Ye'll have to get an emergency rest centre set up."

Douggie just pointed doon the road to the ruins of the Schools. "That's the nearest one."

"Aye, well, ye'll think of something." I got on the bike and Douggie held it while Sergeant Dorothy sat on the saddle. I pushed off and we wobbled aboot a bit before I got me balance. The bike was solid but Sergeant Dorothy was a lot heavier than wor Jackie had been – not that I was thinking of her, like.

I'm not much for thinking anyway, as you've probably gathered, but I now wonder how we managed that neet. Bombs seemed to be coming doon all ower – the ARP building had been hit but the people inside were still working by candle light and hurricane lamps. Things were happening so fast that as soon as one message was sent then a different one came oot five minutes later. I learned when I eventually got back to the nick that the Harton Laundry had been bombed oot and five houses in Harton Lane had been demolished. Gas and watter mains had been burst but luckily there was only one casualty - a sentry at the Brinkburn field who was keeping guard near the ack-ack gun was injured when a bomb fell close by.

The Power Station at West Holborn was reet by the river by the Harton Coal Staithes so I went doon Pan Bank and we were soon there. The building was in pitch darkness and all the workmen on night shift were stood outside. I skidded to a halt and we both nearly came off. I'll not write oot what Sergeant Dorothy said but ye can have a guess.

One of the men ran forward and put a steadying arm oot.

He was a big fellow with broad shoulders "I'm the night shift foreman, Bernie Mackridge. I'll take ye in." We all just followed on. It was pitch black inside and we had to gan doon a corridor to get to the boiler room, but Bernie and the Sergeant both had torches. There was a geet big hole in the roof and there was rubble everywhere – the bomb had made a mess of the insides. It had smashed through steel girders and demolished a lot of machinery and there it was, a geet big'un, twice the size I'd seen at Mount Street, balanced on top of the boiler's manhole cover. "Looks like a thousand pounder or bigger," said Alec. "Nae wonder it did so much damage." He shone the torch on it. "It looks pretty well knocked aboot itself - the tail and the fins have gone."

Mr. Mackridge said something aboot the steam pressure being very high on that boiler.

"We'll have to evacuate the whole area," Alec replied. "It didn't explode when it was ripping through the building, but the heat from the boiler could set it off any minute. Can we get the fire brigade to douse it with watter?"

"I wouldn't like to try it – the whole thing could gan up and the place would be full of boiling steam. The only way to cool it doon safely is to draw the fires – it will still take a while to bring the heat doon but it will ebb away gradually – with the roof off there's plenty of cold air circulating, which will help."

"There's a high risk of the bomb going off, Mr. Mackridge. Would one of your men volunteer to do the drawing?"

"Ay, I'll pick one."

Alec looked roond – I dain't think he'd realised that we'd all followed him in. "Oot the lot of ye'se! This thing could gan up any minute with the heat that's under it."

We didn't need much telling as we'd heard every word they'd said. As soon as we were ootside Mr. Mackridge went ower to one of the men - a stocky bloke. He nodded his head and went into the building with Mr. Mackridge. Bernie Mackridge came oot in a couple of minutes. "Geordie Leggett's drawing the coals. He's a steady man. He's worked here years." He looked at Alec and said very quietly, "He's a bachelor."

Sergeant Dorothy got everyone to move to a safe distance. "Mossie," he said looking at me, "can ye get to the nearest telephone? There's one in the office but I'm not risking ringing from there. I dain't kna' whether ye'll get through – the Exchange has got a back-up generator but they have a job keeping it gannen for more than ten minutes at a time. If ye can get a line tell Ernie to get on to the bomb squad. It's a category "A" without any doubt, and they should get here as soon as they can although it will be a good couple of hoors before the boiler's cooled doon enough. You'd also better say that we don't expect the electric to be back until the morra'. We'll need barriers put up all round this area to at least two hundred and fifty yards, and if it's possible a couple of fire engines on standby. If it does go up then there'll be a fire with all those red hot coals flying everywhere."

I was off. Laygate nick was not too far away and I managed to get through on the phone to Sergeant Leadbitter. The line was not very good and I had to repeat everything twice. I was then sent up to the Market. I learned after that it took Geordie Leggett an hour or more to draw the fires. He just got on with it, even though there was a dirty geet bomb dangling ower his heed.

If the Power Station had gone up it would have been a disaster – apart from the damage it would have caused doon there, all of Shields would have been without power for months. When he came oot Geordie got a handshake from Sergeant Dorothy, a pat on the back from Bernie Mackridge, and was then sent off to the nearest shelter.

When I got to the Market, the rescue squads, the fire engines, ambulances and first aid cars were there at the far corner. When I got close I could see that the entrance to Union Alley was all blocked off, the front of the *City of Durham* was blown in and the Market Café was completely demolished. I recognised the bulky figure of Sergeant Cummings and went ower to him. I told him what was gan on doon the Power Station.

"It's bad here an' all, Mossie. They've not found any bodies yet but they think that there's people in the café cellar – they used to gan doon there when there was a raid, but we can't find a way in. Ye can give them a hand if ye want." I didn't need much telling and was soon in amongst the bricks and masonry helping Matty Lightfoot clear away as much as possible. Since the raid on the Lawe Top in April when I'd cut me hands to shreds digging Davey Corbett oot, I always had a pair of gloves in me pockets – I'd got them from Saleem – fireman's gloves that they wore when they were stoking the ship's boilers. They were an auld pair and well worn, but they came in handy noo. We were lifting a door oot the way when Matty's foot went doon a hole. "Ower here!" he shouted. Mr. Scott came across. He got doon on his hands and knees and started moving as much rubble as he could. He had a crow bar with him and started prising up the ends of the floorboards around the opening. They were all sagging under the weight of the three storeys of building that had come doon. Just then there was another shout from ower the alley. One of the auxiliary firemen had found the cellar trap in the *City of Durham* – the pub had not been damaged as much as the café, and in a couple of minutes a dozen or so folk walked oot. They looked very unsteady on their feet.

Mr. Scott looked up. "If they're injured or in shock you'd better get them to a first aid station to be checked over."

Sergeant Cummings went across and then we heard his big gob. "They're not injured, they're pissed as farts, the landlord as well. They took their drinks with them and when they'd finished those he put a tap in a barrel, and they've been helping themselves."

I heard another voice – it was the landlady, "It was for the shock, Jack." She then looked back at the ruins of the pub. "Eeh, what we're ganna de?" and burst into tears.

"Get them away to the shelter. They might have sobered up a bit by the time the all clear gans." There were two underground shelters in the Market – if you were in the flicks when the sirens went off ye went there. Sergeant Cummings came back and asked Mr. Scott whether he'd be able to get doon to the café's cellar. "I'll have a look." He shone his torch doon the hole. "Naw – it's all dust and rubble – part of the ceiling must have come down." He then heard something. "Quiet," he shouted oot. He shone his torch doon again and we heard a young lad's voice calling for help.

Mr. Scott stood up and started taking his coat off. "I'm gan' doon. I can't see a bloody thing and I don't know how deep it is so I'll have to gan heed first." Nae one said owt. "Reet," he looked at Jack Cummings, "can ye hold one leg, and ye, Matty, take the other. Had on tight mind. If I can see owt, and can find somewhere to take me footing I'll give a shout." He put his heed and then his shoulders into the hole, then Jack Cummings and Matty Lightfoot lifted his legs into the air and slowly lowered him doon. He was all the way in when he shouted up that he could touch the ground and to let him go. His legs slithered doon after him. We heard nowt then we saw a heed covered in dust being pushed upwards. "Put your hands oot, son," shouted Mr. Scott from doon below to the young lad he was pushing up, and we had him. He was aboot twelve. "Are ye all reet?" asked Matty who was dusting him doon. The lad started shaking.

"Here, take him to the first aiders and get him a blanket, Mossie."

By the time I returned Mr. Scott had got another two fellas oot. He'd not let anyone else gan doon as there was an awful smell of gas - a main must have burst. They'd had to pull the auld fella oot from above – he couldn't move his leg - it turned oot to be broken - and he had a nasty gash on his heed, but he didn't groan or owt. He'd been a whaler in his younger days and they were hard men. There was another wait of aboot five minutes and then Mr. Scott poked his heed oot. After a fit of coughing and spluttering he drank in the fresh air.

"There's an auld woman and a young lad but I can't get them oot on me own. We're ganna have to be quick as it could all come down any minute and there's a strong smell of gas – I'm only asking for volunteers." He needn't have said it. Matty said he'd de it and I said I would, but then two auld fellas came up and said that if Mr. Scott had asked for volunteers because of the gas the last thing he'd want was two bright sparks like us doon there.

It took them another ten minutes before they pushed the auld woman up – she was covered in dust and groaned a bit when we pulled her oot. She didn't seem too bad and was walking all reet as Matty helped her ower the rubble, but then she suddenly crumpled up and fell to the ground. Gertie and Glenda who were there managed to get her into the ambulance. She had fractured most of her ribs. There was another shout from doon below and then a hand came up and we pulled up a young lad aboot wor age. He was coughing and wheezing but could walk. As he stumbled ower the rubble he suddenly stopped and looked back.

"Me Mam's doon there - will she be all reet?"

"Mr. Scott will get her oot, son." I didn't kna' what else to say but just then Gertie came ower and took him. "Glenda's worried aboot Jimmy – do you know where he is?" Gertie asked.

I shook my head. "He'll be oot somewhere," I replied. "There's bombs all ower the neet."

I then heard Mr. Scott's voice.

"I can't see anyone else and the roof could cave in any minute. We're coming up."

I ran back, nearly falling doon as I tripped ower a bit of

masonry. "The lad says his Mam's doon there, Mr. Scott."

"Reet. We'll have one more look, but if I can't find her we'll have to wait until we can make it safe."

He was away a good five minutes and then he shouted up. "We've got her. She's buried up to her neck and she's barely conscious. The roof above her heed's sagging reet doon – every time I move something bits start falling doon on to her. She's in a lot of pain. Can one of the first aiders come doon to give her a shot of morphine."

I think he expected a fella but Gertie came ower. "Glenda's looking after the ones in the ambulance; I'll have to do it." Although she was a big lass she got her body into the hole and we lowered her doon. She stayed with them and after a while there was a shout from the hole that they'd need a stretcher with straps on to get the woman oot. I ran ower to the ambulance for the stretcher and we passed it doon.

Just then Freddie Skee came tearing ower the cobbles. He jumped off the bike while it was still gannen but his feet had hardly touched the ground before Sergeant Cummings who was close by ran up to him, grabbed him and stopped him deed. Freddie was just gan to say something when the Sergeant told him that there was a gas leak and if the segs in Freddie's boots had made a spark then we'd all have gone up.

"I'm sorry, Sarge, I've just come from Keppel Street – a bomb's gone off in the back lane between Morton Street and Livingstone Street. Henry Milburn who rang it in says there's lots of casualties. They've already got all the rescue squads oot everywhere else – is there any chance of anyone here gannen along?" Jack Cummings looked roond and called ower the chief ARP warden for the Market. He had a few words and then said that as soon as Mr. Scott and his men came oot they'd talk to them. "I dain't think there's anybody alive left in there noo apart from the woman. As soon as she's oot I'm ganna' suggest to

Jimmy Scott that we cordon this lot off and leave it to morning - he can get ower to the Lawe and the other squads can de what's needed here. We'll need to get the gas mains turned off." He rubbed his chin. "Where ye away to next, Freddie?"

"I'm to report back to the nick to keep them posted."

"Reet, Mossie lad, ye can gan ower to Mile End Road and see if you can help Henry. I'll be across as soon as I'm finished here." We were away. Freddie shouted to me that he was trying to get Gertie to gan to the flicks with him one neet. Then we split up as he turned doon Russell Street.

I heard first hand from Matty what happened at the Market doon the café cellar after I left. The air was so thick with dust that you could hardly see a thing even with the torches and breathing was difficult with the coal gas as well. Mr. Scott stood ower the woman with his shoulders holding up what was left of the roof and which looked as though it could come crashing doon any minute. The poor hinny was reet up to her neck and they had to take the bricks and wood off her bit by bit. She had started moaning something terrible before Gertie had calmed her doon with the morphine. Gertie stayed with them and helped the men who were using only their hands to clear the rubble – they were breathing in coal gas all the time - and they didn't want to use tools in case there was a spark. It took them nearly half an hoor and the poor woman had regained consciousness and was whimpering as Gertie held her hand. They managed to free her and tied her to the stretcher – they went as quickly as they could and lifted the stretcher up to the hole where Jack and Matty pulled it up. Gertie came up next, then the two fellas, and then came Mr. Scott. He was breathing heavy and coughing but he just dusted himsel' off and says, "Thank God that's ower," then wipes his brow, puts his coat back on, has a word with Jack Cummings and then he's off in the lorry to the Lawe. Before Sergeant Cummings went off shift later the next morning he wrote a report and gave it to the Super, who gave it to the Chief. Mr. Scott was awarded the George Medal for his exceptional courage, and total disregard for his own safety. When word got roond aboot what he'd done they started calling him the human pillar.

When I got up Mile End Road I saw Henry Milburn on the corner of Livingstone Street - he was pacing back and forwards. "Are ye the only one they sent? It's bloody murder doon there." He pointed to the back lane with Morton Street. "We haven't even had a fire engine come yet. I dinna' what I'm gan' to de on me own. I'd just patrolled doon Morton Street. The blast nearly knocked me off me feet."

I couldn't see his face in the dark but he didn't sound too good – he'd had a couple of weeks off for shock after the bombings in April but he'd seemed all reet since then. "Let's get a bit closer," I said, "and see if we can help. A rescue squad from the Market should be along in a few minutes."

He nodded but he didn't move. "I can't de anymore, Mossie. I've had it." Henry Milburn was a big man. He'd worked doon the pits before the First World War and had spent three years in the trenches. He'd been aboot to retire when this War broke oot.

"Hey. It's all reet, man," I said. I put my hand on his arm and I heard him sobbing. It must have been the shock of the bomb – I'd heard that in the Great War people got shell shock. I knew that he lived in Moon Street just ower the road. He wasn't gan to be any use the neet. "Why dain't ye gan yem, and have a nice hot cup of tea. I'll tell the Sergeant, and ye can come back when you're feeling better."

"Aye." He didn't say owt else but just walked away. I pedalled up the road to the police box that was just opposite St. Stephen's and tried the phone on the outside. Nothing happened. I tried again and then heard Ernie Leadbitter's voice. He sounded a long way off and there was all sorts of crackling on the line. "It's Mossie here, Sergeant."

"Can you speak up, Mossie – we can't always get a line and when we do it's a bad one."

"Officer Milburn's had to gan yem. He's got shell shock."

"You'd better hold the fort then, Mossie, until I get someone else there."

"The rescue squads should be here soon enough."

"Can you see if you can find out how many casualties there are? I've just had Douggie Errington on the blower and a bomb's demolished most of Cormwallis Square – a lot of folk are trapped in the ruins. We'll need rescue squads there an' all." There was a loud cackling noise and the line went dead.

I got on my bike and rode back to Morton Street - a fire engine and a couple of first aid cars were reet behind me. There were half a dozen houses doon, and you could see that there were a lot more severely damaged at the back with roofs blown off. There were two ARP wardens, a fire watcher and aboot half a dozen folk standing roond. One of the wardens tolt us that the bomb had landed in the back lane and the blast had blown up most of the backs of the dwellings. Nearly all would have been occupied. Some of them had small shelters in their back yards but they could have been hit or buried in debris. The public shelter in Mile End Road had been demolished after the big April raid. The rescue squads would have to go through the fronts of the houses which could collapse at any time or gan up the back lanes and work their way over all the debris.

I'd learned something of how Mr. Scott worked so I suggested that the wardens and the firemen should first gan to each hoose to see if anyone was in there who could be got oot easily, or who knew who else had been at home. The driver of the fire engine said that made sense and said that the polis should cordon off the road. "Aye, I've got to report back on how many casualties we've got here. Cornwallis Square's been hit as well."

"Aye and I heard that they'd hit George Potts Street hard an' all," the warden replied.

The firemen went off to gan up the back lane as the wardens started shouting from the front to see if they could find anybody who was trapped. I went straight to the Duggans' hoose where Frank and Tommy were staying - it was one of those that had been flattened. I climbed ower the bricks, and, as I got further in, I thought I heard something. I shouted again and then heard a dog barking and then a little lad's voice. I shouted oot that I'd found someone and two firemen appeared from the back lane. I very carefully clambered ower the roof tiles and then we all started trying to clear away the bricks with wor hands. After aboot ten minutes we found two deed bodies – Mr. and Mrs. Duggan. They were lying where the doorway used to be. We could now hear little Tommy calling oot. I'd shouted back and he said he was all reet, but Frank wasn't saying owt. We then heard the rescue squad arrive and I clambered back to meet them. The air raid wardens had already pulled two or three people oot, and they now had a good idea of where there were folk in the ruins. I told Mr. Scott that there were two lads trapped, and he got Matty and a couple of others to gan ower to the back of the hoose.

"Hadn't ye better get back to Keppel Street to see if they need you anywhere else, Mossie?"

"Frank's me mate, Mr. Scott, and I kna' little Tommy – he was bombed oot up at Robertson Street in April. I'll stay till I kna' they're all reet."

After we'd moved the bodies we started tunnelling into the back room where Tommy and Frank were. We managed to make some progress and Matty gave oot a shout that he had hold of Tommy's hand. We shone wor torches in and could see that Tommy and Biddy were lying next to Frank who had a wooden beam resting on his back - and that was holding up most of what had been the upstairs flat. It was lying at an angle and Matty managed to pull little Tommy away. Frank opened his eyes.

"Are ye all reet, Tommy?" Matty asked. Little Tommy coughed a bit and said that his leg hurt. I took Tommy from Matty.

"How aboot ye, Frank?"

"I've got a terrible pain in the back, Matty, and I think I've got something through one of me arms." He groaned, his eyes fluttered and I thought he was gan to pass oot, but he groaned again. "Have you got any watter?" Then he did pass oot.

"When ye take Tommy oot will ye get one of the first aiders to come with some morphine and some watter." The first aiders always had bottles of watter. He shone his torch on the pile of bricks, plaster and wood that was piled on top of the wooden beam pressing doon on Frank's back. "We'll have to clear most of that first. It could be hoors."

I had to half carry Tommy ower the bricks to the ambulance. The driver's helper had a good look at him and said that his leg was badly bruised but she didn't think it was broken. I said that I knew someone who might take him in. "Can I gan to Mrs. Pells?" he said. That's who I had in mind. "Do you want us to drive him there?" she asked, but I said I could take him on the crossbar of me bike. There were others who would need looking after.

I was just aboot to set off when I saw Inspector MacTomney coming up the road with a couple of Special Constables. I pushed the bike towards him. "It's bloody murder tonight," he said. "They're still coming down. The ferry's been sunk and the railway line's been blown up. Westoe's been hit bad. You look as though you've been busy," he said, patting Tommy on the heed.

"I was first here," I said, "and Constable Milburn had to gan yem."

The Inspector shook his heed. "The Sergeant told me."

"We tried to find oot where people were trapped and noo Mr. Scott and the rescue squad's here we're trying to get them oot." I tolt him aboot Tommy and Frank.

"You'd best get the little fella to Mrs. Pells then, and let's just hope the Germans bugger off soon. I'll take over here and you get back to the Station as soon as you can. I'm sure that Sergeant Leadbitter will have need of you. I'll try to get any news of your mate Frank back to the nick."

Mrs. Pells was in at Cockburn Street, but I had to knock a long time on the door as they were all hiding under the kitchen table, and nae one wanted to come oot. After five minutes I tried the door handle and it opened – they hadn't locked up for the neet when the sirens had gone off. I pushed Tommy and Biddy under the table and they just pulled them in. "He'll be all reet with us for so long as he wants to stay," Mrs Pells shouted oot – I could hear Ernie laughing as Biddy jumped all ower him.

I could still hear planes gannen ower as I pedalled back doon Mile End Road, and I heard a couple of big explosions. They turned oot to be the last of the bombs – one fell in Harton Cemetery – no one was injured but the roadway was blasted up, and it meant that the lorries taking the deed to the mortuary couldn't get through so the bodies had to be carried ower the graves – aboot twenty folk were killed that neet and some were lying in the streets for ages before the lorries could get back for them.

When I went into the Charge Office it was very quiet. Everybody was oot on the streets and the phones were deed again. Ernie Leadbitter was relieved to see me. "They've just got an old generator for emergencies, and it can't run for more than ten minutes at a time - the wires are down at Westoe and Commercial Road as well. All the lads are out apart from Norman." Norm was sitting in a chair with a cup of tea in his hands. He'd been crying or someitt because his eyes were all red. Ernie leant ower to me to talk quietly. "A big un' fell on Grosvenor Road and blew up six houses and killed an air raid warden. Norm took the call – he was helping out on the phones when they were working – they told him the warden who was killed was called Proudlock – his Mam." Norm must have heard as he started crying again. I went and sat beside him.

"Any chance of a cup of tea, Sarge," I said.

I didn't kna' what to say to Norm so I said nowt – just sat beside him drinking my tea. It had sugar in. "Where'd ye get the sugar from, Sarge?"

"John Burgess dropped in this evening - he said they'd managed to get hold of some, but not to ask where – and dain't tell anyone about it – it's Sergeants only – but I'll make an exception for you, Mossie."

John Burgess was one of the old timers doon at the Nook. I said to Ernie, "Last time I was at the Nook they tolt me that Sam Beecroft had it from a widow woman he knew who made jam."

He chuckled. "I'll tell you a story aboot Sam Beecroft, Mossie, when we've got a bit more time."

It wasn't long after that that the phone rang – they were back on for a few minutes. It was the ARP HQ – they'd been told to sound the all clear but the electric was off – could the local polis blow their whistles, and those in cars let the sirens off. The next ten minutes I was on the phone contacting those police boxes and other sub-stations that I could reach. Then we had a call in from the bomb disposal squad – they were just leaving from Low Fell and could someone meet them at Dean Road. They'd go to the Power Station first as that was the most urgent.

"Will ye go, Mossie?" said Ernie. "I know you've been out all neet but there's nae one else."

As I was gannen oot I asked the Sarge if Norm would be all reet. "I'm going to ask him if he's got any relatives. His Da's away at sea." Norm's Da' was a master mariner and Norm reckoned he was away in the Atlantic somewhere. "Sergeant Duncan sent a message down with Freddie half an hour ago – there's a UXB in Tynedale Road – he reckons it's a big un and they're going to have to evacuate all the houses within a quarter of a mile – that would include Norm's house so we can't let him go back."

"He can stay at wor's if he's naewhere else to gan," I said.

I went off. I took the bike and hoped that they'd have enough room in the back of the lorry for it. It was nearly midnight by the time they arrived but I'd not been standing aboot. A call had been put oot for mutual aid and, although the Sunderland squads had not been able to come yet as they had been bombed heavily as well, there were lorries and cars from Newcastle and Gateshead waiting directions. The Army had been called oot as well because of the number of folk who were now homeless or had had to be evacuated. A couple of ARP messengers had turned up and had taken the first ones off doon to Cornwallis Square and up the Lawe Top so I sent half of those waiting to the Westoe area as they had been bombed last and the others to Keppel Street. Then a lorry and trailer pulled up and I heard Lieutenant Brook's voice. "Jump in, Messenger, and you can take us to the Power Station."

"Can I put me bike in the back?"

"Might not be enough room for that – ask Big Jock and he'll try to sort you out."

It only took two ticks. There was a pile of wood on the trailer and he managed to put my bike underneath a couple of planks that would hold it in place. "Isn't it past your bedtime, Mossie?" He laughed.

"Wye aye it is, but there's a war on ye kna!" and we both laughed. I liked Big Jock and I'd already worked oot that it was better to have him as a friend than an enemy.

As I was seated beside the Lieutenant he asked me what I knew aboot the two bombs. "There's four," I said. "The bomb at the Power Station's dangling on top of a high pressure boiler. Geordie Legget drew the coals so it should be cooled doon a bit noo."

"Well done that man."

"Sergeant Dorothy reckons it's a thousand pounder or more. There's another one in someone's bedroom in Commercial Road

– we think it's a five hundred pounder. Then there was one that came doon in the Middle Docks. I dain't kna' anything aboot that but there's a dirty geet big un' at Tynedale Road wedged between two houses. Everybody's been evacuated up to a quarter mile by Sergeant Duncan."

"You have had a night of it then."

"Aye and they're hundreds oot of their homes."

Chapter Row ARP HQ

When we arrived doon at the riverside there were barriers all ower the place manned by the Home Guard. They let us through and we were met by Sergeant Dorothy and Mr. Mackridge. The Lieutenant and the Subaltern went off with Alec and Bernie. The Subaltern came back two minutes later and started giving orders. They were going to have to construct a platform alongside the bomb so that the Lieutenant could work on the fuses. The Lieutenant thought that there were two of them although the bomb had been badly knocked aboot and he wasn't certain. He'd also need some lights rigged up. There was nae electricity so they'd have to use their own batteries. Although I was allowed to help them carry things to the Power Station door I was not allowed any further. The sappers worked in teams of three – fifteen minutes each. In aboot half an hoor they were ready and then everybody left apart from the Lieutenant. He'd taken his tool kit in and we could hear him banging and knocking even though we were a good hundred yards away behind sandbags.

He came oot after aboot half an hoor. He was in his shirtsleeves and was dripping wet with sweat. He had one of those long tubes that doctors listen to your chest with dangling roond his neck. "It's not ticking but I can't get either of the fuse covers off, it's been smashed about so much. I'm going to have another go but I need a breather. If I can't defuse it then we're going to have to try moving it. I don't think it's got a Sus in it or it would have gone off by now with the hammering I've been giving it."

He wiped his brow and went back in. Bernie Mackridge followed him and came oot a few minutes later. "I've given him a hand towel from the washroom."

I tried to keep my voice doon as I asked Big Jock if the Lieutenant was a doctor, like, having a stetho' whatyecallit roond his neck – I didn't want the others to think I was stupid, but Dekka heard and started mouthing off that I should ask the Lieutenant for a check up next time he came oot. "Shut it, Dekka," said Big Jock, "the lad's not to know." Dekka shut up straight away – ye didn't argue with Big Jock.

"When a bomb doesna' gang off, it's either a dud or it's got a delayed action fuse with a clock in it. If you put a stethoscope on you can hear the ticking."

"And what's a Sus?"

"That I'm not allowed to tell you, son, but if it had one inside then it would have gone up as soon as the Lieutenant hit it with his hammer." Big Jock paused. "It's a special hammer too – the fuses can be set off by magnetic fields so you can't use anything with iron in it. They have special tools that are non-magnetic."

Alec Dorothy and Mr. Mackridge had both edged closer as they knew aboot as much as I did. Then Sergeant Dorothy realised that I was there. "You still here, Mossie?"

"Aye, is there anything else ye want deein' before I get back to Keppel Street?"

"Just had on a sec," said Alec as he had a whispered conversation with Subaltern Coxon and Mr. Mackridge. "When ye get back to Keppel Street tell Ernie to let the ARP HQ know that the power's not likely to be back on for six to eight hours depending on how long it takes to move the bomb. Then can he ring Fenham barracks and warn them that they might have a live thousand pounder coming in later this morning."

It was nearly two o'clock by the time I got to Keppel Street. The phones were off again but Ernie said I could gan yem. The rescue squads were only working at places where they knew someone was buried. They couldn't plug their lights into any electric sockets and the batteries wouldn't last all night. They were reluctant to use hurricane lamps because of leaking gas from broken mains. They were gan to come back in the morning. Barriers had been put up at most sites and officers were manning them. Ernie was making a list of roads that were blocked, and where we would need officers to direct traffic. He made me a cup of tea. Sergeant Cummings had looked in aboot an hour before and had taken Norm upstairs to his house for the neet. "We'll try and sort something out for him tomorrow. The trouble is he hasn't got his ration coupons, and no one wants an extra mouth to feed with nae tickets. There'll be others in the same boat so something'll have to be done. His Mam was very friendly with the

Corbetts – Davey's parents – and he thinks they might be willing to look after him for a few days."

Just then Inspector MacTomney came in. "Any chance of a cup of tea, Ernie." The teapot was still hot so Ernie poured him one – nae sugar – he was keeping quiet aboot the bag from John Burgess. He asked Ernie if they knew how long the lights would be off for and I told him about what was happening at the Power Station. After I'd finished I asked him whether they'd managed to get Frank Foster oot.

"You're the messenger that took his young brother away?" I nodded. "I'm sorry, lad – I didn't recognise you - it's so dingy in here. You've been busy tonight then." He took a sip of tea and groaned. "I'll never get used to tea without sugar. I've just come away now. He was the last one we could get out tonight. The batteries on the big lamps went half an hour ago and we just had torches, but Mr. Scott said they'd dig him out in the dark if they had to. It took nearly four hours. He'd had as much morphine as they could give him but he was still groaning. They eventually got enough rubble off so that they could lift the beam that was pinning him down just a few inches. But when they started pulling him out he shouted blue murder. One side of a window frame had gone right through his arm and they couldn't pull him free. They had to saw it off."

He heard me draw me breath in, and Ernie said "Ye bugger."

"Not the arm - the wood."

"Thank Christ for that," Ernie muttered.

"Mr. Scott shone the torch while young Matty sawed it through either side of Frank's arm. Matty did it as quickly as he could but the wood was moving and poor Frank was telling him to stop, but Matty had to do it. Then they got him out and put him in the ambulance." He looked in my direction. "He's not good, lad, but they'll do all they can for him."

"Do you think I could visit him tomorrow?"

"You can try but you know what hospitals are like about visitors. It's normally relatives only."

"He's got none. Just his brother, Tommy, who's only a bairn." Children weren't allowed to visit.

"Aye well, go in your uniform and if you have any trouble tell them you're on official police business and if they still aren't happy ask them to ring me."

He was a canny fellow, MacTomney, even if he talked funny – Freddie reckoned he was a scouser and I kna' that Jock didn't like him, but then Jock wasn't keen on Inspectors generally.

CHAPTER 9
OCTOBER 1941

Me Mam let me sleep in that morning – we didn't gan doon to the warehouse every day noo as we only delivered once or twice a week to save on the gas for the van, and some days we only had spuds anyhow. I was up at nine and away to the shop. The trolley buses were still not running - the electric didn't come back on until ten in the morning – I took me bike. It was Wednesda' and half day closing so me and Jasmin both came back to Frederick Street for dinner – she sat on the saddle behind me and held me close with her arms roond me chest. Jasmin's Mam always cooked a stew on Wednesda's. Sometimes it was just vegetables, but she'd managed to get hold of a bit of mutton – she never told me how, but whenever we got any fruit or vegetables in, you would always see her popping doon to the butcher's with a little paper bag in her hand. I suspect he returned the favour.

I went up to the Ingham Infirmary after me dinner. I'd gone yem to put me uniform on. At first the Sister was a bit sharp as visitors were not allowed until four o'clock, but I said what the Inspector had told me and she let me have a quick look in. Frank was conscious but only just, and kept drifting off – the Sister tolt me that most of his ribs had been broken. He had bandages all roond his chest and his right arm was hoisted up in the air in a sling. He managed to ask aboot Tommy and I tolt him that he was with Mrs. Pells. Frank mumbled something about seeing if Tommy could be evacuated. The Sister asked me if he had any

relatives and I said naw – but that I would look in and see him.
She said he might be in for a good few weeks.

I was just gannen and Frank started saying something else.
"Can you tell the Dock that I won't be in for a while?"

The first thing I did after I'd left the hospital was to pedal up
Mile End Road to call in on Mrs. Pells to see if Tommy was all
reet. He was quite happy playing with Ernie and Biddy but Mrs.
Pells said that he'd hardly said a word. I told them that I'd been to
see Frank, and that he was deein' well but that he'd be in hospital
for a while. Children weren't allowed to visit so Tommy wouldn't
be able to see him. Mrs. Pells said that she was gan' to wait until
things had settled doon after the raid and then see someone at
the Council aboot Tommy, as he had no relatives now and Frank
couldn't look after him. I told her what Frank had said aboot
Tommy being evacuated and she said that she'd been thinking the
same thing aboot Ernie.

As I was pedalling doon Mile End Road I saw someone
standing on the corner of Morton Street. It was a mariner and
he had a big sea bag ower his shoulder. I recognised him as I got
closer. It was Billy Duggan, Matty's cousin. I pulled up next to
him. He looked at me as though he was a bit dazed. I could smell
the beer on his breath and he'd no doubt had a few pints on the
way. "I got paid off this morning and I was just gan' yem. What
are all the barriers for, Mossie?"

"Has nae one tolt ye?"

"I've just got here. I was gan' to have a word with the bobby
ower there." An officer was standing on the pavement by the
barrier that was across the road – you could see the rescue squads
at work trying to clear the rubble.

I didn't kna' what to say, but somebody had to tell him. "A
German bomb landed in the back lane last neet and blew up
the street. I was one of the first here, Billy. Your hoose was
completely destroyed. Your Mam and Da' were killed."

He just stood there and said nowt, so I asked, "Did ye kna' they'd taken in Frankie Foster and his brother Tommy?"

He just shook his head.

"We had to dig them oot. Tommy's all reet but it took four hours to get Frank and he's badly injured."

"Wharraboot the neighbours?"

"I dinna' – if they were in a shelter they may be all reet, but they'll be in a rest centre or with friends or relatives."

"I'll gan to me Auntie Ellen's in Fort Street first and see what she kna's. One of me brothers works at Redheads' and the other's away at sea, but his lass lives doon Taylor Street. Do you think they'll kna'?"

I shook my head. "The Shields Gazette Office was blown up last neet and there's nae paper the day."

"I'll be away then, Mossie. Ta." And he turned on his heel and walked off up the road.

I then remembered that Frank had wanted the Middle Dock to kna' that he wouldn't be in so I decided to gan there straight away. When I arrived I could see a crowd standing roond at the dock gate. I tolt one of them why I'd come and he said to gan to the office and pointed to a big white building. It was nearly as busy there with a lot of people to-ing and fro-ing. A big hefty fellow in a boiler suit and a cap came ower and asked what I wanted. When I tolt him he said there was not much point waiting to see one of the office staff.

"We were bombed last neet. One of the bombs blew up the canteen and sunk the ferry. It went doon with four hands aboard. There's a lot of damage needs fixing but the other bugger is lying at the bottom of number three dock. It went strite through the ship's side and hit the bottom but didn't gan off. The bomb squad didn't get here until an hour ago – we've had to keep the docks closed but they said we could keep the office open." He took a dog eared note book oot of one of his pockets.

"Tell me the lad's name again." I gave him Frank's name and his last address. "Aw I kna' him – he was a canny young lad. Ye'll have to tell him to put in a doctor's note as soon as he can. And ye said he was lodging with one of wor fitters who was killed."

"Aye. Mr. Duggan, the address is the same."

"Aw, ye bugger, I've known him for years. There'll probably be some money due to him. The family will have to contact us."

"I kna' one of his sons – I saw him this morning. He's a seaman and he'd just been paid off."

"It's a bad time for us. We're as busy as we've ever been what with the War an' all, and it's a devil getting new men, and we've been tolt we might have to take lasses when they start calling them up. The apprentices are deein' men's work if they're any good." He took a good look at me. "You look like a strong lad – if Frank's gan to be off for a while we could take someone else on and we'd keep Frank's job open for him if..." he paused for a sec. "I mean for when he gets better. Are you working noo?"

"I'm a police messenger but that's only when the sirens gan. I work at Bates' Fruit and Veg during the day."

"Aye, well, if ye came here you'd be in a reserved occupation and you wouldn't be called up – some lads still want to gan and get killed though. How auld are ye?"

"Sixteen and three quarters."

"You'd have a good year before you had to decide. It's good money – you'd get £2 and 6d a week in your first year. If you're interested come roond and ask for me – I'm Sid Mordue, shore side manager for rivetting and fitting."

"I'll think aboot it, but I'm quite happy where I am for the minute and I was thinking of gannen to sea, anyway." I got on me bike and then asked him where the bomb disposal squad were. "They might need a message getting back to Police HQ."

"Ye can't just gan riding up – I'll take ye there." It wasn't far and I saw the bomb squad's lorry well back from the dock. Big Jock and the sappers were stood round, and I could see the Lieutenant crouched doon behind some sandbags on the dock side. He had a piece of twine in his hand and was pulling it very slowly.

Big Jock waved me ower. "Are ye keeping an eye on us, Mossie?"

"Naw, I had to come doon to the dock anyway – one of me mates who works here was hurt bad last neet when his hoose was blown up. I wondered if ye needed any messages carrying anywhere."

"I'll ask the Lieutenant when he's finished. There's a thousand kilogram bomb on the dock bottom. He's opened the fuse cover and he's trying to pull the fuse out."

Just then the Lieutenant gave a shout and pulled the twine hard - it came up ower the edge with the fuse attached. He laid it doon and then shouted ower that he was gan' doon to check everything was all reet, and then they could start lifting the bomb.

"He'll no' be long noo."

"What happened last neet?" I asked.

"It was hard work, Mossie. The Lieutenant was on the bomb for nearly two hours, but he couldn't get to either of the fuses. He tried everything. So we had to move it anyway. We were lucky that they had pulleys already installed above the boilers for maintenance - so we used them but once we got the bomb doon we still had to manhandle it oot of the Power Station and on to the lorry."

"With the fuse still live?"

"Aye. But with the bouncing aboot it had done before it landed on top of the boiler, and the knocking the Lieutenant had given it, he didn't think it would gang off – but we had to get it oot of the Power Station. He hadn't heard any ticking but these clocks can start up any time. Once we'd got it on the lorry the Lieutenant said that he'd gang up with it and stay in the back of the lorry – he'd lay alongside it with his stethoscope

and if it started ticking then they'd head for somewhere oot in
the open and scarper. Young Dekka was to drive the lorry. He
didn't like that but he's the only one that can drive apart from
the Subaltern and the Sergeant and they were to stay here. There
were other bombs to deal with and if anything had happened to
the Lieutenant then they would have to stand in for him. There
was a polis on a motorbike leading the way, and a car behind to
get them away quick if needed. They went to Fenham Barracks.
They'd told them what to expect and Major Stringfellow was
waiting with his squad to take over. They were going to try to
steam the explosives out. We got our heads down here until they
got back."

Dekka walked ower.

"You're looking a bit pale and thin, Dekka," I said, "Jock was
telling me you were shitting yoursel' all the way to Newcastle this
morning."

He made a grab for me but I hid behind Big Jock. "Well ye
would have been too if it had been ye. Every time I went ower a
pothole I had me heart in me gob. I should get a medal ye kna'."

"Aye, the Geordie Cross," laughed Jock.

"Anyhow, Lieutenant Brookes patted me on the back when
we'd got rid of the bomb, so I thought I'd ask him if I could
billet with wor Audrey at the café while we're in Shields and he
agreed."

"Ye jammy bastard," muttered Big Jock.

"Aye, I'll be sleeping in a proper bed, having bacon for breakfast
and fish and chips for dinner, and as much ice-cream as I can
shovel into me gob."

Sergeant Hopkirk came ower. "Get the sheer legs ready,
lads, we're going to pull it out now." He looked at me. "The
Lieutenant wants to go over to Tynedale Road to recce a category
"B". Could you lead the way for him on your bike?"

I rode ahead with the lorry following – I took him up Claypath

Lane and then up Westoe Road. Once we'd got through the barrier, and the officer had parked the car, he said, "Thank you, Messenger, that will be all." Then I tolt him that the mutha' of one of the PAMs had been killed by the other bomb that had gone off further up Grosvenor Road. His house was within the evacuated area and he had no ration tickets or anywhere to live. "Can I stay until you've finished your recce and I might be able to tell him when he can get back in."

"Of course," he said straight away, "although I can't guarantee that I can give you much of an answer." I thought to mesel' that he might have been a canny fellow oot of uniform. He went off with Jock Duncan who had been waiting for him.

Ten minutes later he was back. "It's wedged in the party wall between two houses – it's not in the ground but we're going to have to demolish two walls to get to it. We'll start this afternoon so you can tell your friend that he should be able to get home Thursday or Friday. I'm off back to the Middle Docks."

I said, "thank you very much, sir," and pedalled off mesel'.

I decided I'd had enough and headed back yem rather than gan doon to Keppel Street. I was starting to feel tired so I had a cup of tea and then sat in the chair by the fire and fell asleep. The next thing I knew me Mam was shaking me arm. It was seven o'clock.

"I thought I'd better wake you up, Mossie or you won't sleep tonight. I've kept your tea warm." It was scrambled egg made from dried egg and it tasted like cardboard, but me Mam had managed to get some brown sauce the other week so it wasn't too bad. She'd made a rice pudding for afters but it didn't have much sugar in. Mary wanted to kna' all aboot Frank and Tommy and I was just starting to tell her when Bella Rutherford knocked on the back door and came in. With no Gazette, folk only knew aboot what had happened from what others had tolt them, and Bella knew that I'd been out most of last neet. She wasn't the only one who called in and by nine o'clock I was worn oot with talking so I went to bed.

It was up as usual in the morning and off to work. I'd always looked forward to gan' in, but noo I could hardly wait to get there to see Jasmin. We were starting to get really close and each night before I dropped her off at home we would normally try to find a back lane or somewhere we could have a kiss. I tried not to let me hands wander, but I couldn't always stop mesel'. I didn't think of Jackie so much noo, and I was gan' to try to get Jasmin into the air raid shelter in wor back yard. I'd like to have it again with a lass, and although Jasmin was a bit young I was beginning to think that she might say yes if I said I was really desperate for it. I'd asked her if she wanted to gan to the Sutton Hall dance with me one Wednesda' or Sarrada' and she'd said all reet. We could ask Edie if we could stay to tea, and then walk doon – there were fields on the way and we might be able to have a cuddle or someitt. We'd come back on the trolley bus as well, although I wasn't planning to de what Freddie had done with Gertie. I'm not trying to give the impression that that's all I thowt aboot, but after the bombing the other neet we were all realising that if your name was on a bomb then that was it; and that it could happen if you were oot on a bike, or in a shelter, or at home tucked up in bed. So if I had a chance of having it with Jasmin I'd be daft not to take it, and I hoped she saw it the same way.

I put me uniform on and went oot on the bike aboot half past six that evening. I wasn't expecting any raids that neet but you never knew, and I wanted to see Norm to tell him what the Lieutenant had told me. I'd been too tired to gan oot the neet before. A smaller version of the Shields Gazette was oot – it had been printed with the help of the Sunderland Echo and the Newcastle Evening Chronicle – so folk could read aboot what had happened. One of the Gazette's own reporters had nearly been blown up when the bomb hit, and he told his own story first hand. He'd been knocked doon the stairs when the bomb struck

– he was a bit dazed and nearly stepped oot a hole in the wall two storeys up.

I wasn't sure whether to gan to Keppel Street and ask where Norm was or to gan straight to Hepscott Terrace where Davey's parents lived - they had one of the big houses at the Sunderland Road end. I decided that I would be bound to see Davey and Jackie some time so I might as well just gan there noo – if Norm wasn't there, they'd know where he was. It was Davey who opened the door. He was pleased to see me. He asked me in, but I said I just wanted a quick word with Norm and had heard he might be staying there. Davey said he was and to hang on a sec, and then Norm came to the door. When I tolt him what I knew he said that he'd heard the same thing himsel' – the Corbetts had agreed to take him as a lodger until his Da' came back from sea so he only needed to go back yem for his things. He was thinking of gan' doon to DiBresci's – he'd heard that the lads were gan' to meet there the neet - did I want to come?

"Wye aye, I can catch up on all the news."

All the lads were there apart from Matty – he was either oot, still working, or at yem and too tired to come oot. All the rescue squads were working full pelt and there were also teams from all ower the north east that had come in under mutual aid. They had to find all the bodies first, and then make sure that the sites were safe to work on. Then they would de what they could to repair houses that could be lived in again – so folk could be moved oot of rest centres. There'd been so much damage done that Jimmy Clay reckoned that they'd be fully occupied for a couple of month at least. I looked roond. "Is Dekka not here?" I asked Wally.

"He might be still working – he said they would like to finish the Tynedale Road bomb the neet and they've got two more to sort oot before they can gan. Some of the squad have had to gan ower to North Shields to help oot with a category "A". Even if he's finished he'll be in the *Woodbine* or the *Marine* before he comes yem."

"Tell him I want to see him, mind," said Freddie.

"Aye, I kna'."

I noticed that Wally was blushing. "What is he after - some johnnies?" I asked and Wally blushed even more. I wondered what he'd done with the ones I'd got him from Johnny but then I decided that I didn't want to kna'.

"Keep your voice doon, ye stupid nowt," whispered Freddie. "I'm gan' oot with Gertie on Sarrada' to the Majestic dance. If it's not too cad I'm ganna see if she'll come for a walk in the Marine Park afterwards. Ye might get lucky with Glenda too, Jimmy."

"I dinna'," Jimmy replied, "she always says she's not that sort, but we were in the Park last Sunda' and I got me hand reet up her thigh and she was getting all hot. Then she pulled away. I'll be eighteen in a month's time when I'll be getting me papers, so I'm thinking of asking her if we can get engaged. She might let me have it before I gan away to the RAF."

Lenny and Norm were taking it all in. The café door opened and Billy Duggan walked in. He came and sat doon and ordered a coffee. "Wor Matty's just got in. He asked me to tell ye he wouldn't be oot the neet. He's having his tea and then he'll be in the tub, and off to bed.

"I'm away to South Eldon Street in a minute to see Annie. I'd promised her that I'd be roond as soon as me ship got in, but I couldn't last neet, like. Do ye want to come, Jimmy – or ye, Freddie? You look a lot older noo."

"Naw it's all reet, Billy. We've both got lasses and we might get lucky at the weekend. Hey, could ye de us a favour, Billy?" said Freddie, and whispered something in his ear – nae prizes for guessing what. Billy took thre'pence each of both of them and said he'd see them the morrow. He didn't stay long and went off to catch the trolley bus doon to the Dock.

"He likes that Annie," I said.

"Aye," Freddie said, "Matty reckons that Billy's gan' to ask her to give up the game so he can have her all to himsel'. He says that she only ever took on young lads that she fancied, not like the other two who'd de it with anyone who'd pay. She should be called up to de war work soon anyway."

Not long after the sirens went – it was aboot eight o'clock. We all piled oot and got on wor bikes. Wally would have to put his uniform on and was the last to arrive at Keppel Street.

We heard the planes coming ower and the ack-ack guns start to gan off just before nine o'clock. Then came the first explosions, and the phones started ringing – there seemed to be bombs coming doon all ower. We had reports of bombs at the Deans and at Brigham and Cowans on the riverside, and two rows of houses had been blown up at Marlborough Street and Albany Street – the Special who called that one in reckoned that his mate, who had been on patrol with him, had been caught in the blast. Ernie sent Jimmy and Len to check things oot there. "It looks like it's going to be a busy night again. Mossie, you and Freddie get up to Chapter Row and just check that the ARP HQ have had the same reports we have. Then head up to the Market. Jack Cummings is on duty there the night – if there are problems at Brigham's he might need your help."

There was still a lot of bomb damage that hadn't been cleared up from two nights ago, and we had to wend wor way very carefully. The ARP were hard at it when we arrived - they knew of all the bombs and were sending oot rescue teams and fire engines. As we turned the corner into the Market Place we saw an ambulance and a first aid car heading very slowly up the road just in front of us. "I think that's Gertie's ambulance," shouted Freddie - I didn't kna' how he knew, as it was pitch black and I could only see them because of their white bumpers. I could just make out an ARP warden standing by the entrance to one of the underground shelters.

King Street and Market Place

"I'll cut them off," Freddie called oot as he tore strite across the Market Place standing on his pedals. I was way behind, and riding ower cobbles is bad enough when you're gan' slow. He was past the auld Town Hall and took one hand off the handle bars to wave to the ambulance driver, and then the bombs came doon. I dain't kna' how many there were but the last thing I saw was Freddie flying through the air, and then the blast caught me. I was oot for a couple of minutes and didn't kna' where I was. I came to, feeling a bit sick, and couldn't hear owt. I was just behind the auld Town Hall and that must have saved me from the full force of the blast. All I could see was flames all roond. Me bike was on top of me and I pushed it away and got to me feet. I had a stab of pain in me left leg and had a job putting any weight on it, but that was all. A trolley bus ootside the *Tram* was alight. I then saw Gertie get oot of the ambulance. You couldn't mistake her. She was running towards where I'd last seen Freddie. Then she was doon as there was a geet big explosion from Dunn's Paint stores, and blazing tins of paint and oil were gan' up like rockets and then coming doon like fire bombs. She got up and ran forward and I limped across as quick as I could. I saw her bend ower and pick something up – it looked like a pile of rags. I was nearly there and realised that it was Freddie – I was reet beside her but she was strong enough and then something dropped doon. I bent ower to pick it up and it was the bottom part of a leg with a boot on. Gertie had stopped as well. "What should I de with it?" I started puking. "Bring it with you, Mossie. We'll keep him all together. He's still breathing."

We got to the ambulance and Glenda and the other first aiders were all ower him for a minute sticking needles into him, and then Gertie said that she'd have to get him to the Ingham as quick as she could, and Glenda was to stay with him in the back. I was just standing there and I put me hand doon to feel me leg. One of the first aid team asked me if I was all reet. It was a woman of aboot forty. I could hardly hear her but I just pointed to me leg. She moved me ower to the car and sat me doon – she took off me bicycle clip and then pulled me trouser leg up – there was a nasty gash and you could see the bone where the flesh had been cut. "You'll need to get that stitched."

Just then I heard someone come ower and heard Jack Cummings' voice. "A bomb's landed on the entrance to the north shelter and another's hit the south shelter – we're ganna have to see if anyone's alive. I've just rang from the box for the rescue squads and fire engines but we'll have to manage until they come." He paused a sec and then said, "Is he all reet?" He must have meant me.

"His leg's badly gashed and he seems a bit dazed. He might be in shock – I was going to have him taken to the first aid post in the clinic at the Chi."

"I'm not gan' to nae clinic while there's work to de." I wondered whose voice it was, then realised it must be mine.

"He's reet, ye kna', the car might be needed for worse than him. Bandage him up quick as ye like and then get ower to the shelters the both o' ye'se."

It didn't take the first aider five minutes – she'd already cleaned

the wound with something that stung like mad, and she then
strapped it up really tight with a bandage.

"You'll do for now," she said as she grabbed her bag and went
off. She'd done a good job because I could put most of me weight
on it without it hurting too much. Sergeant Cummings and
the two lasses who'd gone with him to the north shelter came
running back.

"It's too dangerous there with all the cans of paint flying
roond. We'll have to wait until the fire tenders come. We'll start
on the south shelter." I was beginning to come to me senses, and
it was a scene I've never forgotten. In the corner of the Market
Place Dunn's Paint Store was blazing like an inferno – you could
feel the heat where we were, and cans of paint and anything
else that would set alight were flying through the air in every
direction. The *City of Durham* which was next door was already
alight and then I saw what was left of Crofton's catch fire. Then it
was the *Locomotive* and Campbell's lodging house – in Union Alley
the roofs of the *Imperial* and *Metropole* were ablaze. Doon the road
from where we were, a gas main just by the Water Company's
offices was shooting flames all ower – they'd jumped East Street
and I could see the *Grapes* and Jackson's the Tailor's take light.

I'd followed the others, and they were gathered roond the
entrance to the south shelter – they'd pulled oot the ARP warden
who I'd seen standing there and he was being put onto a stretcher
– Jack Cummings was in the entry pulling away bricks and timber
and then a couple of people walked oot coughing and spluttering.
But they were the only ones who could manage under their own
steam. "It's nae good," I heard Jack shout. "The rest are gan' to
have to be dug oot."

We helped the two that had survived ower to the first aid car.
The woman had blood all ower her face from a cut in the heed,
and the man needed to lean on me – he couldn't put any weight
on his leg, it was stickin' oot at a funny angle. I had to de all I

could not to fall doon mesel, mind, as me own leg wasn't that
sound. Then the first fire engines arrived followed by two rescue
squad lorries. Two engines went strite ower to the north end to
tackle the blaze at Dunn's, and the other tried to douse the flames
from the gas main. One of the firemen came running ower – he
knew Sergeant Cummings. "We can't get any pressure on the
hose – the mains must be broken. We'll try further ower but
we'll need a lot more watter to put all this oot. We'll need more
fire tenders – I kna' calls have gone oot from other parts of the
toon, but this will need everything we've got. We'll have to try to
relay watter from the ferry landing – and there's a static tank in
North Street. Can you send someone doon to the ARP HQ and
get them to send oot a request for mutual aid. As many tenders as
possible."

I knew that I wasn't gan' to be much use here now the rescue
squads had arrived.

"I'll gan," I shouted, "my bike's ower there."

"Are you sure, Mossie?" Jack asked.

"Wye aye, I'm as right as rain noo."

"Tell them the shelters have been hit and we'll need rescue
squads and first aid teams as well. Then get back to Keppel Street,
and get Ernie to organise someone to meet the teams coming
in up at Dean Street." I was dragging me left leg a bit as I went
ower to me bike which wasn't damaged – it was solid. I was just
pedalling off when the Sergeant waved me ower. "Now mind ye
take care, Mossie, and get to the clinic as soon as ye can to get
that leg seen to..." I was off before he could finish.

I was the first to tell the ARP HQ aboot the damage in the
Market, and that two shelters had been hit. The woman on the
counter took me straight through the main room where they
had tables, message boards, and loads of phones to an office
where this auld fella with white hair was sitting behind a desk. I
think it was Major Todd, the head warden. He asked me to tell

him exactly what I had seen – he then very politely thanked me very much and then walked oot into the main room and started barking oot orders in a voice they would have heard ower on the fish quay. Then everybody was on the phones or if they couldn't get through, writing oot instructions for the messengers to deliver.

I was asked to tell Sergeant Leadbitter that mutual aid would be coming in from all roond and that the PAMs would have to be used to take them to where they had to gan – the civil defence messengers were already oot passing messages from one place to the other. It was vital to ensure that help got to where it was most needed. The Market Pace was to be top priority.

When I got to Keppel Street it was a lot quieter – only Ernie was in the office and Wally and Norm were on the switchboard. Everybody else was oot – there'd been bombs gannen off all ower Shields – the Micah Lubricant Works in Candlish Street had been badly damaged, the Harton Coal Company cutting in Erskine Road had been blown up and an electric cable had been set on fire. This had lit up the area, and in Hyde Street and Wharton Street aboot twenty houses had been demolished by enemy aircraft dropping bombs where they could see the light of the burning cable. Broughton Road and Winchester Street had also taken a hammering.

"We've not had any new calls for a while – everybody must be out at the bomb sites – I'll see if I can get through to the ARP to find oot when we can expect the outside help." Ernie picked up the phone and then tapped the receiver a couple of times. "Ye bugger – the phones are dead. Reet – there's no point in you two staying here – " he was talking to Wally and Norm. "Get yoursels' up to Dean Road with Mossie."

"Mossie – on the way up see what's happening where bombs have come down – speak to the officers in charge and see what help they need. Tell them the phone lines are down and to use the messengers." Ernie looked very pale and then sat doon holding his chest.

"Are ye all reet, Sarge?" I asked.

"Aye. Me chest's a bit tight that's all. Nowt that a good strong cup of tea with two spoonfuls of sugar won't sort out. Off you go now. Keep your helmets on and watch out for bombs."

On the way up Fowler Street we turned down Percy Street – aboot a dozen hooses at the corner of Redhead Street were nowt but ruins, and it was the same further doon near the bridge. There were only a couple of ARP wardens and Special Constables trying to dig people oot with their hands. Then I heard a voice I recognised – it was Sergeant Duncan. I shouted ower and he came towards us – as he got closer he saw Wally. "Who sent you lot out in the middle of an air raid?" He sounded resigned as much as angry.

"We're gan' up to Dean Road to fetch any reinforcements that come from other toons," I replied, "but Sergeant Leadbitter asked us to stop off to tell folk that the phones are doon, and you're ganna' have to rely on us messengers."

"Aye – we've got casualties here and dozens are trapped in their shelters. Can one of you get over to the rescue squad depot and then to the ambulance yard and tell them we need urgent help here. Even if they're all out they'll know where they've gone to. Ye might have to do a bit of pedalling tonight."

"Reet, Sarge. Norm, off you gan. Me and Wally'll gan up to Dean Road – if any squads have arrived we'll send one doon here. The Market Place is top priority, Sarge – it's all ablaze and they're having to pump watter from the river. Did ye kna' that Freddie Skee got blown up?" He shook his head. "I was lucky; I was just behind him."

I was just aboot to gan but I thought I better tell him aboot Ernie. "He said it was nowt but he didn't look too good and he's on his own at the minute."

"Thanks for telling me, Mossie. As soon as we get help here I'll go back."

It was the same up at Hyde Street and Wharton Street but the need there was for fire engines as gas mains had burst and little fires were breaking oot all ower. People who'd survived the raid were forming chains to pass buckets of watter across the ruins of their homes to try to put as many fires oot as possible. I sent Wally oot to try a couple of the auxiliary fire brigade out-stations but I reckoned they'd already be doon at the Market.

When I reached the Chi I met up with Jimmy and Len – they'd been helping oot at Marlborough Street. "One of wor Specials was killed in the blast," said Jimmy. "They've still not taken his body away. When the houses came doon they trapped a lot of folk in their shelters in the back yards. We were one of the first there and were helping to clear away as much of the bricks and rubble as possible, but it wasn't easy. We'd got one family oot and then a rescue squad and a first aid car turned up. They said that there were bombs all ower, and that more squads were coming in from neighbouring toons. We were sent doon here to fetch one of them back there, and take the others to where they're needed." He looked at me leg – ye could see the bandages where me troosers had been torn. "What ye been up to, Mossie?"

"Me and Freddie were sent to the Market Place – well ye kna' what Freddie's like – he just went pelting ower the Market cobbles and a bomb landed reet on top of him. Gertie had to carry him to the ambulance – I picked up one of his legs."

"Wor Freddie?"

"Aye – he's in the Ingham noo, but he caught the full blast and he was more deed than alive when they carted him off."

Lenny had said nowt but he looked at me. "Are ye sure ye're all right, Mossie?"

"Wye aye, but I was sent flying off me bike – me leg's cut a bit but a first aider bandaged it up. I've got to gan to the clinic ower there." I pointed to the clinic – there was already a queue of ambulances and first aid cars dropping off folk who were not too badly injured.

Just then Bobby Lawson, one of me auld mates from Laygate Lane School who was a PAM doon at Laygate, came pedalling up. "Ye all reet, Mossie? I've been sent up to fetch the relief squads when they arrive. With the phones doon Douggie Errington came ower on the motorbike from the Dock to see if one of us could get up here – all the polis are oot at the bomb sites. There's hooses blown up at H.S. Edwards Street and two bombs have come doon at South Eldon Street – the Dock Police have called oot the rescue squads from the shipyards but they'll need all the help they can get." The yards and some of the big factories and warehouses had their own volunteer fire and rescue squads.

It was aboot then that the first convoy arrived from Sunderland. They'd come doon Mortimer Road and had pulled up by the clinic and sent a man ower. When he asked where they were wanted the other PAMs just looked at each other, so it was left to me. I sent all the fire engines to the Market with the exception of one that was to gan' to Hyde Street and then doon to the railway at Erskine Road. Jimmy took them as well as half of the rescue and first aid teams – he was to direct one of the rescue squads to Percy Street. Len took a rescue team up to Marlborough Street and Bobby took another doon to H. S. Edwards Street, at Tyne Dock.

I stayed behind and there were three of us there when the Gateshead teams turned up. I'd heard nowt else aboot any raids so I sent the fire engines to the Market and the rescue teams to the other bomb sites. Norm, who'd been to Hyde Street and back, said he'd heard that Winchester Street had been hit. I decided to take one mesel' doon the Dock to South Eldon Street as Bobby had not come back. I was just gannen when Inspector MacTomney turned up in one of the cars.

"Who's directing the reinforcements?" he called oot as he got oot of the car.

The lead driver from Gateshead shouted oot, "The young fella's in charge," pointing at me, "and he's deein' canny."

"There was nae one else, Inspector. Sergeant Leadbitter tolt me that the Market Place was the priority, but I had to send some teams to gan where there were fires or where people needed digging oot of their shelters."

"Good lad. I'll take over here – the car's going to go back to Keppel Street and then come back to keep me up to date. Be steady how you go, son."

I pedalled as fast as I could – me leg was starting to hurt but I held it up off the pedal and used me right leg as much as possible - I dain't think the cars would have gone much faster – it was pitch black and once or twice the lead car tooted its horn for me to slow doon. They didn't kna' the roads, and in the black oot they could hardly see owt with their headlights half covered – they could easily have driven into a trolley bus pole.

Two bombs had come doon in South Eldon Street – the first had just missed the railway bridge but it must have been a Satan because it had damaged the wall holding the bridge up, and there was a dirty geet crater reet in the middle of the road – it must have been 70 foot across. It had broken the gas and water mains, and had brought doon the phone lines and the trolley bus wires. The other bomb had come doon a few minutes afterwards and had blown up aboot ten houses just in front of the bridge. The ARP wardens and a couple of polis were in the ruins trying to get to people trapped in their shelters but some of them were dangling on the edge of the crater. The Gateshead lads got everyone organised as best as they could - it was not long before the first bodies came oot, and then they were pulling oot the injured. I stayed there to help for a bit and was there when they hoiked Billy Duggan and Annie oot. They were dead lucky – half of their flat had been completely demolished, but the room they were in had just crumbled slowly doon and although the roof had fallen on top of them Billy had had time to pull himself and Annie reet up against the wall to save them from serious injury. The fella who got to them first shouted oot, 'Can someone fetch some blankets.' I was handy so I went to one of the first aid cars. I didn't kna' then that it was Billy, of course, and thought that it was an auld hinny who was cauld, but when I stumbled ower the rubble I could see that Billy and Annie had nowt on. Billy had just got in the flat when the sirens went and the other two lasses had gone to the shelter – he wasn't gan' anywhere until he'd had what he came for, so him and Annie stayed in the flat and got doon to business. He was still at it when the bomb went off. I gave them each a blanket and then helped them ower the rubble – they had nae shoes on. They managed but Billy came oot with a few words I'm not ganna' repeat here. Even with the blanket Annie was shivering so I took me overcoat off and gave it to her. "Where we ganna' gan in nae claes?" said Billy. "Can ye take us to Fort Street – that's where I'm staying?"

"How far away is that?" asked the lass who was the first aid car driver.

"It's reet on the other side of toon."

The driver of another car came ower. He'd been listening and looking – you could still see quite a bit of Annie's legs. "I'm just off to the first aid centre at Chichester if it's near there."

"Naw, but my hoose in Maxwell Street is just doon the road from the clinic." I thought I'd help oot – I didn't kna' Billy that well but he was Matty's Cousin so I says to him, "Me Mam'll look after ye for the neet and she'll have claes for Annie and ye can borrow some of mine or Saleem's."

I then said to the driver, "I'll show ye the way. I've got to gan back up there anyhow to fetch more rescue squads doon."

The first aid car dropped them off at Maxwell Street and I gave the driver directions to the clinic. I had to leave Billy and Annie on the front step while I went round the back and got me Mam oot the shelter. There hadn't been any bombs for a while so she went through the house and let them in. She said she'd find them something to put on and they could stay the neet. As soon as the all clear sounded she'd make them something hot.

I went straight off to the Dean Road pick up point. The Inspector sent me back doon to Eldon Street with two more rescue squads and a fire tender. With the gas mains broken there was always the risk of a fire.

We'd just turned into Barnes Road when I saw a bike coming towards us. It was Bobby Lawson.

"Is that ye, Mossie?"

"Aye."

"Can you pull up a minute?"

Stopping in front of one the rescue lorries in the black oot could be dangerous. They didn't always stop as quick as ye, even if they did see your hand signals, but this time they pulled up with aboot two inches to spare.

Bobby came ower and spoke to me and the driver.

"Is that a fire engine?" he asked, pointing doon the convoy. "Aye, we're taking it to the Eldon Street Bridge in case the gas main sets afire."

"Has it got a pump aboard?"

"Wye aye," replied the driver as though it was a stupid question.

"Can it come doon to Lytton Street? There's a big crater and there are people trapped on either side but the water main's burst and the hole's filling – we're worried in case any of those under the rubble might droon. We need a pump."

"Aye of course, lad. Come with me." The driver took him back to where the tender was and told the firemen to follow Bobby. After I'd taken the rescue squads to the bridge at South

Eldon Street I decided to pedal ower to Lytton Street in case they needed any more help.

Crater between Lytton Street and HS Edwards Street

When I arrived there it was mainly deed bodies that they were dragging oot of the ruins either side of the crater - it had been a big bomb and had landed reet on top of the terrace ending up in the back lane. The firemen were just starting to pump, but after five minutes it was clear that the watter was still rising, and that it was coming in faster than they were pumping it oot.

"We'll need some more pumps," one of the firemen said to Sergeant Dorothy who was the officer in charge. "We could send one of the messengers to look for another tender," Alec replied.

"They'll be at the Market," I said. "It's all ablaze and they're having to pump watter from the river. I'll gan if ye want but even if they let me have one it'll be a good half an hoor at least before I can get back."

One of the ARP wardens was listening. "They've got some manual pumps at the Middle Docks." He paused a minute and then said, "I work there. The night watchman will let you in if you can wake the drunken bugger up but you'll need someone who kna's where the pumps are."

"I kna' Mr. Mordue," I said.

"Aye, Sid would be all reet. He just lives roond the corner in Palmerston Street."

"Reet," said Alec, "ye, Mossie, gan in one of the lorries – put your bike in the back. Pick up Mr. Mordue and then get doon the docks and fetch us a couple of pumps." The ARP warden came with us to show us the hoose. When we knocked at the door an auld hinny with her hair tied up in a scarf opened the door.

"What the devil d'ye want? - there's an air raid gan' on ye kna'."

"We're after Mr. Mordue. We want him to come doon to the Middle Dock with us."

"He's beat you to it. He's all ready doon there. He's on fire watch duty the neet."

The ARP man left us to it, as he wanted to get back to Lytton Street. Once we got to the Dock the night watchman opened the gate and we drove up to the office. Sid Mordue came oot. I explained to him what had happened at Lytton Street and that we needed more pumps.

"Nae bother – ye can have all three if you've got enough hands to work them." We went ower to the shed where the pumps were kept. The rescue squad lads carried them to where the lorry was and then lifted them into the back. While they were deein' that Mr. Mordue asked me if I was the lad who'd been roond the other day. When I said I was he asked if I had me bike handy. "Aye it's in the lorry."

"Reet you get on your bike and lead the way – I'll get in the lorry with them and once we've got the pumps working ye can bring me back here on the back of your bike – there are a couple of other fire watchers but I can't afford to be away too long."

I kna' that people said afterwards that us PAMs were either brave or daft for riding aboot in the middle of an air raid – I dain't kna' aboot the others but I just didn't think aboot that – and it was exciting an' all. It was like the cowboy films with me riding ahead as a scout. The ARP had messengers as well but if they were under eighteen they were only sent oot after the all clear had sounded – us PAMs went oot when we were needed.

We got there all reet and Mr. Mordue showed the rescue squad lads how to work the pumps. With the fire pump and the three other pumps all working together the water started levelling off a bit. Sergeant Dorothy then asked me what I was deein' standing aboot. I said I was ganna take Mr. Mordue back to the Docks - he let oot a laugh and tolt Sid to had on tight.

"As soon as you've done that ye better get back to Keppel Street. With the phones doon ye PAMs are the only means of communication - God help us."

He put his hand on me shoulder. "Ye did well, Mossie. Watch oot for bombs, mind."

Me leg was starting to hurt a bit so I asked Sid if he could ride a bike. He just laughed and straddled the cross bar while I got on behind. He reckoned that he used to ride his bike to Seaham Harbour and back when he was courting his wife, so a little trip doon to the Docks with me on the back was a doddle.

The last bomb had landed at 10 o'clock – it had demolished all the north side of Queen Street between Mile End Road and

Station Approach. Many people were trapped, and they had the same problem there as at Eldon Street when the crater started filling with watter because of a broken main – I dain't kna' what they did aboot pumps.

National Fire Service Canteen in Market Place

The phones didn't come back on until the next morning and us PAMs were to-ing and fro-ing between the bomb sites, the ARP

HQ, the emergency rest centres and anywhere else that needed a message taking. We were lucky – when we went back to Keppel Street we might have a cup of tea in the Charge Office. If ye were working with the rescue squads or with any of the emergency services ye'd de withoot. Sometimes folk in a street would get together and make a big pot of tea for the workers but they might not have enough milk for everybody and there was never any sugar – better than nowt.

Ernie had had to gan yem and naebody else was allowed to touch his sugar bag. His chest pains were getting worse and he would have called a doctor oot any other neet but they were all on call anyway looking after the raid victims. Superintendent Lamont had taken ower in the Charge Office – everybody else was oot at the bomb sites.

Police from neighbouring forces were due to arrive in the morning as well as detachments from the Army and teams from the Naval base in North Shields who would help with demolition and making the sites safe. There'd be more rescue and demolition squads as well and all these men and women needed feeding. The WVS came oot with their mobile canteen and they opened the Hedworth Hall as a big canteen as well.

We'd all come back into Keppel Street for a last cup of tea and it would be light soon.

"Why don't ye knock off now, lads," said the Super. "Get your heads down. If you want to come in later on there'll be plenty to do. All these new helpers will need showing around." He paused. "Don't all come in – if there's another raid tonight we'll need some fresh legs."

"You don't think they'll come again do ye, Super?" asked Jimmy – it was aboot the only time I'd known him serious.

"I hope not – but the town's on the ropes, and the Germans don't back off when their enemy's weak."

The others left but I had been the last in, and still had half a

cup of tea to finish. My thoughts had turned to Freddie as I'd
been sipping the strong black tea. Freddie would never drink black
tea even if that was all there was. "It makes your teeth gan black
and folk think you've been chewing baccy," he would say.

"Has any one told Freddie Skee's Mam that he's been injured?"
I asked the Super.

"Ye bugger, I don't think they have. We couldn't ring to find
out how he was and with everything else going on...." He didn't
finish what he was saying but asked, "Could you go, Mossie, and
tell her?" He paused. "I should really go round myself but I can't
leave the Station unattended."

"Aye, I can gan."

I didn't rush oot the door and the Big Fella looked at me. "Is
something the matter, son?"

"When Gertie...I mean the ambulance driver picked him up he
wasn't moving, and I had to carry one of his legs that had been
blown off. Gertie looked as though she wasn't sure if he'd make
it." I didn't like to say what I was thinking but the Super was no
fool.

"You mean that it would be unfortunate if you told his Mother
that he was seriously injured and he was aleady ..." That was the
second sentence he hadn't finished – he normally rattled them off.
I was hoping he wasn't coming doon with something as well. I
didn't say owt.

Sergeant Cummings walked in. He was covered in dust and
sat straight doon in the nearest chair. "They've just aboot put the
fires oot in the Market but the gas main by the Water Company's
offices is still blazing away – they can't find the f****** stop cock."
His voice was quiet and he didn't try to crack any jokes.

"Could you look after the office for ten minutes, Jack?" asked
the Super.

"I was hoping to get me head doon, Super."

"Mossie here's just reminded me that no one's told young

Skee's family that he's been injured."

"Nae bother then – do ye kna' how he is?"

The Super shook his head. "We're going up to Ingham first, and then we'll have a better idea of what to say."

We went in the Super's car – he normally had a driver but this time he drove himself. It was aboot half past five when we arrived at the Ingham. Ambulances were coming in - they were still digging people oot although not so many noo. We walked in and the Super asked a nurse if they knew what ward Freddie was on - he told her who he was and she said she'd see if she could find oot. She came back with the Matron.

"We were wondering when someone would come. We need to inform the next of kin. He's very poorly."

"We're just going off to see Mrs. Skee now but wanted to check how he was first. I'm sorry no one came sooner - we've been preoccupied with other things."

The Matron looked as though she was thinking and so have we, but she just said, "I'd tell her to come and see him as soon as she can, and not to wait for the visiting hours. We didn't know what religion he was but he's been given the last rites. He's lost two legs, and his left hand is badly damaged. The Surgeon may have to amputate that too but the poor lad's not strong enough for any more surgery just yet. All his ribs are broken and one of his lungs is punctured; he's got other internal injuries and they had to remove his spleen. The Surgeon says that if he survives the next twelve hours he's got a chance, if only a slim one."

She was a very stern looking lady but when she looked at me, she half smiled. "Are you a friend of his?"

"Aye I was only aboot twenty foot behind and I was blown off me bike, but I'm all reet apart from a cut on me leg." I wished I'd kept me gob shut.

"Well, we'd better have that looked at."

"I'd like him to come with me to see Mrs. Skee – I can bring her back here in the car and I'll bring Mossie as well."

She nodded.

Freddie lived in an upstairs flat in Edith Street. It took his mutha' a few minutes to come doon – she'd popped her heed out of the winda first to see who it was. The Big Fella told her at the door that Freddie had been injured. He didn't tell her everything the Matron had told us but he said she ought to come back with us to the Ingham. She asked us in and made a cup of tea while we waited for her to get ready. There was milk and sugar, and she even put oot a couple of broken biscuits. We sat doon, drank the tea, munched wor biscuits – the Super let me have the two halves of the bourbon, and we said thank you very much.

When we got to the Ingham things had quietened doon a bit. Mrs. Skee had to give all Freddie's details to a nurse, and then we were taken to the ward. There were curtains roond Freddie's bed. He had a tube sticking oot of his arm and most of what we could see was covered in bandages. He hadn't come roond from the anaesthetic. The nurse brought up a chair for Mrs. Skee and said she could sit with him and the doctor would see her when he could. The Super said he'd stay until the doctor came but I was put in a side room until someone could have a look at me leg. The doctor who saw me was an auld fella and said he was retired but he came oot when there was an emergency – he looked exhausted. The nurse had taken the bandage off and it didn't look good – you could see the bone reet doon the middle of the leg and there was a lot of dried blood that had turned black. "When did this happen?" he asked. He tutted when I told him. "Were you told that you should have it seen to straight away?"

I didn't want to get anyone into trouble so I said yes, and that with everything gannen on I'd forgotten aboot it. "Stand up," he said – as soon as I put me weight on it I gave a squeal. "Whoever bandaged you up did a good job, but we'll need to get it x-rayed to see if you have a fracture. And you've been working with it all night?"

"Aye well I was on me bike most of the time and I could pedal all reet."

He gave me some strong tablets for the pain.

The Super had looked in to see me before he left. He said that he'd call in on me Mam and tell her where I was. "I've asked them to give us a ring if they need help in getting you home. Let us know how you get on, Mossie."

It turned oot that I had what they call a greenstick fracture – they thought I must have been hit by a cobble stone or something when the blast caught me, or it could have been the bike getting caught up in me legs. There was a break, but it had not gone all the way across the bone. "You're still growing," the doc said, "so the bone bent a bit and saved it breaking all the way across. We'll have to stitch you up and then we're going to have to put a cast on but it shouldn't take too long to heal up – it's normally about four to six weeks. You'll need to keep the weight off it for a couple of days but you should be able to get round with a crutch."

They would have kept me in for a day or two but the beds were all full so I was sent home in an ambulance after dinner - it was worth gan' into Hospital for – steak and kidney pie, with mashed spuds and carrots. As soon as I got yem I went to bed and didn't wake up until the next morning. Me whole body ached and I didn't want to de owt so I just sat in the chair by the fire with me leg resting on the cracket stool. Me Mam was away at the café and Mary was at the shop so Bella Rutherford kept looking in to see if I needed owt, and brought me in a bowl of soup for me dinner, but I wasn't that hungry. Sergeant Duncan called roond aboot three o'clock. He'd been up to the Ingham to see how Freddie was. He'd ridden up on me bike and was dropping it off – they'd noticed it against the wall in the yard that morning and realised whose it was – mine was the only delivery bike there.

He asked if I wanted a cup of tea – his tongue was nearly

hanging oot so I said aye, so long as he made it. He brought the
sugar oot from the cupboard as well – we normally didn't have
it in tea for worselves although me Mam would give Saleem a
spoonful, and sometimes two, so I said that we normally only had
half a spoon each and hoped me Mam wouldn't notice.

Jock told me that the Market Place was completely wrecked –
King Street was closed to traffic and the Corporation was trying
to get some auld trolley buses from other Councils to replace
the ones they'd lost. The emergency teams from other toons all
roond the north were still here and Jock thought it could be a
good few months before they left. Inspector Mullins was back
and lodging with Jock again. He had more or less taken ower the
Station Sergeant's job leaving Jock and Jack Cummings to make
sure the other officers that had been brought in were properly
supported. Ernie Leadbitter was still at home in bed. The doctor
thought that he might have had a slight heart attack, or it could
have been just exhaustion and stress, but he wouldn't be back
soon if at all. Henry Milburn had been signed off sick with shell
shock for a month.

As the Sarge slurped the last of his tea from his saucer I told
him about Mr. Mordue's offer of a job at the Middle Docks. "I
was thinking I might gan and see him but after the other neet I
think I might be safer gan' to sea."

Jock laughed. "There's nowhere completely safe, Mossie, but if
you get an apprenticeship you'll have a steady job for life and you
could still gang to sea at the end of it if that's what you want. If
you sign on now as a fireman or trimmer that's all you'll ever be."
He put his saucer doon. "Is that right that you're courting young
Jasmin?"

Jock didn't say much but he knew everything that was gan' on.
I nodded – I would have blushed a bit if I could.

"Well if you're thinking of getting wed in a few years' time
she'd much rather have you at home than sailing the seven seas,

and a job in the shipyards is better than labouring or going doon the pits."

He was right and I knew that I couldn't stay a delivery lad all me life. Besides, Mrs. Hussain had always made it clear that Peter Boyle, who had worked at the shop since he was a lad, would get his job back when the War finished, and her husband Geordie would be coming yem too.

"Well, even if I wanted to I'll be oot of action for a month and Mr. Mordue will want to fill the job as soon as he can."

"Don't ye worry yoursel', Mossie. I've got to go down to Tyne Dock nick tomorrow to check that Alec's got all the help he needs – I'll pop into the Middle Dock and see Sid Mordue. I want to thank him personally for the use of the pumps."

As he was gan' oot of the door he turned back and said, "I almost forgot, Mossie, Wally said to tell you that the lads were going to meet up at the café tomorrow night about seven, and that a couple of them'll come and pick you up – if you feel up to it."

CHAPTER 10
OCTOBER 1941

Lenny and Norm came roond just after seven. They put me on the back of Len's bike. I managed to lift me left leg ower the crossbar, and then Norm held me steady while Len pushed away – he was gan' all ower the shop and if Norm hadn't ran alongside keeping us steady I dain't kna' what would have happened. Me Mam had come oot and I could hear her shouting blue murder, and what she was ganna de to them if I came to any harm. Once we were on the road Lenny let Norm get ahead so that he could be ready to catch me if I fell off when we stopped.

That wasn't the only shouting we heard that neet. I was gan' through the café door with me arm roond Len's neck, when I was nearly knocked ower by Dekka being chased by his sister Audrey. I think she would have killed him if he hadn't jumped on Norm's bike and made a getaway. She was calling him every name under the sun and some that I'm not ganna repeat here. She stormed back in and went back ower to the fish and chip counter still muttering under her breath.

All the lads were there. After I'd sat doon Wally came ower to ask what we were having. "What was all tharaboot?" I asked in a quiet voice. Wally wouldn't say owt but just looked sideways at where Audrey was standing and made a face. After he'd gone back to the counter Jimmy Clay whispered that when Wally had gone doon the cellar that afternoon to get sugar for the next mix of ice-cream, it had all gone apart from a couple of two pound bags

– he hadn't noticed it before because they always put an auld sack ower it so that if anyone happened to come doon to the cellar they wouldn't see how much there was doon there. Apparently Tony DiBresci's Da' had started stockpiling sugar before the War, and that's why they'd always had ice-cream even if they did limit you to how many you could have a week. The only one it could have been was Dekka – Audrey had confronted him when he'd come in to borrow some money for a pint. He'd given her some lip and she'd gone for him. Wally came ower with me ice-cream. "Has Jimmy telt ye?"

"Aye."

"That might be your last one for a bit. We've got an order of sugar coming at the end of the month but what we get officially doesn't last long. Dekka's been getting away with a lot since he's been here but the sugar was the last straw."

"I can't de withoot me ice-cream," I said.

We were quiet for a while and then I asked if anyone had heard anything more aboot Freddie.

"He's still hanging on," said Norm. "Davey and Jackie went up the other evening but the Matron wouldn't let them see him. It's family only. She told them that he slept most of the time, and that even when he was awake they were having to give him so much morphine for the pain that he wouldn't be saying much. He was still on the danger list but she said that his mother and his fiancée would sit with him as much as they could."

"His fiancée?" I nearly shouted.

"Dain't get too excited, Mossie," said Jimmy, "it was the only way Gertie could get in to see him. The hospital knew that if she hadn't got to him as quick then he wouldn't have made it, but they have strict rules on visiting so she's noo his fiancée."

"Does he kna'?"

"What d'ye think?"

"Well, I was with her as well, dodging the bombs and the flying paint cans, and with a broken leg, so will they let me visit him?"

"Wye aye," said Matty, "ye can be the best man!"

We all laughed. "And wharaboot ye and Glenda, Jimmy?" I said. "If Freddie's engaged to Gertie, then Glenda's gan' to feel left oot."

Jimmy didn't say owt for a minute. Then he spoke – but very quietly. "I think we are engaged."

"Ye only think ye are?"

"Aye, well yesterday morning, I went roond to the hostel. I'd not seen her since the raid – we had been gan' oot on the Sarrada' but I worked late as there was so much to de with all the new bobbies, and I'd been up all the neet before so I was exhausted.

"I waited on the other side of the road until I saw the Matron gan oot to Church aboot quarter past ten, then I sneaked in. Gertie was just gan' oot up to the hospital so we were on wor own. We were talking aboot Freddie – and ye, Mossie, with your broken leg – and Glenda said that it could have happened to me. So I put me arms roond her and started kissing, and then ten minutes later we were in the bed and she was letting me have it.

"She was on call and we couldn't gan oot anywhere so I stayed with her till Gertie got back and then sneaked oot. She's off duty on Wednesda' neet so I'm gan' to take her to the flicks. I'll have to ask her then. I'll be eighteen in a couple of weeks and I'll be off in the RAF." Jimmy had been in the Air Cadets with Davey. "While I'm deein' me air-crew training I'll be able to get some home leave but once I'm posted I could be away for months."

The café door opened and Big Jock walked in. He came ower to the table and asked in his gruff voice. "Which one of ye is Norm?"

Poor Norm looked petrified and half lifted his hand. "I brought your bike back – Dekka says thanks. I'm to collect his bag as well if I can."

Wally had heard and came ower. "I'll gan upstairs and get it.

Do ye want something while you're waiting?"

"Aye, a cup of tea would do fine." He pulled up a chair and was just putting it beside mine when he noticed me leg.

"What ye been up to, Mossie?"

I tolt him the story – they already knew aboot Freddie but just that he'd been blown up. I realised that none of me mates had heard everything that had happened that neet and so I tolt them aboot digging Billy Duggan and Annie oot both stark naked and also aboot the pumps from the Middle Dock.

"And all the while ye had a broken leg and ye didn't kna'?" asked Matty.

"Well, I knew it hurt but I just got on with it, and it was well bandaged up."

Wally came ower with Dekka's bag. Jock took it and said, "Thanks, laddie. Can you bring another ice-cream over for oor Mossie – he'll need his strength building up."

"Naw, I can't – he's had his one for the week, and Mrs. DiBresci says she's not serving any sappers in future, either."

I thought for minute that Big Jock was gan' to grab Wally by the neck as he half got oot of his chair. "It's all reet, Jock, I've got to get back anyway."

I went oot with Jock. Matty helped me along and said he'd give me a lift yem.

"What was all that aboot, Mossie?" asked Jock, "Dekka said that he'd had a row with his sister but I didna' think it was anything too heavy."

"They keep a load of sugar doon the cellar. They were stockpiling before the War but naebody's supposed to kna' aboot it – that's why we can get wor ice-creams whenever we want them. Dekka's stolen all of the sugar apart from a couple of bags."

"He's stolen from his own sister. And you lads won't be getting your ice-creams!"

Jock was aboot as clever as me but he was slowly getting there.

"Weel, we'll have to see aboot this. Can you get aboot all reet, Mossie, I mean with your leg an' all?"

"Wye, aye, I can, so long as I have some help getting on the back of Matty's bike."

"Reet, let's gang and have a word with oor Dekka. He's in the *Woodbine* with the lads." With Jock to steady me I got onto Matty's bike nae bother, and we headed off to the *Woodbine*. I didn't kna' much aboot pubs but everybody knew that you didn't make any trouble there – the landlord was Bill Spyles – he was the auld bobby who was doon at the Nook with his two marras John Burgess and Sam Beecroft. When he'd been called up as a pensioner reservist his wife took ower the running of the pub, but Bill was still aboot if there was any trouble.

Jock went in and came oot with Dekka, then held him up against the wall and punched him a couple of times in the kidneys. The other lads had come oot as well. Dekka admitted taking the sugar, but said he had no choice. While they had been doon at Marsden he'd got in the habit of dropping in at the *Nook*, and he'd got in a card school with Bill and the others. He'd lost a bit and had tried to get it back by playing three card brag with Bill after hoors in the *Woodbine* whenever he was allowed to stay ower at the café. He'd lost a packet and he ended up owing him ower five quid, and it was either pay up or a thumping. He knew that Bill had had a little racket going with black market sugar - Sam Beecroft got hold of it from a widow woman who was supposed to make jam with it - and Bill had agreed to take sugar instead of cash.

"Is there any chance of getting it back?"

"Not unless you've got five quid and besides I doubt if Bill's got much left. I was taking it a few bags at a time and he was selling it as he got it. Most of it's gone to Nobby Bates who runs the fruit and veg shop at the Nook."

"Well you'll have to get some from somewhere else."

There was a muttering as one of them said something and then another voice spoke up – it was Sergeant Hopkirk.

"You can count me out on that one. It's all right for you lot - you'd just do a week in the glass house but I might be reduced to the ranks."

Big Jock answered him with a hardness in his voice.

"Dekka'll do it on his own, Sarge. I'll gang along to make sure none of it ends up anywhere else."

Big Jock came back ower to where we were standing. "Drop in at the café on your way back, Mossie. Tell Mrs. DiBresci she'll get her sugar back – it might take a few days and she's not to ask where it comes from. It'll cost her nowt but I'll need a bottle of whisky to sort things oot."

"I'm not sure aboot whisky but I know they've got a few bottles of grappa."

I couldn't see Jock's face in the pitch black but I could hear him muttering something aboot what the f***'s that.

"It's Italian – Wally's Da', Sergeant Duncan, used to drink it when auld Mr. DiBresci was still alive. They've got bottles of it in the cellar." I stopped a minute, and then whispered, "Unless someone's nicked it."

There was nowt wrong with Dekka's hearing. "If you make any more cracks like that I'll break your other f***ing leg for you, Mossie Hamed."

"Shut it, Dekka. If you can get any, Mossie, take it home tonight. We'll call in on the way back to Low Fell. If what I have in mind works oot we might need to drop the sugar off at your hoose – I don't want people seeing the lorry outside the café."

I told him the address in Maxwell Street and we were off. Little Audrey had calmed doon a bit and said that she hoped they weren't gan' to de anything stupid, but I said that Big Jock would see that everything went all reet. She told Wally to get two bottles of grappa – one for Big Jock himsel'. "Nae one else drinks it since Giovanni left. And ye can tell him that I'll serve the sappers so long as they dain't bring that miserable little sod of a brother with them."

I'd got the knack of getting on the saddle noo, and even with a bottle of grappa in each hand, I had an easy trip back to Maxwell Street. We went doon the back lane and Matty slowly pulled up against the back wall, and then put his arm roond me to support me as I got off. We went into the back yard and Matty pushed open the door as we went in through the scullery. He suddenly just stopped. I pushed mesel' forward – all I could see was Saleem's bare arse going up and doon on top of me Mam who was in the chair by the fire with her legs in the air, groanin' and moanin' and digging her fingers into his back. I forgot aboot me leg and ran forward to hit him with a bottle, but just fell ower. I had to hold the bottles up because I didn't want to break them and I nearly knocked mesel' oot. I vaguely heard me Mam asking Matty what the bloody hell was he looking at, and he was away off.

It took a few minutes for me Mam and Saleem to straighten their claes, and then they helped me up. I'd flattened me nose and it was bleeding, so me Mam got a cad flannel to dab it with. Saleem just stood there looking very shifty eyed and keeping his hand ower his groin so I couldn't see the geet lump in his trooser.

"I still love your Da', Mossie and I always will, but I like Saleem as well and he likes me."

Saleem then spoke to me in Arabic. He said that he loved me Mam and that he had no wish to bring dishonour on the house. He would marry her and then I would be his son. He only said that because he knew that a son wouldn't stab his fatha' in the back when he wasn't looking. I said he should ask me Mam so he did in his broken English. I was looking at them and I realised that they'd make a good looking couple – me Mam had had me when she was just sixteen so she wasn't much older than Saleem – it still felt funny kna'ing that your mutha' was having it off with another fella, though.

"You don't have to, Saleem," she said.

"Aye he does and ye have to say yes – if not I'll have to fight him." I kna' I'm British, but I've got Arab blood and he'd dishonoured me Mam – I was heed of the house and dishonour meant a blood feud.

She looked at Saleem and then at me. "Mohammed's the heed of the hoose, Saleem. I'm willing, but Mohammed will have to give his consent." It was the first time I could remember her calling me by me proper name.

Saleem broke into a big smile – he came towards me and used the traditional Arab words. We then embraced like Arab men do. I couldn't say naw – I'd always liked him, and I couldn't see how it would change things much.

"I'll make some tea," me Mam said.

"Aye and we might be getting some sugar an' all," and I started telling them aboot Dekka, Little Audrey and Big Jock.

There was a knock on the front door - it was Dekka and Big Jock. I brought them in and Big Jock shouted to the Sergeant who was driving to wait for them at the corner.

"This is me Mam and Saleem, wor lodger," I said. Jock stuck his big paw oot and shook hands. Dekka stood where he was just inside the doorway.

"There's the grappa. Little Audrey says ye can have one for yoursel'."

Jock took them – the dark broon bottles were still dusty. "They look braw, Mossie. Would you like to try a drop noo?"

"Naw, I dain't drink. Nor does Saleem."

"Och, I should have known, you being a Muslim." He then spoke to me Mam.

"Mrs. DiBresci has run oot of sugar for young Mossie's ice-cream thanks to Dekka there - so we're gang to help him get some back. They keep a warehouse full o' it at Fenham Barracks – we use it to make a mix of brine and sugar that stops the time delay fuses on the bombs – but that's top secret and ye havena' to tell it to anyone. Well we're gang to redistribute some o' it for a good cause – your laddie's ice-creams." He chuckled. "I dinna' want anyone to see oor lorry ootside the café so I was gang to ask if we could bring it here. Ye can then transfer it to smaller bags and one of Mossie's mates can take it doon to Mrs. DiBresci on the delivery bike."

"I'm not sure," said me Mam. I spoke quickly and quietly to Saleem in Arabic – I could see from the look on his face that he hadn't understood a word that Jock had said. His eyes lit up when I said sugar and then he whispered someitt to me.

"Saleem says we should help, so long as we can have a couple of pounds for worsel'," I thought I'd better explain. "He can only drink tea if it's got at least three teaspoons in it."

"Aye well," said me Mam, "in that case, we better have a couple of punds for the Rutherfords upstairs – they're bound to find oot what we're deein' – not that they'd tell anybody, mind."

"Once we drop the sacks off here we won't be coming roond checking the weights of the bags you make up," said Big Jock, "just so long as Mrs. DiBresci gets enough to make up what Dekka took. But the less people know the better."

Me Mam offered to make them a cup of tea but Jock said that the other lads were waiting for them. I suggested that they gan oot the back door – they should then count the doors to the street and when they came with the sugar they could pull the van in at the corner and bring it doon - we were only six doors along.

"If it gangs to plan it'll be Friday neet aboot ten o'clock."

When Mary came yem from Jasmin's we tolt her aboot me Mam and Saleem. She didn't say much but she seemed happy enough. I couldn't stop mesel' from looking at Saleem's crotch and he still had the horn on – I didn't fancy getting into bed and waking up in the middle of the neet with that thing sticking into me back, so I says does anyone fancy any fish and chips.

"I'll gan – it'll give me a chance to practise with me crutch, but Mary'll have to come with me to carry them yem."

Saleem hadn't had any tea so me Mam went to her purse – he beat her to it and gave me half a croon.

"I think I'll gan to the chippy in Regent Street. It's a bit further than the one in Cuthbert Street but Matty telt me that they were using whale meat there and it makes the batter all soggy."

As we walked oot the door I said in Arabic to Saleem that we'd be half an hoor so he'd better make the most of it. He nodded and gave me a toothy grin.

"What you're saying to Saleem?" asked Mary as we went into the back yard.

"Aw, I was just checking that he wanted salt and vinegar."

I had a word with Mary on the way back aboot how I was fed up with Saleem snoring every neet, and that I was gan' to suggest that he sleep in with me Mam now they were engaged. She just shrugged her shoulders.

That neet I was alone in me bed and the next day me Mam was doon the Registry Office. They were married before Saleem's next trip away. She had to pay a bit extra for an emergency dispensomeitt or other as he was a mariner aboot to gan to sea. It was a quiet wedding - we all went oot for dinner at Said's Café and then we had the wedding cake at wor hoose. Bella Rutherford had made it – Alice Hussain had provided the fruit, Said had given the flour, and you dain't need to guess where the sugar came from.

It had been brought in to wor backyard that Friday neet as Jock had promised. Jock and Dekka carried the half dozen or so hundredweight bags on their backs. They put it in the air raid shelter and were straight off. Every Friday the Lieutenant and his Subaltern went across to Fenham Barracks for an officers' mess dinner. Dekka usually drove them and Big Jock had asked if he could gan along to meet up with an auld mate of his. They arrived aboot half past seven, and unless there was an air raid they'd stay until well after midnight. After they'd gone in the Mess, Dekka parked the lorry at the back of the warehouse. Big Jock then went roond the front and got into conversation with the warehouse sentry – pulled the bottle of grappa oot of his pocket, and there was no risk of Dekka being disturbed. There was an office at the back - it only took five minutes for Dekka to glue on a bit of broon paper to a small pane in the winda' and tap the glass oot with a toffee hammer. He then clambered in and found the key to the back door. After a bit Big Jock left his new found friend after making him a gift of what was left in the bottle, helped Dekka lift the bags oot, and they had plenty of time to get to Shields and back.

I spent the next couple of days putting the sugar into bags and tins Little Audrey had provided, and then Mary who was deein' me job as delivery lad would put them in the basket and deliver them to Audrey. Those in the kna' got a bag of sugar but had to keep stumm.

Me Mam gave up her job in the café as soon as she was wed. Saleem bought me a racing bike with Sturmey-Archer gears, Mary took ower me job as delivery boy permanently and as soon as me cast was off, I started doon the Middle Docks as an apprentice fitter. Jock Duncan had been to see Sid Mordue – he'd had to employ someone else to de Frank's job but there was need of fitters and I was taken on. I would have to gan to neet school but Sergeant Duncan said that it wouldn't de me any harm to put me brain to work for a change.

CHAPTER 11
NOVEMBER/DECEMBER
1941

Freddie Skee pulled through but he stayed in hospital – he had a couple more operations. Gertie went in to see him every day - as she was an ambulance driver they let her see him whenever she was up at the Ingham even if it wasn't visiting hours. Once me cast was off and Freddie was oot of danger, me and Matty would gan up of an evening – we'd get Wally to put a big dollop of ice-cream with plenty of monkey's blood in a pudding basin and we'd tear up to the Ingham on wor bikes so that it was still solid when we got there. He was just the syem, making stupid comments and saying what he was gan' to de with Gertie when he was oot. He hated being in bed. They were talkin' aboot getting him fitted with false legs but he might have to transfer to one of the Army hospitals doon Sooth where they specialised in treating soldiers who'd lost their legs.

Jimmy Clay was away training as air-crew in the RAF, and was gan' to marry Glenda as soon he could.

I was working hard in the Docks and enjoying it, but still went in to Keppel Street when the sirens went. We didn't have any raids in Shields for nearly three months but we still had air raid warnings when planes flew doon the coast.

Norm was lodging permanently with the Corbetts and so I knew that Jackie was expecting to have the bairn in the middle of January – it came early and Jackie was taken to hospital as an emergency in December.

It was on the 15th December at aboot half past seven that there was a knock on the door. I was sitting at the table trying to make sense of some algebra homework so I got up and answered it. "It's Mrs. Corbett," a voice said. Ye didn't keep folk waiting on the door step in the blackoot or ye'd have an ARP warden shouting blue murder.

"Ye'd better come in then."

She came through, and as soon as we were in the kitchen she handed me someitt wrapped in a blanket.

"That's yours," she said. She then took some things oot of a bag. "That's milk powder and bottles to keep you going a week. You'll have to register the birth. It's a boy, and you can name him yourself. We're having nothing to do with it, and Jackie's mother won't either. David won't throw her out, but he's not bringing up another man's bairn in our house." She turned roond and left.

Me Mam said nowt but came ower and took the bundle – she pulled the cover away from the face. It was a new born bairn – with black hair, brown eyes and brown skin just like mine.

"Oh Mossie, what have ye gone and done," she said.

POST SCRIPT

Shields Gazette – 20th December 1941

"*Police are still searching for Mrs. Jacqueline Corbett who went missing from her home at Hepscott Terrace on the 18th December at about ten o'clock at night, dressed only in her night clothes and a dressing gown. A woman matching her description was seen walking down Mowbray Road near the junction with Tadema Road in the direction of the sea front by a pitman coming off shift at Westoe Colliery. Mrs. Corbett, who was said to have been depressed, had only recently given birth but the baby had been given up for adoption. The Police have, as a precaution, alerted coastal authorities in case a body is washed up. Her husband Mr. David Corbett is too distressed to make any comment.*"

Historical Notes, Sources and Acknowledgements

Blitz PAMs is a work of fiction in that the main characters, and their story, are fictional but the backdrop of the Blitz of South Shields is fact.

At the outbreak of war there was a great fear of air raids and possibly invasion. A whole new apparatus of civil defence was set up – in embarking on research for a final chapter of what was intended to be a sequel to the Five Stone Steps I discovered a new world of home front heroes – air raid wardens, street fire watchers, Special Constables, War Reserve Police, auxiliary fire fighters, ambulance drivers and first aiders, rescue squads, home guard, WVS (it had not yet been made Royal) who set up mobile canteens and then I discovered the Police Auxiliary Messengers (the PAMs). Police Forces recruited young lads aged 16-18 with bikes whose job was to take messages when there were air raids. Practice varied between forces – some lads were given full time jobs, very much like Police Cadets – others volunteered to come out when there were raids. The idea of young lads riding their bikes to pass messages on when the phone lines were down and with bombs flying round their ears stirred my imagination.

I set my PAMS tale in South Shields but it could just as well have been in any of the towns that were blitzed - I do not know how the PAMs were organised in Shields and it is here where the fiction takes over.

The action takes place between September 1940 and December 1941, the height of the blitz. I have tried to give as accurate a picture as possible of the air raids. My main sources were, first, the photographic archive of South Tyneside Library Service using their web site South Tyneside Historic Images made up primarily of the photos of Miss Amy Flagg, a librarian and a keen amateur photographer who recorded the aftermath of all the raids; and second the web resource NE Diary – Pears and Ripley which gives a narrative of all war time activity in the North East.

Unexploded bombs were a particular hazard and the fictional bomb squad that appears in these pages is based on the activities of No 27 Bomb Disposal Section of the Royal Engineers based at Low Fell under the command of Lieutenant Brookes. Thanks to Chris Ranstead, who could not have been more helpful, I had access to their War Time Diaries (in note form and extremely brief – well, they were very busy!). My own Lieutenant Brookes has only the name in common with the eponymous Lieutenant – I know nothing of his character but he was one of the many unsung heroes of bomb disposal. The bomb on top of the boiler incident is almost beyond belief but all he records in his diary is:–

"1/10/41 01.30 After …enemy air attack Cat 'A' at Shields Power Stn. 1000 kg recovered at 5.50 hrs."

The raids on Shields mentioned in the book took place very much as described but I have tried to portray the true devastation and horror using my fictional characters to bring the scenes to life. Any mistakes are down to me!

Historical Characters

At the beginning of the book I have made the usual disclaimer about characters being fictitious with certain exceptions:

Lieutenant Brookes: commanded No 27 Bomb Disposal Section of the Royal Engineers based at Low Fell.

Sergeant Tom 'Jock' Duncan – based on Sergeant Thomas 'Jock' Renton Gordon whose memoirs inspired my first book 'The Five Stone Steps'.

Miss Amy Flagg – librarian and amateur photographer who took most of the photos used in this book.

Minchella's – still going strong – the DiBrescis are completely fictitious but their ice cream and its red sauce, or monkey's blood as it used to be called locally, is inspired by Minchella's award winning ice cream.

Ernie Pells – my Dad's cousin – his narrow escape during an air raid is a true story and Ernie, who loved telling the old stories, would always end this one by pointing to his face where you could still see the scar on his cheek where the piece of glass had cut it.

James Thomas Annis Scott GM: the rescue of people from the cellar of the Market Café is based on the citation for James Scott's award of the George Medal.

Major Stringfellow: No 1 Bomb Disposal Co. Fenham Barracks.

Ralph Thorburn: one of the Sunderland Firemen who came to help under the mutual aid scheme. He gave his life trying to put the riverside fires out.

Major Todd: Chief Air Raid Warden

Sources

I list below the web sites and books that I have used.

www.southtynesideimages.org.uk/newsite
www.ne-diary.bpears.org.uk/

CD – South Tyneside: The Blitz. Six-T Media

Disarming Hitler's Weapons – Bomb Disposal – the V1 and V2 Rockets – Chris Ranstead – Pen and Sword Books

Danger UXB – The Heroic Story of the WWII Bomb Disposal Teams – Owen James - Abacus

South Shields Pubs – Eileen Burnett – Amberley Publishing

The Trolley Buses of South Shields – G. Burrows – Trolley-books

Put That Light Out – Britain's Civil Defence Services at War – Mike Brown – Sutton Publishing

Sunderland's Blitz – Kevin Brady – The People's History

Songs

Keep Your Feet Still Geordie Hinny – 1856 – Joe Wilson
Cushie Butterfield – 1862 – George Ridley

Acknowledgements

Thanks to: Marilyn Gordon, Dave Kerr, Chris Ranstead, Catrin Galt of South Tyneside Libraries, the team at UK Book Publishing

CPSIA information can be obtained
at www.ICGtesting.com
Printed in the USA
BVOW06s1027011216
469298BV00019B/119/P